Acknowl[illegible]

I regret that my [illegible] to see the publication of this [illegible] ing from my earliest scribbles to [illegible] she ran out of library books and an [illegible] ovel which she painstakingly typed. Thanks, Mum.

Thanks to all who gave feedback, advice and morale-boosting at various stages, including Emily, Dan, Paul, Hannah, Jane, Cathy, Chris, David, Juliette, Alan, John, Tim, Scratch, Peter and all my friends at Writers Talkback. And I mustn't forget teacher Paula and fellow writers at the Coventry University 'Writing Novels' class of 2006.

Special thanks to Kay Green, my wonderful editor and publisher at Circaidy Gregory Press, for her belief in this book and her patience with me. And thanks to all at the Earlyworks Press Writers' and Reviewers' Club for excellent criticism and welcome diversion.

Finally, much love and gratitude to Paul for his never-failing support. You have given me a safe place to write.

About the Artist

Cover artist Catherine Edmunds was born in Kent in 1959, and won her first art competition as a small child with a charcoal drawing of a Christmas tree. Something of a Renaissance woman, she has since worked professionally as a violinist and published a novel, as well as a variety of poems and short stories. Her artwork embraces such diverse themes as delicate portraiture and exploding beetroots. Recent commissions include cover art and illustrations for Earlyworks Press, BeWrite Books, TWI Publications, and her own poetry collection *wormwood, earth and honey* (Circaidy Gregory Press). Catherine will tackle anything 'arty', and has designed an African shamrock tattoo for a client of Afro/Irish descent, as well as more traditional illustrative work for ezine *The Mad Hatter's Review*.

Catherine has three grown-up children and lives with her husband in North East England, between the grey North Sea and the windswept High Pennines.

www.freewebs.com/catherineedmunds

About the Author

Rosalie Warren has two grown-up children and lives in Coventry with her partner, Paul. She has a PhD in Cognitive Science and at various stages of her life has taught English, maths, chemistry, hairdressing science, linguistics and computing, as well as running her own gardening business for a time. Writing under the name Sheila Glasbey, she has published articles in the following academic journals: *Natural Language Semantics* (Springer), *Journal of Semantics* (OUP), *Metaphor and Symbol* (Lawrence Erlbaum Associates), and contributed towards a number of books such as *Recent Advances in the Syntax and Semantics of Tense, Aspect and Modality* (Mouton de Gruyter) and *Non-definiteness and Plurality* (John Benjamins).

Charity's Child is her first novel. She has also written a number of short stories, some of which can be seen on her website at

www.rosalie-warren.co.uk

Dedication

To my father, George,
and in memory of my mother, Betty,
with love.

PART 1

Chapter 1

"Joanne – I *can't* be."

I barely caught Charity's words before the wind whipped them away. We were standing outside the public toilets on Castlehaven High Street, the east wind off the sea hurling hailstones the size of gravel into our faces.

Charity had a blue cardboard packet in her hands. She clutched it as though it was something precious, while the fear on her face suggested it might explode any second.

I'd begun to shiver and couldn't stop. My voice came out weak and shaky. "It says you *are*."

Charity's long, bright gold hair had been dragged and twisted into knots and tangles by the wind. Red strands caught the light from somewhere, God knows where – certainly not the sky. She raised a hand to wipe her face. As usual, she had no jacket and her arms were bare, purple like bruises. She claimed she never felt the cold.

I wanted to be somewhere I could study the result again, somewhere quiet where I could make sure, without having every sensible thought torn out of my head by the force eight gale. I tried to push Charity towards the entrance to the public library but she stood still on the pavement, like a boulder parting the stream of shoppers.

"Can they sometimes be wrong, these tests?" she asked, her voice a little stronger – hoping.

"I don't know."

"Shall I buy another one and try again?"

Boots the chemist was halfway back along the High Street. The assistant who'd served us, the elder sister of one of my classmates, had given us a funny look the first time. I didn't want to go back.

We dug out our purses: mine from the inner pocket of my fleece-lined jacket, Charity's from her beaten-up khaki shoulder bag. We counted up just under three pounds between us. Not enough for another kit.

Charity was just sixteen and I was almost exactly a year younger. We'd been friends for just under five months.

It wasn't possible, I told myself. Perhaps the freak result had something to do with the cold? It had been icy in the toilet block.

Neither of us had been with a boy – that's what I'd thought. Neither of us wanted to. We had each other. I'd believed that until this morning, when we met outside WH Smith's and I saw right away that something was wrong. Charity had lost her usual bounce and her features were frozen up in a way that had nothing to do with the cold.

I'd taken off my woollen mittens to scrabble in my purse and my hands were numb. I didn't know what I'd done with the mittens but it didn't seem right to look for them.

Charity was staring out to sea.

"Perhaps you should make a doctor's appointment," I said. "They'll be able to give you a proper test, to make sure. Make sure you're *not*, I mean."

I wanted to comfort her, but I had what felt like a gunshot wound in my chest, throbbing harder with each heartbeat. I could believe my blood was running out of me onto the pavement, that I would collapse any second. It was a different pain to the one when my dad died, and it shocked me to realise that this felt even worse.

Charity didn't reply but she turned her eyes to me. They were brown with glimmers of green. They'd held such warmth for me, so often, that it was impossible to believe she'd betrayed me, been with someone else.

Her pale pink t-shirt was soaked.

The sky was still darkening. The hail was thicker and faster than ever, bouncing up several inches when it hit the road. I thought of how excited I'd been by hailstones as a small child. Now I found them downright nasty.

"Come on, let's get some hot chocolate in Brown's." I gave Charity's arm a tug. She was unresisting now and I began to steer. "You look awful."

She didn't, as a matter of fact, look awful or anything like it. I have only seen Charity look awful on a couple of occasions, and they came later. Most of the time she looked wonderful, even soaking wet and in circumstances like these. Her hair was sodden now and stuck to her face and neck, but it still found a way to gleam. While my cheeks were no doubt blotched red by the stinging hail, hers had a healthy pink glow. Her eyes had the emerald glint of the sea around the rocks in summer. Her nose was a little too long, perhaps – though who decides these things? Her upper lip dipped in the middle in what my mother called a Cupid's bow.

She was tall – a good three inches above me. Built on the heavy side, rounded but not plump, or not in a wobbly way. Her skin retained a suggestion of the tan she'd arrived with in September. I'd assumed it was the result of some overseas holiday with her father. She'd told me he travelled a lot.

But her colour hadn't faded. The Castlehaven wind had so far failed to scour it off her skin and I was beginning to think it must be permanent.

She had no trace of the acne that colonised my chin. Her hair displayed no grease, ever, as far as I could see.

She let me manoeuvre her along the street, the hail now coming at us from the side and easing off a bit. We turned into Brown's Tea and Coffee Stop. When the new owners took over and the sign went up we'd assumed it was a mistake; before that it had been The Little Tea Shop. But they never changed it and the name, whether it had been deliberate or not, began to make sense.

It was shabby inside, like most of Castlehaven, but comfortingly hot and steamy. We found a table in the window and I wriggled my toes, beginning to think that the horror of the situation might just be a result of the cruel weather. Perhaps things would be better now we were in the warm.

Charity remained silent but her face had relaxed. I got up and joined the queue, then remembered that I had less than a pound on me. Not enough for two Brown's special hot chocolates with whipped cream. I settled for two mugs of tea, remembering to put one-and-a-half sugars in Charity's. My change was just enough for a chocolate éclair, which I would let Charity have. Perhaps the nourishment would bring on her period.

Or maybe I'd take just a bite.

As I put the red plastic tray down on the table she pushed a tissue into her bag and gave me a hint of a smile. "Thanks."

She picked up the éclair and bit off more than half. Her face took on a glazed look as she tasted the soft fudgy chocolate and the sweetened cream. Brown's did a good éclair. Forgetting my good intentions, I took a big bite from what was left.

For a moment or two, while she was eating, you could almost believe this was the same Charity who regularly jumped onto a chair at our Crabbie meetings, waving her arms, squealing with joy and begging the Spirit to descend on us.

Then she swallowed, the delight left her face, and we were back to reality.

Someone had left the door open a crack and a piercing draught blew into our faces and around our legs.

My piece of éclair, once swallowed, seemed to wedge in my gullet. I thought, for the second time that morning, of the day we got the news my dad was dead. I'd forgotten the throat-ache, how it was impossible to swallow.

I cleared my throat and took a deep breath. "Char, you can be honest with me." Where had I got that line from – some book or film? It sounded stupid. "Is it one of the lads from school?"

Her mouth fell open, revealing a piece of yellow choux pastry on her tongue.

"Joanne, you know it isn't."

"*How* do I know? If you're pregnant, it has to be someone."

"I'm not pregnant. Like I said, I can't be."

"But the test says you are. I don't think they can be wrong, not if you do it properly." I knew she had done it properly – I'd helped.

"It must be wrong."

"Will you go to the doctor's, then? Do you want me to come with you?"

"There's no need." Her voice had risen several tones. "My period will come any day. It has to."

We both knew it wouldn't.

As we sat drinking our tea in silence, swallow after swallow, Alan's face, his big white gleaming teeth, came into my mind and I couldn't banish it.

Alan was our assistant pastor, in his mid-twenties, married with two small children. Alice and David.

I'd seen the way his eyes followed Charity in our meetings. I'd tried not to think about it, not to mind. I'd reminded myself, over and over again, that Charity belonged to me. Didn't she?

She had stayed for a few nights in Alan and Louise's home, just after Christmas, when her father went on a business trip and the heating failed. I did a bit of mental arithmetic.

The timing could so easily be right.

Surely not Alan? He was always speaking out against immorality. He saw it everywhere, even on children's TV. Even on Coronation Street. You could believe, from what he said at meetings, that he didn't approve of sex at all, not even in marriage. In spite of the fact that he had two kids.

I'd been scared of him for years. He looked at me as though he could see what was in my head. As though he knew about the nail varnish I'd shoplifted from Woolworth's and never dared to take back. And, in recent days, as though my love for Charity was something bad.

Surely it couldn't be Alan? A creamy burp rose in my throat and I tasted sick.

Charity had been in Castlehaven since mid-September. She'd turned up at one of our Thursday evening prayer meetings, held in a couple of rented rooms above Peter Nevis Accountants on Harbour Crescent. That evening, as usual, there were only seven or eight of us. I was the youngest by over ten years. Everyone except Alan looked either bored or sleepy or both, and even Alan lacked his usual energy and bluster.

"Welcome, everyone," said Tom, our pastor, catching each of our eyes in turn and submitting us to a checking-over. He did this every time but I never minded.

Tom had proved his worth on his arrival in Castlehaven a couple of years earlier. He'd been the only person to understand that, although I didn't show it, I was missing my father like hell. Mum, Aunt Daisy and the other Crabbies all assumed that because I never cried (I couldn't) and went on exactly as I'd been before (good little swotty girl, coming top in all my school tests), I didn't really care.

Or, as I heard someone say, I'd 'emerged unscathed' – whatever that was supposed to mean.

Mum told me I was her comfort and support and she didn't know what she'd do without me. After that, I was stuck with my role.

Tom, the second time we met, asked me about my father and the things we'd done together. After a few minutes of this I was able to have my first proper cry. I met up with Tom once a week after that, for what he called counselling. I was only eleven and had never heard of it. I still don't understand what he did, but I will always love him for it.

So he was more than welcome to scrutinise me. I was fine, of course, just wondering, as always, why I was there. Why I continued to go to Crabbie meetings when there were no other young people except, once in a blue moon, the Bond twins, Ray and Tony. At one time I'd been in love with both of them and the thought of seeing them had been enough to get me to a Thursday meeting. But that was last year and my tastes had changed.

"Any special requests for prayer?" asked Tom.

No-one spoke up and I considered mentioning my geography test next day, for which I should have been revising. But it would be just my luck if, after I'd mentioned it, someone remembered about a sick baby or a famine.

"Okay then." Tom, his hay-bale of hair uncombed and wild as always, gave his big grin. He was not a good-looking man; that was part of his appeal for me. "Let's bow our heads and ask the Lord to prompt us. Don't be afraid to pray short prayers. Just mention someone's name, if you like."

Before I shut my eyes (I never kept them shut for long) I glanced at Alan, sitting across from me. He was, I decided, angry – and trying very hard to keep a lid on it. His face was set in grim lines and I hadn't seen a glimpse of those fearsome teeth. He had a bent nose from a fight he'd been in years before, in the days before he joined the Crabbies, when he'd been involved with motorbike gangs and minor crime.

My mother said Alan had spent some time in prison. She didn't like him at all, not even when he spoke about how God had blotted out his sins and made him a new man. Especially when he spoke like that. She didn't quite believe him, I suppose. Or perhaps she spotted a kind of boasting when he spoke about his former life. She had been a school dinner lady in the distant past and remembered Alan as a sullen eleven-year-old.

Maybe I caught my mother's distrust of Alan, although I disagreed with her on most things. Or perhaps it was because of Louise that I didn't like him. She'd been my friend for years, in spite of the twelve-year age gap. Before she married Alan she was studying physics at Newcastle University. When they got married she gave it up. She insisted it was her own choice, or rather that "the Lord had led them both together to the decision" – but I never really believed it. She'd been crazy about physics and loved astronomy, too.

It was because I'd plucked up the courage, aged ten, to ask to look through Louise's telescope that I'd first got to know her. Then she shocked me by leaving university, suddenly, in the middle of her second year, after getting a brilliant result at the end of year one. Nowadays, she was rarely to be seen without her children. She and Alan no longer held hands and she often looked stressed or sad.

Anyway I was glad, that evening, that Alan was subdued and not giving us the benefit of his enormous grin while telling us the latest thing that the Lord was doing with him. God seemed to pay a lot of attention to Alan. I was a little piqued, but in the main relieved, that He didn't take the same interest in me.

None of the other Crabbies spoke about God in the way Alan did – a sort of over-familiar greasiness. If they had, I'd have stopped going long before.

Perhaps Alan's anger was the result of a row with Louise. I hoped not, for her sake. I'd never seen him lose his temper but I could imagine it.

A few late rays of sun slanted in through the grimy, sand-streaked window. There was a smell of something starting to go off (food in the kitchen? Only biscuits were ever kept there. Perhaps someone's socks). The air was dusty, giving the atmosphere a sultry weight that would have been unpleasant if it hadn't been so familiar.

I'd shut my eyes and was trying to focus my thoughts on prayer, when Charity burst in.

It was customary to keep our eyes closed, or at least half-closed, when latecomers arrived, and pretend not to notice them. But, since Charity was new, that wouldn't have been right. No-one could have ignored her, anyway, since she tripped over Mrs Pinderfield's outstretched bandaged leg and nearly fell on top of Tom and old Mr Streatfield. Tom held out his arm and managed to save her.

Charity apologised in an accent that wasn't quite Castlehaven, but wasn't so far off. Still Yorkshire, but perhaps inland or further south. I'd ask her later.

Her most noticeable feature was her hair. The weak sun seemed to make a special effort to light it up, and it gleamed like a torch.

"Hello, everyone. I'm Charity Baker."

I marvelled at her lack of shyness, imagining how paralysed I'd have felt in a group of strangers.

Tom shook her hand as she sat down in the chair he'd pulled out for her, next to him. "Good to meet you, Charity. I'm Tom. You're very welcome to our meeting."

"Sorry – I didn't realise you'd started or I wouldn't have barged in," she said. 'You were so quiet. I didn't think you could be praying."

Charity's comment struck me as odd. Wasn't quietness what you expected in a prayer meeting?

"No problem at all," said Tom. "I'll introduce you to the others when we've finished, if that's okay."

My stomach began to churn. I couldn't wait for the hour to be over and to have the chance to speak to her. If I dared. And if I got the chance – newcomers were so rare in Crabbie meetings that there was a tendency to mob them.

The room was quiet for about five minutes, apart from Mrs Pinderfield's asthmatic breathing, the occasional cough from Mr Streatfield and a few sighs from Alan. He gave a series of long, slow breathings-in, followed by a short, sharp expulsion of air from his nose, as though trying to clear a blockage.

I studied Charity. She sat like the rest of us, head bent slightly forward. One hand was on her lap, the other fiddling with the ties of her cheesecloth top. I'd noticed when she first came in that it was thin, see-through enough to suggest a red bra underneath. Her trousers matched the top and were rather grubby, especially the knees. She wore un-trendy, non-label trainers not unlike mine. Her feet, I noticed, were large, possibly size eight or nine. Perhaps they'd suddenly grown and that was why she tripped over things.

I guessed she was a year or two above me at school.

Could she possibly be a new friend? A girl close to my own age, in the Crabbies, was something I'd given up hope of years before.

I dug my fingernails into my thumbs, willing the other Crabbies to behave themselves, not to say anything stupid that would put her off coming again.

A crooning sound started, quiet at first but increasing in pitch and volume to a kind of controlled wail. A bit like a child pretending to be a ghost. At least, I need no longer fear that one of the Crabbies would do something embarrassing. Charity, it seemed, could hold her own in that respect.

The spooky sounds continued for a minute or so. Then Charity was singing – a familiar chorus that began. "Send, Lord your Spirit now, upon your waiting flock."

Alan's eyes were open. He was watching Charity and starting to sing along. He had a strong, tuneful voice and they harmonised well. Before long, Tom's off-key Geordie croak could be heard, together with Mrs Pinderfield's whine and some squeaks and snuffles from the rest. I mouthed the words, in case anyone was watching me. Though that was unlikely – Charity had got everyone's attention.

When the chorus finished there was silence for a few seconds. Then Charity's voice rang out. "Oh, loving Heavenly Father, please hear us and send Your Holy Spirit to fill our hearts and make us overflow with praise. Fill us from Your everlasting fountain of joy. Lift us up into the heights of adoration. Make us vessels of Your holy love."

I'd never heard words like this from someone my own age. It should have been incongruous, but somehow, coming from Charity, it sounded natural and sincere. I could tell she wasn't trying to impress anyone. In fact, she seemed to have forgotten the rest of us were there. Her eyes were shut and she held her hands in front of her, palms up as though ready to catch the Spirit falling from above.

Tom had a slight frown – the bemused look he got sometimes when Alan was ranting on. Alan gazed at Charity with his eyes glazed and unblinking, eyebrows raised, a slight shake of the head as though he could not quite believe this apparition.

Mrs Pinderfield was less affected. She was deaf and had probably not caught Charity's words. She fiddled with her bandage. Perhaps her leg was sore where Charity had fallen over it.

I could so easily have been irritated by this girl, seen her as some kind of religious crank. But I didn't. I suppose her looks helped. My main feeling was one of admiration – how *dare* she? There was curiosity too – I'd never met anyone like this. And a desire to protect. She looked so vulnerable in her cheesecloth outfit, which I noticed had a couple of holes in the side-seam.

Charity stopped, and everyone except me and possibly Mrs Pinderfield expressed their agreement with a loud "Amen".

I saw Alan draw breath, no doubt ready to launch into an echoing prayer of his own. But he was beaten to it by Mr Streatfield, who had suddenly remembered his sister's neighbour's hip operation. Mr Streatfield liked to supply a lot of detail. We heard the diagnosis, the likely outcome, the location of the hospital and the name of the surgeon. Then he added the number of the ward and the fact it was the left hip. Finally, he remembered that the woman in question was seventy-three years old and had a birthday coming up in two weeks' time.

All this came out in a slow, monotonous rhythm, with long gaps between sentences so you thought he had finished, and smaller pauses while he looked for exactly the right word.

I heard Alan do his abrupt breath expulsion at least twice during Mr Streatfield's prayer. Mrs Pinderfield's breathing became even heavier and I suspected she had gone to sleep.

Alan tried to jump in during one of the pauses. But Mr Streatfield ignored his "Lord, we praise you" and resumed his medical dossier. Alan's face went purple and I felt sorry for Louise again. What must Alan be like to live with?

I knew Mr Streatfield was drawing to a close when he gave a short summary of his request. It was kind of him, I supposed, to remind God of the salient points.

After the final "Amen", Alan wasted no time. "Dear Lord, I can only echo the prayer of this – of our beautiful sister here – this angelic stranger You have sent to remind us of our need of Your

Spirit." He continued in this vein, alternately praising God and Charity, for at least ten minutes. Halfway through, he stood up and raised his hands above his head. No-one had ever, to my knowledge, got to their feet in the middle of a Crabbies prayer meeting, other than to visit the loo.

Charity stood up, too, and she and Alan locked eyes for a few seconds.

Tom was watching them, still bemused but now with a more pronounced frown, almost like my mother's look of exasperation when I refused to make up a guest's bed.

Then Charity started to pray in tongues. I only found out afterwards that that was what it was. She began with a deep hum, interrupted every three or four seconds by a splutter like a car engine failing to start. Alan fell silent. He remained standing and stared. Charity, oblivious to everyone, eyes still shut, continued with the humming and spluttering for a few minutes. Then she started to say a word which sounded like "ardoo", or perhaps "armoo", over and over, with varying intonation.

Tom's head was down, his shoulders hunched.

I felt as though I was watching a good film. This was by far the most excitement I'd ever seen at a Crabbies meeting.

Mr Streatfield kept giving his head a little shake, as though he thought he was imagining it all and wanted to dispel the picture.

Mrs Pinderfield slept on.

Tom closed the prayer time with his usual blessing, jumped straight to his feet and shook Charity's hand again.

"Charity – let me welcome you properly now. Let's all introduce ourselves." He was doing his pastoral bit but I could see he wasn't happy. Tom has one of those transparent faces that reveal his every thought.

We told Charity our names. Alan, of course, added an extra bit about how delighted he was to meet someone who, like himself, was "thirsty for a massive outpouring of God's Spirit."

Charity smiled at him but turned quickly back to me and said, "Joanne – you go to my school, don't you?"

"Castlehaven High?"

"Yep. Thought I'd seen you there. Whose class are you in – Mrs Morris's?"

I was pleased – Mrs Morris's class was the year above mine. Charity thought I was older than I was.

"Miss Carter's."

"Ah. Fourth year."

The other Crabbies, bored by this interchange, had started to drift towards the adjoining kitchen, where Mrs Pinderfield was boiling the kettle to make tea.

"I was so relieved to see you," Charity said. "I thought at first I was the youngest here. How do you stand it?"

"What, being the youngest? I don't like it much."

"Well, no. But I meant, how do you stand it, being in such a..." she lowered her voice, probably not quite enough, "... such a dull group?"

I felt miffed. She was right, of course, but it was a cheeky remark for a first meeting. I wanted to defend my Crabbie companions.

I must have shown my feelings. Perhaps I was as transparent as Tom.

"Sorry," she said. "Didn't mean to be rude. It's just a bit quiet, compared with what I'm used to."

Alan, mug of tea in hand, was now listening in. "May I ask what you're used to?" He showed his teeth in a smile that gave me the shivers.

"At my old church in Barnsley we had a manifestation of the gifts at every meeting," she said. "It was very exciting, though it could be a bit too much at times. And it led to some terrible arguments. That's one reason Dad and I left Barnsley to come here."

"The gifts?" repeated Alan.

"The gifts of the Spirit." She looked surprised. 'Haven't you heard of them?"

Alan hesitated. "I'm not sure."

I said, "I haven't. What are they?"

Tom had joined our little group now. I couldn't see his face but I could feel vibes of discomfort coming off him.

"They're what you get when the Spirit comes upon you – when you have the Special Blessing," she said. "It's God's free gift to all believers. But you have to ask for it."

"I've heard of that," said Alan. "But I've never quite understood it."

It was unlike Alan not to know something.

"Oh, it's easy," Charity said. "Like I said, all you have to do is ask. It's such a shame that lots of Christians don't know about it. It's a whole new dimension of worship. Puts things on a higher plane, my dad says. A whole new level of relationship with God."

"So, what are these gifts?" I asked.

Her expression became more normal when she looked at me. A girl again, not some super-spiritual being. "Tongues, prophecy, interpretation, healing… those and a few more. You can look them up in the Book of Acts."

"May I ask which church in Barnsley you went to?" asked Tom.

She reeled off a long name I didn't catch.

Tom nodded.

"Have you heard of it?"

"Just in passing."

"It's a wonderful place. At least it was, before the split. Things haven't been the same since."

"The split?" asked Alan.

"Yes, the big argument we had. Some of our members didn't agree with the Special Blessing." She looked round. Everyone was listening now. "Can you believe it – people not wanting to receive the Holy Spirit? Rejecting God's precious gifts?"

"I've heard of it happening," said Tom. "It's a question, sometimes, of how you interpret the Bible. Some people think that God gives His Spirit to all believers, as soon as they believe. That it's not an add-on extra you have to ask for later."

"But that's so wrong!" cried Charity. "Isn't it sad when people just refuse to accept the truth? My dad used to practically tear his hair out after some of the meetings. People putting up so much resistance to God's will. He used to wonder if some of their doubts were inspired by the devil."

"Hey, steady on," said Tom. "That's a bit strong. I happen to believe, myself, that there's no Special Blessing. Not as such."

Charity was looking at him in alarm, her eyes huge. "Really?"

"Yes. Really." His voice was gentle but had a touch of firmness.

Charity's eyes darted among us as though she was looking for a gap in the group around her, keen to escape. I feared suddenly that she would dash out of the room and we'd never see her again.

I tried to smooth things over. "Surely it doesn't matter if we don't agree on everything? That's what you always say, isn't it, Tom? That the most important things in a fellowship are love and support?"

Tom grinned at me. "That's it, Joanne."

I was pleased to have got things right for once.

"Well, of course, that's true in a way," said Charity. Her voice was flat, but at least she hadn't made a run for it. "But our pastor in Barnsley used to tell us that Christian love can only flow once the Spirit has released it."

"I wouldn't argue with that –" began Tom.

Before he could continue, Alan jumped in. "Charity, I'm beginning to think God has sent you as the answer to my prayers. You wouldn't believe how much I've been asking Him – imploring Him – to send an outpouring of the Spirit, to wake us all up. I've sat in these meetings, feeling the deadness all around me. I've –"

I looked at Tom's face, to see how he was taking this. He was biting his lip like a three-year-old and I didn't blame him. He was the pastor, after all, and someone was attacking his flock.

I wanted to help him out but couldn't think what to say.

Tom put a hand on Alan's arm. "Let's not overstate things," he said. "We can end up devaluing ourselves too much. There's a lot of good in our fellowship, as well as a lot of things we need to work on. Charity – let me get you some tea and a biscuit."

"I like Tom," Charity told me as we left the meeting hall together, twenty minutes later.

"Me too."

I'd discovered she lived over a mile away, towards the town centre.

"There's a bus every half hour into town," I told her, looking at my watch. "It goes from near my house. I'll show you. There's one due in seven minutes."

It was dark now, with a chilly breeze blowing off the sea. Charity hugged her arms to her chest as though cold, though she insisted she wasn't.

"Do you like Castlehaven?" I asked.

"Haven't made my mind up yet. It's very quiet. I'm used to a lot of stuff going on, especially in our church. We had meetings nearly every night. Is it right what Tom said, that you only meet up on Thursdays and Sundays?"

Wasn't twice a week enough? "There aren't enough of us for any more meetings."

"That'll change, too, when the Spirit comes," she assured me.

After a pause, I asked, "What got you into it all? Did your parents – your dad – take you to the church from when you were small?"

"No, not at all. My dad was converted when I was ten. Before that he was just a businessman, involved in lots of shady deals. Lost in sin. Then someone dragged him along to hear an evangelist and he heard the Good News for the first time, about salvation in Jesus. He gave his life to the Lord and it all went on from there. He joined the church and started taking me along."

"What about your mother?"

"She's in France."

We were almost at Sea View, the guest house run by my mother and Aunt Daisy which was also our home.

"You mean with her work or something?" I knew from the way Charity's cheeks reddened that it wasn't that.

"No. All the time. She lives there now."

"You mean she and your dad are divorced?"

"Well. Not quite. Separated. For a long time. They might as well get divorced."

"That's sad."

"I'm used to it."

"This is where I live." I pointed to Sea View, which didn't look particularly welcoming – a grey looming shape with only one light visible. All our summer guests had gone. There might be a few more at October half-term but after that we would be on our own until Easter. I couldn't wait.

"It's huge!"

I explained that we lived in only a small part of it and that the rest was used for guests.

"Does your bedroom look out over the sea?"

"No, I've got a view of next door's dustbins. We save the good rooms for the guests. Do you want to come in for a few minutes?" Mum wouldn't be pleased, I knew – it was after ten and I hadn't finished my homework. But she would have to be polite to Charity and I could deal with her recriminations later.

"No, I'd better get home. My dad doesn't like me staying out too late."

We stopped at the bus stop, a few yards further on. I wanted to tell her about my father and the accident that killed him. Partly, I suppose, to show I understood about losing a parent – so she would be able to tell me about her mother. But also because I wanted her to know me.

There was the worry, however, that the bus might arrive any time, and I didn't want to tell her only half the story. So we talked about school, comparing notes on the various teachers.

As the bus appeared, she said, "Joanne, I think you and I are going to be very good friends."

"I hope so. I'd like to be."

"And I believe that God is going to do great things among the Crabbies."

"Do you?"

"You've only got to look at Alan to see how much he wants the Spirit. Where there's longing like that, God always answers."

I wanted to warn her about Alan, tell her I didn't trust him. But it was too late – the bus had stopped and Charity was climbing aboard.

I waited until it had disappeared around the corner, veering inland from the cliff top, before I went inside.

Tom's journal, Thursday 15th September 1983

Interesting meeting tonight – much livelier than usual. Rather worrying, too. Of course it's always good to have someone new along, especially someone young. Just wish I could get rid of this nagging anxiety.

Tried to tell Pattie about it when I got home but she was in a huff because I was so late. If only she could understand. I'd much rather be home with her and the children than hanging about in a draughty meeting hall trying to calm Alan down. But it's my job and I don't have much choice. Why does she always have to see it as a personal affront?

I'll come back to Pattie later. For the moment, I need to sort out my thoughts about Charity Baker, our newcomer. A charming girl – warm, friendly and enthusiastic. Dear little Joanne could hardly believe her eyes. I do hope they make friends – Joanne has needed a girl her own age in Crabbies for so long.

So why am I so worried? Two things, I suppose. The first is her championing of the Special Blessing. Oh yes, it may be new and exciting to someone like Alan, but I'm old and cynical enough to have seen it all before. Something similar did the rounds when I was at Bible college.

I'm not saying there's anything wrong with a desire for a closer walk with God – I'm sure there isn't. But things can so quickly turn into gimmicks. Divisive gimmicks that split a band of believers into the haves and the have-nots – those who have received it and those who haven't. Those who have are seen as proud and gloating, puffed up with their own importance. Those who haven't come across as weak in faith, lacking adventure and heart, lukewarm in their love for God.

All Alan can see is the answer to his prayers – in the form of a beautiful young girl arriving out of the blue to lead us into a closer relationship with God. What could be more appealing?

Perhaps I am an old cynic and being far too hard on Alan – but the way he looked at Charity disturbed me. I shall have to keep an eye on all this.

Now Pattie. I must do something to close this deepening rift between us, but what? If she could bring herself to show a glimmer of interest in my work, it would help. While she bores

me rigid every tea-time telling me how badly things are going at work.

I try to understand, but what more can I do? I've suggested she look for another job. I know she would like to leave Castlehaven, but how can I, when this is my calling?

I'll see if she's still awake and wants to make love. Maybe it will help. It always used to.

Chapter 2

Louise banged the giant-size paint tin down on the meeting room floor. "Alan, you've gone and got two different shades of yellow."

"That can't be right. I bought them all in one batch. Dewhurst's DIY store had them on offer." Alan didn't look at his wife as he spoke, or at the cans of paint. He was struggling to set up a stepladder.

"This one's Misty Lemon and the other is Soft Primrose. Completely different."

A couple of weeks had passed since Charity's arrival at the Crabbies and we had become friends.

I'd already been allocated my paint, poured into a plastic container that bulged alarmingly when I lifted it, almost spilling over. Fortunately for my favourite jeans, my mother had insisted on giving me one of her ancient overalls, an unflattering flowery polyester garment that buttoned down the front and reached to mid-calf.

"Let's see." Tom came over, looking even more like a scarecrow than usual. It had been his idea to redecorate the meeting room. He'd managed to get nine Crabbies to give up their Saturday afternoon to come along and paint. There was a rumour that he'd brought cream cakes to reward us at the end. One of the boys, Mark, had spotted the boxes in the fridge.

Tom had already managed to get a splash of yellow on his cheek and a bit more in his hair. He wore a green t-shirt with the name of some long-ago pop festival on the front. It was daubed with paint of various colours.

"You're right, Louise. Alan – any chance of getting them exchanged?"

"The guy told me they were all the same." Alan's cheeks were red, his eyes starting to bulge. He hated being wrong.

"How about mixing them?" suggested Pattie. She was a foot shorter than her husband, Tom, and comfortably plump. She never seemed to worry what she looked like or what she wore. A full-time employee of the local council's housing department, she didn't take much part, as a rule, in Crabbie activities. I didn't know her very well but I liked the way she was always smiling.

“Tricky,” said Louise. “We’d need a huge container. Otherwise, if we’re not careful, we’ll end up with lots of different shades.” She turned to Alan. “Is it worth seeing if Dewhurst’s will take them back?”

“They won’t,” Alan replied. “It was a special deal. And they won’t have any more of either colour, you can bet.”

“I’ve got an idea,” said Charity, who was beside me, tugging at the bristles of her paintbrush as though trying to pull them out. “Let’s splash it on at random. The different yellows swirling together – it’ll look amazing.”

Mark pulled a face. “Sounds disgusting to me.”

“No, no – it’s an interesting suggestion,” said Tom. He put on his head one side. “Though I’m not convinced.”

“How about having the paler shade above the dado rail and the darker one below it?” said Louise. “Though I don’t really see why Dewhurst’s should get away with conning us.”

Tom put his head on one side. “That might just work. If you’re sure, Alan, that we can’t get them exchanged. What does everyone think?”

I liked Louise’s idea but I didn’t want to go against Charity, so I kept my mouth shut. The rest agreed to accept the proposal. Tom reallocated pots and containers of paint and we were finally ready to begin.

Charity was wearing a short blue cotton dress that had seen better days. Tom had assigned both of us upper sections of wall, probably because we were young and agile. This was unfortunate where Charity was concerned, as it gave those down below a clear view of her legs, almost to the top.

I don’t suppose Mrs Pinderfield, picking her way around the skirting board with a tiny brush, thought anything of it, but Alan, who kept coming down his ladder and admiring his handiwork, certainly did. I saw him looking up Charity’s skirt more than once and my disgust towards him deepened.

Louise, painting on the opposite wall, kept looking across at her husband. Was she keeping an eye on him? It was the kind of thing that had recently begun to fascinate me, although I had, as yet, no inkling of the pain of sexual jealousy.

I should have made the most of those last few carefree minutes.

Charity appeared to be wholly oblivious to Alan's attention. I wondered whether to say something – but what could I say? It would only have embarrassed her, and there was no real evidence of anything untoward.

Charity's paint, I noticed, was going on in streaks. She overloaded her brush and substantial globs kept dropping off it onto her clothes. It was just as well she was wearing an old dress. The smears on her exposed thighs could soon be scrubbed off as it was water-based emulsion. I pictured Charity at home in her bathroom (which I still hadn't seen), rubbing her upper leg with a flannel. She was the same golden colour all over. The image disturbed me.

"How do you get it so smooth?" she asked.

"I've done it before. You have to make sure you don't put it on too thick. Look, like this."

I showed her how to dip her brush a third of the way up the bristles and give it a twist against the top of the can to remove excess paint. Mum and Aunt Daisy had first roped me in for redecorating duties years before. Although I pretended to object and had considered demanding payment, I secretly enjoyed painting, especially with bright colours.

Charity observed me closely and tried the technique herself.

"That's better," I said. "Now, once it's on the wall, don't just leave it there. Smooth it out. A nice light touch. But don't try to go over what you've already done. It's half-dry already. You can give it a second coat later."

"How come you know so much?" she asked.

"I've got a mother who uses me as a child slave." This made her giggle. Charity always laughed at my jokes, however feeble. It was one of the things I loved about her.

Tom was on his way round the room, inspecting. "Good work," he said to both of us. I think he'd overheard our interchange. "That's much better now, Charity. You're both doing an excellent job. It's very good of you to give up your Saturday afternoon."

I saw him catch sight of Charity's thighs and give a quick frown. His eyes didn't linger. After a few words with Mrs Pinderfield, he crossed to the other side of the room.

After twenty minutes or so, Alan finished his patch and had no alternative but to move on. He was out of earshot now, leaving Charity and me free to talk.

We'd had a few conversations but so far I had discovered very little about her home life. I'd seen the outside of her flat, walking home with her a couple of times after school (half an hour out of my way but I didn't mind that). She'd apologised about not asking me inside. Her father often dozed in the afternoons, she said, after a late night meeting with colleagues, planning new amusement arcades on the South Bay down in Scarborough.

Their flat was on the second floor in a dank grey sixties block. It was a cheap, two-bedroomed property, rather surprising considering Mr Baker was a businessman who flew abroad for meetings. Perhaps his business was failing. I didn't like to ask.

While I was hunting for a tactful remark that would get Charity talking about her family, she said, "Joanne, have you thought any more about the Special Blessing? Whether you'd like to receive it?"

My brush-stroke faltered, scuffing a patch I'd painted earlier. This was the last thing I wanted to discuss. She'd told me a few days before that I should think about it hard. God wanted the best for His children and at the moment, she told me, I was making do with second-best.

How could I tell Charity I wasn't even sure I was still a true believer? – not since she had told me about her relationship with God. He, it appeared, was at least as important to her as her father, probably more so. She spoke of God the way other girls talked about their boyfriends – with intensity and passion, but also with a kind of matter-of-factness. He was someone she chatted with every day, and He spoke back.

"I'm not sure," I replied, trying to repair my brushwork. "I don't think I'm quite ready. I don't understand it properly."

"You don't need to understand it. Receiving the Spirit isn't like solving a maths problem. Think of it as accepting God's embrace. He is waiting to take you in His arms."

If she'd been anyone but Charity I'd have hated this. I'd have run a mile from Crabbies and never gone back, if I hadn't been so fascinated by her.

"But if I'm not a real Christian…" I heard myself say.

"Of course you are! You told me you gave your life to the Lord when you were a little girl."

"I thought I did. But I'm not sure now. It doesn't seem to work the way it does for you. I don't feel God beside me the way you do. He doesn't speak to me. Maybe I've been kidding myself."

I couldn't believe I'd said this. I took a quick look round, but no-one seemed to be paying attention. Thank God Alan hadn't heard.

"You can always make sure. You know, ask Jesus into your heart again, just in case."

"But that would mean…"

"What would it mean?"

It would mean telling God all sorts of things – not least the feelings for girls that had grown in me these last few months. My feelings for Charity.

"Oh… nothing."

"You can tell Him anything at all, you know."

"I'm not sure that's true."

Tom had happened to mention to me a few weeks earlier, just before Charity came, that one of his friends at Bible college had been gay. I didn't know why he'd told me. I was tempted to believe he might, by some magical process, have guessed about me. Whether or not that was true, his words had made me feel better.

I knew that a number of the Crabbies 'disapproved'. Alan, for one. Not that I cared what Alan thought. But there were others who shared his views, whose opinions I couldn't dismiss so easily. My mother was one. I wasn't sure about Aunt Daisy. And I wasn't entirely convinced that being gay was okay with God.

Charity gave me a look I could have sworn showed full knowledge of my thoughts. Her eyes held mine for several seconds. It was easy to believe she saw right inside me.

The surprising thing was, I didn't mind. I liked it. If she wanted to invade my brain, she was welcome. Unlike Alan.

"You can tell Him anything at all," she said. "God knows all our secrets already. We can never surprise Him."

"So what would I have to do?" She had told me on a previous occasion but I hadn't taken it in. I had a frightening mental image of tongues of flame, a sort of mini-bonfire, bursting through the ceiling and landing on my head.

"I could pray with you. There's nothing to stop you asking for the Spirit on your own, but it seems to work better if someone else is with you."

I pictured Charity in my bedroom. She'd already been there twice, while I helped her with some maths. I thought of my mother and Aunt Daisy downstairs.

"Does it make a noise?"

"What a funny question!"

We had both stopped painting. I was sitting on the flat top of the stepladder, cradling my tub of paint, stirring it with my brush. Charity had taken up the same posture and was doing the same thing. I don't know who had copied whom.

"It's just that if my mum heard any weird sounds she'd come barging in. It could be embarrassing."

"Why? Your mum's a Christian, isn't she? Maybe she would start wanting the Spirit herself."

I wriggled with discomfort, almost spilling my paint. I couldn't imagine anything more awkward, more excruciating. "No – she wouldn't understand. She's not like that. She's not into anything emotional. She hates it when people cry at meetings."

"It might be good for her – help her to release her grief."

I'd told Charity about my dad, about the bus crash that had killed him and seven nine-year-old girls. He'd been the driver.

I gripped my tub of paint harder. She didn't understand. Perhaps it came of not living with her own mother.

"It's not that my mother *can't* cry," I said. "She often does, when she thinks no-one can hear. But she can't do it in public – not even with Aunt Daisy and me. And she can't bear to hear anyone else cry."

"Is that since your dad died?" At least Charity was able to speak of my father's death in my presence. This was more than some people managed. And she didn't use the silly hushed voice that many did.

"I don't know. I can't remember what she was like before."

"Okay. Well – perhaps we can find a time when she's out. Sometimes when people receive the Spirit they yell with joy. Or speak in tongues, or sing, or even cry. A happy kind of crying."

I didn't like the sound of this. Or, rather, I liked the idea of Charity praying with me in my bedroom, perhaps touching my head – all her attention on me. But I was afraid of the rest.

"I need a bit longer to think about it."

I noticed Alan looking across at us. It was time to resume painting.

"That's up to you," said Charity, with a trace of hurt in her voice. Or perhaps I'd imagined it. "Just let me know, whenever you feel ready. But don't leave it too late. God is going to do great things among the Crabbies and I want you to be in on it from the start."

And, I realised, I wanted to be. Whatever Charity did, I wanted a part in it. It was my fear that there might be something in it that stopped me. Something true, something genuine that came from God. If I'd been able to dismiss it all as superstitious fancy, I might have gone along with it there and then. Any excuse to be close to Charity, to share moments of high emotion with her. But what if God was real – what if, when I asked for the Special Blessing, He answered me? That was too scary to contemplate.

Alan must have heard something – perhaps he'd been listening for a while. He came over, in the grubby grey overalls he used for his gardening job. Green stains on his behind.

Without giving me a glance, he said to Charity, "Sorry to butt in. But I heard you mention the Holy Spirit. The Special Blessing. I've been praying for it but nothing's happened. I wondered if you could help me?"

Charity, who hadn't seemed to like Alan much up to that point, jumped to attention as best she could, sitting on a stepladder with a paint pot on her lap. Some paint spilled onto her leg but she ignored it. Her eyes shone as she replied, "Alan, that's wonderful! I've been praying too – that someone in the Crabbies would start to want the Spirit. Would you like me to pray with you?"

That moment was my initiation into the pain of jealousy. The kind that never lets you go. I wanted to cry, No, no – you can't! You can't have Charity, she's mine. She's waiting for *me* to want the Spirit, not you…

But I couldn't say those things. I sat clutching my paint tub, something burning in my throat, down my gullet, all the way to my stomach. As though I'd swallowed the fire I'd imagined earlier, coming through the ceiling. I burned with fury at them both.

I looked at Charity, wanting her to rescue me. But she said to Alan, who was gazing at her as though she was Jesus, "It's no trouble. I'd really like to."

"Would you?" he whispered. "I'd appreciate it so much." He lowered his voice even further. "I've spoken to Tom but he doesn't understand. I suggested we called a meeting, all of us – a special prayer meeting to ask God for the Spirit. But he didn't agree. He thinks we should be cautious. That's the word he used – cautious."

Charity shook her head. "Cautious isn't a word the Spirit uses," she said, "and it's not a word Tom will use, when he is finally blessed."

She gazed at the ceiling for a moment as though seeing the Spirit-filled Tom there. "But it looks as though we'll have to wait for Tom. He's a doubter by nature. God will deal with him in His own good time. Meanwhile, those of us who recognise the work of the Spirit must press on."

I had to say something. "It sounds wrong to me, going against Tom."

They looked at me, both of them, as though I was about seven. Alan gave me an oily smile. "Joanne, God will work in your heart, too, in His own good time." He didn't waste any more attention on me, but turned back to Charity. "When can we do it?" he asked.

I could see Charity working out how it could be done. Obviously she couldn't invite herself into Alan's bedroom.

I looked round for Louise, but she was nowhere to be seen. Tom had left the room, too.

"I tell you what," Charity said. "We could stay behind for a while, after the painting. You and me."

"What – here?" said Alan.

"Why not? When the others have gone. You have a key, don't you, to lock up afterwards?"

"I do. But I'm not sure about Louise."

"She could stay, too. Does she want the Spirit?"

"No. I've tried to talk to her about it but she's not keen. A bit like Tom."

"Some believers are slower than others. When she sees the change in you, she'll come round."

"Do you think so?"

"Oh yes. I've seen it happen with lots of couples in Barnsley. It's often the man who gets it first."

I wanted to speak again, but couldn't find any words.

Alan said, "Louise is leaving early, to pick up the kids from her mother's. They'll stay for tea there. So if I stayed on, that would be fine. She needn't know."

Even Charity was doubtful now. "Shouldn't you tell her? It's a bit weird to go behind her back, isn't it?"

"Oh, I'm not going behind her back. I'll tell her later. When she sees the difference in me, I'll explain why."

Louise was back in the room now, over the other side, talking to Mrs Pinderfield and Mrs Pinderfield's sister, Miss Allen. I stared, willing Louise to look our way, to come over and join us. But it was almost as though she was making an effort to ignore her husband.

"Can I stay behind as well?" I asked.

Charity frowned. "I'm not sure that's a good idea. Receiving the Spirit is a very personal thing. You don't want someone there watching."

"But I want the Spirit, too."

"You told me just now that you weren't quite ready."

"I might be, when I see it happening to Alan."

Alan shook his head. "No, I'd rather it was just the two of us." He turned his eyes to me for a millisecond. "Your turn will come, Joanne. Keep praying, and God will show you when it's time to receive His Spirit."

That was when Charity should have stood up for me, but she didn't. I felt a new stab of pain, this time below my ribs. She didn't look at me but kept her eyes on Alan while they made a few more arrangements. The smell of paint would be off-putting in the hall, they agreed (for them or for the Spirit?) so they would do it in the kitchen.

Alan gave Charity a wink which could have been a leer. She responded with the sort of smile you'd give a boy with whom you'd just arranged a date.

Alan smoothed his overalls with his enormous brown hands and padded across to his own side of the room. His paint, I reflected, would be half dry and would scuff up when he tried to join the new patch with the old. But, I observed, he knew better than to attempt this. Instead he left a gap between the old and the new, to be filled in later. He was a professional handyman after all.

Charity said nothing, but started her own painting again. I was pleased to see that hers *did* scuff. The unevenness would show up, even when dry.

After a few minutes, when I was back in the rhythm of my own painting, I said, "I don't like the idea of you and Alan praying together behind Louise's back."

Charity seemed to have resumed friendly relations with me. Her voice was light as she said, "You make it sound as though we're doing something wrong. I'm only praying for him – we haven't arranged to have sex!"

"I didn't say you had."

'Well, then – why should Louise mind?"

"It just seems wrong."

She gave me a long look. "It's because you're not sure, isn't it? Because you're not quite ready for the Special Blessing, you don't want anyone else to have it?"

"Of course it's not that."

"It sounds like it to me. Don't worry, it's a natural reaction."

"Is it?"

"It shows that God is working in your heart. But it's not a race, you know. It doesn't matter if Alan gets the Spirit before you do."

"No, of course not. It's not that that bothers me. It's what I said – it seems wrong. And staying behind with a man, just you and him, isn't a good idea, is it?"

"Oh Joanne. You're not suggesting I can't trust Alan? That he might try to rape me or something?"

"No."

"You are, aren't you? That's what you're scared of." Charity rested her dripping brush on the top of her can and turned to look me in the face. "Joanne – Alan is hardly a stranger. He's the assistant pastor of the Crabbies. Do you think he'd be in a position like that if he couldn't be trusted?"

"Of course I don't think he's going to rape you." I kept my voice down, wishing Charity would do the same. "It's not that. But wouldn't it be better if someone else was here? I could stay in the hall while you two prayed in the kitchen. I could carry on with my painting."

"Watch us through the keyhole, more like."

"I wouldn't do that," I said, though I'd been planning to.

She shook her head. "No, it's a stupid idea. And as for telling Louise – well, I agree that would be better – but it's up to Alan. We can't interfere between the two of them."

I suppose it was the build-up of anger that made me do it. It was all too easy.

For some reason she came down her step-ladder. Perhaps to pay a visit to the loo. Anyway, she was on the bottom step when I gave my paint container a push.

The result was a yelp from Charity as the container caught her on the shoulder. I regretted hurting her, but not the fact that its contents spilled over her dress, her arms, her legs and her trainers. From the neck down she was yellow.

The 'accident' with the paint tub meant that Charity and Alan were unable to stay behind for their meeting, for their session in the kitchen.

Instead, Charity was given a thorough and painful scrubbing-down by Louise, helped by Mrs Pinderfield, who mewed and fretted as she tipped out long-neglected cupboards looking for vinegar, which she assured us would lift the paint gently from Charity's face.

Charity was crying – at first, I expect, from shock and then from the man-handling. "Let me go home, I'll get cleaned up there," she said after a few minutes, starting to calm down.

"No, we must get it off your face first," said Louise. "Some of it's near your eye – it could do some damage."

"I think I should call an ambulance," said Tom. "Just in case."

"No!" protested Charity. "I'll be fine – please just let me go home."

Did she guess it was deliberate? I kept trying to catch her eye but she wouldn't look at me. Perhaps she assumed it was an accident but was angry at my carelessness? I wanted to run, to be miles away from all of them. At the same time, I was worried about Charity.

After a few minutes of Louise rubbing and Charity squirming, Alan took charge. "Okay, I've decided. My car's outside. I'll drive Charity straight to casualty."

Tom moved his closed lips from side to side, uncertain. He wasn't the greatest of decision-makers.

"I'm not going to hospital," Charity said. "The paint's nowhere near my eye and I'm fine. Just let me go." She wriggled herself out of Louise's grasp and made for the door, but Alan grabbed her.

"Oh yes, you are. I'm sorry, but you're our responsibility while you're here. What's your father's number? – we need to let him know."

"He's in Leeds," said Charity. At last, she turned to me. "Joanne, stop them. Take me to your house instead."

"That's a good idea," I said, my brain beginning to work. "My mum's good at this sort of thing – she can clean Charity up."

But Alan, ignoring us, didn't release his hold.

"I need the car for picking up the kids," said Louise.

"Don't worry," said Tom. "I'll give you a lift."

I followed Alan, who was leaving, his hand on Charity's arm, pulling her. She resisted like an angry toddler, her face red with effort where it wasn't yellow with paint.

"Let me come to the hospital," I said.

"Yes, come with me, Joanne, please." Charity was beginning to realise she couldn't fight Alan.

"Thanks, Joanne – good idea. We'll tell your mother where you've gone," said Tom. Alan had to concede defeat, though I could tell he didn't want me there.

Chapter 3

"There's still a bit of paint in your hair," I told Charity.

"Never."

We were on my bed. Charity sat on the edge, looking at herself in the dressing-table mirror. I was kneeling behind her, pulling my wide-toothed comb through her tangled mass of hair. Its wispy extremities scattered the light from my bedside lamp like dust dancing in sunshine.

The trace of yellow was down among the roots. All other signs of Charity's baptism-by-paint had gone. A fortnight had passed since the incident. The hospital had cleaned her face and Alan had driven her to her father's flat.

"Hang on, I can probably get it out with the comb."

"Don't you dare pull my hair out," she said – not meaning it, not caring. She trusted me. She had no suspicion I'd tipped the paint on purpose. As the days passed I felt more and more guilty.

I abandoned my attempt to remove the offending clump of hair. "It'll come out when you next wash it."

She stretched her legs and arms in turn and gave an enormous yawn. "Use the brush again. I love the feeling of it."

I was happy to obey. We'd tried it the other way round – her brushing my hair – but it didn't have the same effect on either of us. For a start, there wasn't enough of my hair for it to be worth protracted brushing. A couple of flicks and it was smooth. Nor did it have the texture of hers – mine was thin and lank and prone to grease.

I hated my dull, straight mop as I hated my body in general. I made sure, in this position, that my reflection was obscured by Charity's. All I wanted to do was brush her glorious hair, wave after golden wave of it like the sea coming in.

"It's like God's love," she said at one point.

"How do you mean?"

"Your brushing. Over and over, again and again. That's the way He blesses us."

I tried to think of anything like that in my own experience. It wasn't easy. There were times when I'd almost believed God might love me. Sometimes when Tom spoke on a Sunday and made God sound fair, as though He had no favourites. But it was all in my head – I'd never felt it. And the more I saw, the more I was convinced He *did* have favourites.

"Joanne, have you thought any more about the Special Blessing?"

"I've told you. I'm not ready for it."

"Why not?"

Because I'm in love with you, Charity, can't you see? "Because I'm not a good enough Christian."

"All you need is a repentant heart. Throw yourself on God's mercy. We are all sinners."

"You don't understand."

"Look, Joanne – whatever you've done, God is willing to forgive you. As long as you are truly sorry."

"That's the trouble."

"You mean you're not sorry?" Her eyes, in the mirror, widened to popping point.

I was still brushing. Rhythmical, unceasing, more gently now. Aware of my heartbeat, of something new in my blood.

"No, I'm not sorry."

"Are you sure it's something sinful?"

Something in her eyes made me wonder if she guessed. No, I decided, it wasn't that. It was nothing more than friendship of the best kind – compassion, concern, the desire to understand. It would have to be enough.

I stopped brushing for a moment and let my hand with the brush fall onto the bedspread. She turned and looked at me and I saw her eyes were full of tears.

"What's the matter?"

"Nothing. I just want…"

"What do you want?"

"I want you to have the Spirit, like me. Then I'll be able to talk to you. You'll understand about spiritual things. Please, Joanne. Tell God you want to be sorry. I think that can sometimes be enough."

"Charity, please." I reached over for my box of tissues, pulled one out and offered it. She blew her nose hard.

"Joanne, I can feel the Spirit wanting to enter your heart."

"Can you?"

"Yes, He's here. Very close."

I believed her; there was something in the room with us. I was still frightened but suddenly I wanted this, whatever it was, more than anything.

It was almost dark outside. My window was open an inch or so and the draught from it was gritty, sandy and cold. I slid off the bed to go and close it.

"Leave it open a bit."

'Why?' Surely the Spirit wasn't a real, literal breath from heaven which needed an open window to get in? But I did what she said.

"Let's sit like this." She swung her legs round so she was sitting on the edge of bed again and patted the bedspread beside her. When I'd positioned myself, she said, "Shuffle up a bit." I did, until we were touching. Fear flashed through me, leaving behind it an electrical thrill.

"Let God have all your inner feelings, Joanne. Offer them up to Him."

I did, as best I could. I had a mental image of a tray full of objects, like the party game where you have to remember as many as you can. Each object was one of my inner feelings. At the centre was an angel-shaped brass doll which gleamed the colour of Charity's hair.

"Okay, that's good."

How did she know what I was doing?

"Now I'm going to pray," she continued. "I may speak in English or it may be in a tongue. Don't be afraid."

I'd heard Charity pray in tongues before, but this was much more personal, like being invited into one of her dreams.

"Yes, please pray in tongues."

"All right. I expect I will. But you can't make yourself do it – you have to take it as it comes."

She started. Her words tumbled out like light from a firework, raining sharp and silver and leaving a blurry afterglow. Low-pitched and foreign-sounding, with glottal stops and gradations of tone unheard in English. Yet somehow familiar, or at least recognisable, as though I had once known them, perhaps as a small child. Like the Beethoven sonatas Aunt Daisy played on her piano, where if you listened hard you could catch the composer's thoughts, without ever being quite sure you'd heard him right. You were thrilled but also guilty, listening in, as though you'd overheard a private conversation. This was a conversation between Charity and God and they were talking about me. I was the centre of their world, like a baby fussed over by its parents.

I thought, this isn't right, I don't deserve this. I'm Joanne, fourteen, no childhood cuteness left – awkward and spotty and undesired.

Charity's voice went up a tone or two, became urgent. Her language had switched, I realised, to English.

"Dear God, my beloved sister awaits your Holy Spirit."

I did await Him, she was right. And I no longer had any doubts that He was going to come. My nerves spat static. I couldn't hold in my longing, though its object was no longer clear. Charity, the Holy Spirit, something inside me I couldn't name. I bowed my head, eyes tightly shut against the light that was suddenly overwhelming – the fierce green light I imagined a newborn baby might see.

All the time, I was aware of Charity's hand on my head, as though to soothe a fractious toddler.

Some organ inside me expanded as though it would burst out of my skin. But there was no discomfort. It felt like a natural process, a sense of acute readiness for what was to come. A tickling sensation low in my abdomen – my uterus? A deep itch inviting me to poke it with a pencil, as you might try to remove wax from your ear, with caution, aware of the danger. Not quite sexual, closer to visceral.

"Joanne…" Charity's voice was a whisper, holding something that all at once felt forbidden and unwholesome. I kept my eyes firmly shut, sensing an intruder in the room I didn't want to see.

"No need to be afraid. The Spirit is very near."

I started shaking – more frightened in that instant than I'd ever been. Of what? I didn't know, but it was real and I still didn't dare open my eyes.

"It's okay. Open up, let the Spirit come in. Don't try to stop Him."

My body shuddered – its lower half taken up by some concern that had by-passed my brain. Shuddered itself into a relief like sneezing, over and over, or plunging into the icy Castlehaven sea in a May heat-wave. While my brain wrestled with its terror, my body pulsated until the expanding balloon in my abdomen burst. There was, I thought, the sound of an explosion, the smell of scorching hair mixed with some flowery woodland scent that was also familiar but I couldn't place. There was dampness, as though I'd wet myself. Or was it blood pouring out from below? If so, I reasoned, I'd die, and very soon. Perhaps this *was* death and I would see my father.

There was no fear now, nor any hint of embarrassment. I'd forgotten Charity, had no sense of her presence. Didn't need her, it seemed, for these few moments.

"Holy Spirit, I love You," someone said. Was it me?

It must have been me, because Charity said, "Joanne – welcome to the world of the Special Blessing. Now you know what it is to be touched by God's power. Open your mouth, let His praise flow out of you."

But I didn't, it seemed, have any words.

Who was lifting my hair and letting it drop back against my cheek, sending tiny waves of pleasure down my neck, out along my shoulders, a tickling, tingling flicker of current trickling along to my fingertips and deep into my chest? God or Charity or both at once? Had the Spirit come to me or was it simply my body responding to her touch?

"Wow!" said Charity after a few minutes. "That was quite something."

I wriggled, trying to discover whether my pants were wet. It was important to say the right thing. Not to give anything away, in case I'd got it wrong - in case it hadn't been the Spirit at all.

I played dumb. "That was the Spirit, wasn't it?"

She gave a little snorting laugh. I noticed her cheeks were pink. "Of course it was. What else could it be? Joanne, you are well and truly baptised. I wonder which gifts you'll have?"

I couldn't dispel the picture that always came to mind of a stack of presents wrapped in birthday paper.

"Does everyone have gifts?"

She frowned for a moment. "I think so. Some are more visible than others. There's one called 'knowledge' – a kind of wisdom. Deep understanding of things. That could be you."

"Can't I have prophecy or tongues?"

"You'll have to wait and see. I didn't hear you speak in tongues, so perhaps that one's not for you."

All of a sudden, I thought of Alan. I'd been fretting since the day of the painting that he and Charity would get together and she would pray the Spirit down on him. Or something.

"Alan hasn't had it yet, has he?"

She laughed. "No, you've beaten him to it. We've been trying to get together for the past two weeks but something always happens – he has to go and pick up his kids or something."

Triumph. "But why does it have to be you? Can't he get the Spirit from someone else?"

"You don't 'get' the Spirit from someone – it's not like catching a cold. The person with you is just a kind of channel, someone to pray."

"Well, however it works, can't someone else pray with him?"

"There isn't anyone else, not in the Crabbies. Tom would be the obvious person, but he's resistant."

"Resistant? You just said it wasn't like catching a cold."

"Resistant means – well, it means you block the Spirit's work for some reason."

"You make it sound like antibiotics or something."

"Stop trying to be clever, Joanne. The Spirit doesn't respect human wisdom."

"You mean like maths and science?"

"He soars far above them."

"I thought God made the universe. He must know some maths." I was teasing Charity, loving it. Suddenly sure-footed, watching her stumble.

Her lips curled into the beginning of a smile. "Perhaps he relies on a special angel with a maths A-level."

"That must be it…"

We exploded simultaneously into giggles, the room filling up with them like bubbles in a tank. They were in my head, too, giving my thoughts a carefree lightness. The awkwardness I'd felt towards Charity since the paint incident had gone. My feelings for her were no longer a matter of shame.

"Charity – I love you," I heard myself say, my voice unusually firm and clear.

She didn't reply but she pulled me towards her, my head against her chest, inhaling the scent I had failed to recognise earlier, that of Charity herself.

"I've got something very exciting to share with you all," said Alan as the collection plate was passed around. "Could I have just a few minutes, Tom?"

We were nearing the end of the Crabbies' Sunday service, a week or so after my Special Blessing. It was a crisp morning in late October, with autumn-tinted sunshine dripping into the newly-painted hall, highlighting the uneven patches and the bits we'd missed.

Tom looked at his watch, gave a little frown and then a nod. "Five minutes, Alan, no more. The crèche helpers don't like it if we overrun."

Alan bounded up to the front and leapt onto the shallow wooden dais, almost colliding with Tom, who dived out of the way. Alan's teeth looked bigger and more dazzling white than ever, his thick black hair luxuriant, a hint of stubble on his face. Some needle in me hovered between attraction and repulsion (no intermediate position was, it seemed, available), then swung to the latter. His eyes shone, black as his hair. Heathcliff, I thought (we'd just read *Wuthering Heights* at school). I tried to imagine how the others saw him. Louise, his wife – did she still fancy him? Did Charity?

Charity had appeared to accept my declaration of love for her. But it wasn't at all clear how she felt about me. She hadn't said she loved me, too, yet she liked me to touch her, to brush and stroke her hair. We'd even had a gentle kiss or two.

As Alan started to tell us about his latest experience with the Lord, I wrestled once again with the issue of Charity's sexuality. Was she or was she not gay? The idea of her being attracted to Alan was like bindweed twisting itself round my abdomen. No, something more like barbed wire, burning hot.

I tried to distract myself, to focus on Alan's words.

"As some of you will know, last week I went with my family to the Harvest-time Christian Festival in Filey. Our Lord did some great works there, brothers and sisters – healings, conversions and outpourings of the Spirit. Prophecies were given and tongues were heard. I'm pleased to tell you that I plucked up courage and went forward to ask for the Special Blessing."

In spite of myself, I couldn't resist a quick glance at Tom. He was standing to the side of Alan, a few feet away. His body contorted into a shudder, which he tried to hide as he stepped back, folded his arms and gave his head a little shake.

Alan continued. "Anyway, to cut a long story short, the Lord saw fit to bless me with the gift of His Spirit. After weeks of waiting and longing I am now fully baptised."

A pause – did he expect us to applaud or something? There was silence. Tom had himself under control now and didn't react at all. Not outwardly.

No-one but Charity knew about my baptism, though my mother suspected something, I could tell. She'd been giving me funny looks ever since the day it happened. Had she heard sounds from my bedroom? Or perhaps I simply looked happier – I certainly felt it.

Alan waited a few seconds, for whatever audience response he was expecting, then gave up and pressed on. "I wanted to share this with you all because I sense a growing desire in this fellowship for a new touch of God's Spirit. Ever since young Charity here came to tell us what our Lord had in store for us – what treasures we were missing."

He gave Charity an oily grin at this point. I couldn't bring myself to look at her reaction.

"And I can tell you now, my friends, how much my life has changed. Prayer is no longer a chore! I wake up in the morning bubbling over with praise. I find myself getting up before six to spend time communing with my Father. The Bible has come alive to me in a brilliant new way. Every verse seems like a personal message to me from God."

Alan paused again and Tom stepped towards him, signalling that his time was up. But Alan refused to catch his eye and resumed. "I've been late starting work the last few days, because my prayer time went on too long. I just couldn't stop. Just as well I'm my own boss."

There was a titter of laughter at this point. I tried to see Louise's face but it was hidden. She slumped in her seat as though bored. No doubt she'd heard this many times at home.

"So, dear brothers and sisters, let me recommend – if I'm permitted to use such a word – let me recommend fully to you the Special Blessing. It will transform your walk with God. And all you need in order to receive it is a deep longing and a pure heart. That's all God asks of you –"

"Here, hang on a bit, Alan," interrupted Tom. "That doesn't sound quite right. None of us has a pure heart – we're all sinners in need of God's forgiveness. If God had to wait for us to be good…"

Alan beamed round his audience, as though Tom was his stooge and had just supplied the feed-line for his next joke. "Of course, of course. I don't dispute that for a second. But did I say we had to purify our hearts all on our own? No – of course not. Only God can supply us with the pure heart and the deep longing we need, in order to receive His Spirit. But let me tell you, my friends – I detect hearts made ready by the Lord and a fervent desire in this fellowship for the coming of the Spirit. Just ask Him – that's all that's needed. Just –"

"All right," said Tom. "Thanks, Alan, I –"

"One more thing, dear brother. Just a few more seconds, please. Before I stand down I want to express my deepest gratitude not only to our Lord but also to our dear sister here – Charity Baker. The delightful young girl who appeared for the first time a few weeks ago at one of our meetings to tell us about the Spirit. Who awoke me from my stupor and set me on a new path of fellowship with God. A young woman who herself burns with the love of God and the desire to do His will. Charity!"

I gave her a sideways glance. She was gazing at one of the windows and didn't appear, at first, to have heard. Then she gave a little twitch and her cheeks reddened. But she didn't meet Alan's adoring gaze.

"Right – thank you, Alan." Tom had now had more than enough. "Time for the closing hymn. If anyone wants to talk to me afterwards about any of this, you're very welcome. Just ask. Now let's sing *Dear Lord and Father of Mankind*."

I wondered why Tom had changed the hymn from the number on the service sheet, but as we sang the second line *Forgive our foolish ways* I guessed. There was no doubt that Tom was uncomfortable with all of this.

Before the final chord had died away from Mrs Pinderfield's electronic organ, Alan was scurrying down the central gap. He squeezed past several worshippers to reach Charity. Arms out, he invited her to hug him, but she didn't respond. Her face was still red.

"Charity – aren't you pleased I've had the Special Blessing?"

"Yes, it's great."

"I've had it, too," I told Alan, but he didn't appear to hear me.

"Yes, she has," said Charity. "Isn't that good? Tell him, Joanne, how it happened."

I felt awkward in the face of Alan's obvious lack of interest, but managed to say, "Charity prayed for me and I got it."

Alan finally registered my presence. "You got *Him*," he corrected. "Or, rather, you *received* Him. The Holy Spirit is a person – the Third Person of the Trinity."

"I think Joanne may have the gift of knowledge," said Charity, pushing her chair back to make more room for Alan.

Alan gave me a doubtful glance. "We have to be very careful that the gifts are genuine," he said. "It's so easy to be deluded. The devil is always on the prowl, trying to deceive us."

Charity gazed at him, her eyes cool and level. "Joanne isn't deluded. What gift did you receive, Alan?"

"Oh, I spoke in tongues, of course. For an hour or more on end. It was sheer ecstasy. Louise couldn't tear me away. Did God bless you with tongues, Joanne?"

"Only English," I said.

"Your own language hardly counts as a tongue."

"Of course English is a tongue," I said.

"No, it's not. The point of tongues is that you speak in a language you don't understand. One that only God and His angels understand. Except that He may give someone the gift of interpretation – to translate what has been said."

"I like to be in control of what I'm saying." I was worried by what Charity had said about my having the gift of knowledge. It sounded alarming and I wasn't sure I wanted it.

"Did Louise receive the Spirit, too?" asked Charity.

Louise had picked up Alice and David from Sunday School and crèche and was making her way towards us, temporarily waylaid by conversation with Mr Streatfield

"Not yet," said Alan, dropping his voice. "She's not ready – God hasn't put the desire in her heart."

Louise reached us, looking, I thought, exhausted. Her eyes were red-rimmed, her cheeks puffy. Even standing, she hadn't lost the weary, slumped demeanour she'd had while seated.

"Are you all right?" I asked her.

"I'm exhausted. David hardly slept at Filey. He's teething. Kept us awake every night with his crying. And now I've got a cold."

"I've got a cold, too," said Alice. "Listen, I can blow my nose like Daddy." She demonstrated.

Smiling, Charity said, "Well done, Alice."

I grinned, too.

"Alice, you must use a tissue. And try to be more ladylike. A gentle blow," said Louise.

"Well, we must get on," said Alan.

"Hope you feel better soon," I said to Louise.

Alan turned back to us. "What Louise needs is a good dose of the Holy Spirit – to bring healing, along with everything else. Healing from minor ailments as well as major ones. Healing from a fretful, discontented heart."

I was too stunned to speak. Charity said, "That's a bit unfair, Alan. No-one can help having a cold."

"Oh, don't worry about me, I'll be better soon," said Louise. "Come on, let's get home. David needs a feed and a nap."

"You'll be a different person, when you receive the Spirit," Alan told her. "Instead of complaining all the time, you'll be unable to stop praising the Lord. It's like a foretaste of heaven. Charity will confirm that, won't you?"

"The Spirit doesn't stop you getting colds."

"No, but your whole attitude towards them is different."

"I don't want the Spirit," said Louise. "I've no wish to lose control and shriek the place down. One in the family is more than enough."

"Can we go home now?" asked Alice.

"I love that sense of losing control," said Alan. "That's what it's all about. Lost in wonder, love and praise – just like the hymn says. Don't you love that feeling, Charity?"

Charity was not listening – she was examining the grubby embroidered handkerchief Alice had found in her coat pocket and was displaying with pride.

"I'd rather stay in control, too," I said.

Alan looked at me. "It's always possible, Joanne, that you didn't receive the whole experience. Perhaps you were blocking the full extent of the Spirit's power. Is there something you're hanging onto, some unconfessed sin?"

"No."

"Take time to ask the Lord, make sure. The human heart is very devious."

"Come on," said Louise. "Alice, stop pestering. We're going home now. I'm sure Joanne had the experience just as much as you did, Alan."

As they left, Alan shot a glance back at me. I didn't quite catch what he muttered, but it contained the words, "Be careful."

"Don't let him get to you," said Charity. "He's a bit of an idiot but his heart's in the right place. There were people in the Barnsley Fellowship like him. He loves the Lord and that's all that matters really."

"I hate him," I said. "I know I shouldn't, but I do."

Tom's journal, Sunday 23rd October 1983

Alan has finally had it – the Special Blessing. And, as I might have expected, he is overflowing with it.

What's wrong with me, Lord? Alan is my friend and colleague – I've always admired and respected him. Why does every word he says now make me cringe?

I suppose part of it was seeing Louise's face. Can Alan's experience be genuine, when it makes his wife so unhappy?

I should remember that my own wife is not happy with a lot of what I do. That's a sobering thought.

I tried to talk to him after the service this morning. To warn him of the kind of things that can happen. But he won't listen. All he can talk about is his new relationship with God. And who am I to criticise him? Perhaps if my own faith were stronger, Crabbies would be healthy and thriving and not about to plunge into this mess?

I must try to speak to Louise on her own – find out what's making her so unhappy. I suspect it's the implicit criticism from Alan – that she is somehow a lesser Christian because she hasn't received this Blessing. Perhaps it's more than implicit – he may be putting pressure on her at home to seek it, whether or not she wants to. Who knows what he says to her in the privacy of their own home. He's already rubbished my faith – made me feel I'm letting the Crabbies down. I believe he's wrong, but I still feel wounded. How must poor Louise feel?

Please give me wisdom, Father – I need it badly.

Chapter 4

"Do you ever have nightmares?" Charity asked me.

It was my first visit to her home. She'd asked me there after school, promising to cook me a meal. Her father was away on a business trip for a few days. I couldn't imagine being left on my own while my mother and Aunt Daisy went away, though the idea was appealing.

Their flat was small, gloomy and needed a hoovering.

"Every now and then," I replied to her question.

"What's your worst one?"

We were in the living room, Charity on a battered old sofa and me on an ancient armchair that was leaking its stuffing. She had drawn the curtains against what remained of the evening dusk. There was no light on and the TV hummed and flickered to itself in the corner.

The place was cold and Charity had offered me a crocheted blanket, which I wrapped round myself like an old lady. She did the same thing, except her covering was an unzipped navy blue sleeping bag. Even in those surroundings she looked lovely, her hair pulled out of its school-day pony tail, falling messily over her shoulders, catching glimmers of light from the TV screen.

I pretended to think for a few moments, though I didn't really need to. "The bus crash where my dad died. I dream about it quite a lot, or I used to. I haven't so much, lately."

"You weren't in it, were you?"

"No. But I've got memories of it as though I was. I imagined it so clearly at the time, when they told me. It's like I'm one of the girls, trapped between the seats, with blood running along the floor."

"That's awful. Worse than mine, in a way, because it's based on something real."

"What's yours?"

"It's a bit childish. I should have grown out of it by now."

I wished we were sitting closer. "Tell me."

"Promise not to laugh."

"I promise."

With her eyes on the TV screen, which was showing *Tom and Jerry*, she said, "I'm lying in bed, sort of waiting. Then the door creaks open."

I pulled the blanket up to my chest. "And?"

"Sometimes it stops there and doesn't come in. I'm left shivering but I'm okay. It takes a while to go back to sleep."

I waited.

"But other times it doesn't stop. It comes right into my room."

Part of me wanted to be entertained by Charity's fear. A bigger part shrank from it. I would have changed the subject if I could.

"What kind of thing is it?"

"I call it the Terror by Night. It's a cross between a man and a monster. It's too dark to see what it looks like, but it glows a bit."

"Like a ghost?"

"Not really. It's too warm for a ghost. And too heavy."

"Warm and heavy?"

"Yes."

"What does it do?"

Charity's face was white now, staring at me out of the near-darkness. This wasn't a game for her, I realised – she was genuinely frightened.

"Does it touch you?"

"I don't think I can say."

'Tell me.' My voice sounded like my mother's when I was ill or upset as a small child.

"It gets into my bed. Lies on top of me. Squashes the breath out of me. Sort of touches me – you know…"

I couldn't help asking. "Touches you where?"

"You know."

"You mean, like…?"

"Yes. I think so. Everything goes into a sort of blur. The worst is over by then. I wake up and it's just me there shivering. It never actually attacks me, not properly."

"It sounds horrible."

"The worst part is lying there waiting for my door to creak. Sometimes I just know when it's going to. When I'm going to have the dream, I mean."

"Have you told anyone?"

"Not before now. It's not the kind of thing I can tell my dad."

"Why not?"

"He wouldn't understand. You can't say that sort of thing to my dad. He'd – oh, I don't know. He'd be angry. Find some way to make it my fault. Blame me for watching too much TV."

I was silent, taking in what it must be like not to have a parent you could tell your nightmares to.

"Sorry to frighten you," she said.

"You haven't. Well, perhaps a bit."

"I don't get it very often, now. Only once since we came to Castlehaven. I've got a special prayer I wrote out. If I read it aloud before I go to sleep I don't get the dream. But it only works if I get the words exactly right."

"Are you sure?"

"Of course I'm sure. If I miss a word out I get the dream. That time I got it, a couple of weeks ago, was because I fell asleep half way through the prayer. I make sure I read it sitting up now, with the main light on."

"But why would God punish you like that, for getting a word wrong?"

"I don't know. Maybe He's teaching me to be careful – not to take Him for granted."

"But that's so mean."

"God isn't mean. We can't always understand His ways, that's all. He is so far above us."

"Maybe so – but giving someone a horrible dream because they miss a word out. And at night, when you're tired. I don't think God is like that."

"Well, that's what happens. And the prayer must work, because I haven't got it wrong since and I haven't had the dream."

"How does it go, your prayer?"

"I don't like to say it at other times, in case it breaks the power. I've got it hidden inside my pillowcase. I have to remember to take it out when I wash my sheets."

I eased myself from my warm nest and crossed the room to the sofa. "Budge up, let me sit next to you."

Charity shifted along and I sat beside her, one arm round her back. "You must miss your mum so much."

"I miss her how she used to be, before she became an alcoholic. She was awful the year before she went away. I was kind of glad she went."

"Do you hear from her?"

"Birthday and Christmas cards. If I'm lucky."

"It must be worse, in a way, than me losing my dad."

"How?" She wriggled up closer.

"Because my dad couldn't help it. He didn't choose to leave us."

"My mum couldn't help it. She didn't choose to be an alcoholic."

"I suppose not. Sorry. But I can't understand why she doesn't even phone you."

"It's all to do with her and Dad. The break-up was pretty nasty. I don't know much about it. I'm sure she would have taken me if she could. If she'd been able to look after me. She does love me, I know that."

"Did your mum go to the Barnsley church?"

"Yes – she was in the choir. She's got a lovely singing voice. And she's very beautiful."

"Like you."

"More than me. Slimmer. Graceful and elegant. Her nose is a better shape."

"She can't be more beautiful than you."

"Don't be daft."

But I knew she was pleased.

"Maybe you could write me out a copy of your prayer?" I said. "Then I could pray it every night as well."

"To stop you getting your nightmare, you mean, about the crash?'

"No, I mean I could pray it for you. As a kind of back-up. If you miss out a word, then mine will be there for God to fall back on."

Her body tensed against me – doubting. "I'm not sure that would work. But thanks for the offer."

I made up my mind to pray for her every night, anyway, using my own words. The God I knew wouldn't fail to protect her.

Later, as we ate baked beans and scrambled egg, prepared by Charity, I thought of something.

"Why don't you talk to Tom about your dream?"

"Tom? What's it got to do with him?"

"Nothing, really – but he's so good to talk to. He helped me when my dad died. I used to meet him once a week. He understood much better than anyone else."

"I can't tell Tom about something like that."

"Louise, then? Or Pattie?"

"I don't need to tell anyone. It's embarrassing. Don't you dare mention it to anyone."

"Of course I won't."

We finished our meal in silence. The egg had dried out and was burnt in places. I noticed she'd given herself the worst bits.

"What were you and Charity doing upstairs?" my mother asked me one evening a week or two later. Charity had come home from school with me and stayed for a couple of hours.

"Homework," I said. "I was explaining some maths to her. She finds it difficult. And she read through my English essay and gave me some ideas."

"It's good that you can help each other," said Aunt Daisy.

We were at the table, finishing our fish and chips. I'd wanted Charity to stay, but she'd said her father expected her home.

"You were making a lot of noise up there," said Mum.

I tried not to blush, but she gave me a curious look. Charity and I had been praying together and she had cried out in tongues a few times, despite my shushing her. That sort of thing could never be explained to my mother. She'd been a member of the Crabbies years ago, but hadn't been to a meeting since my father died. She'd told me more than once that she didn't hold with all the 'Spirit stuff'.

"We were laughing at something."

"Your maths was funny, was it?"

"Let her be, Jean," said Aunt Daisy. "You know what girls are like – they'll always find something to giggle about. You must remember being that age yourself."

"I'm not sure I do."

I was grateful to Aunt Daisy for rescuing me, but the guilt was still there. Perhaps Charity's prayers had been sincere, but the whole point of it, as far as I was concerned, was to be close to her. Beside her on the bed, propped against the pillows touching all along our legs, my arm round her back or vice versa. The Holy Spirit, if He was there at all, was an optional extra from my perspective.

"I've got one of my headaches coming on," said Mum. She was trailing a leftover chip across the pool of vinegar on her plate. My mother's headaches often coincided with some real or assumed misdemeanour of mine. I felt another pang of guilt.

"Why don't you go and lie down?" said Aunt Daisy. "Joanne and I will do the clearing up."

Mum ignored her. "I wish we knew a bit more about Charity's background. You're spending such a lot of time with her."

"What do you mean, her background?" I asked.

"Where she comes from. I don't mean Barnsley. I mean her family. What sort of people they are."

"I've met her dad. He's okay. And you know her mum lives in France."

"Yes, that's one of the things that bothers me. How can a woman abandon her daughter like that?"

"I told you. She's an alcoholic. She went to France to be near her sister."

"But how did she get into that state in the first place? I thought they were supposed to be a Christian family."

"I don't know. I'm sure she couldn't help it."

"Well, it seems an odd thing to me. A terrible thing – a young girl left without a mother. And her father away so much."

"Charity's used to it. She's good at looking after herself."

"She shouldn't have to."

Aunt Daisy got up and began to pile up the plates. "It takes all sorts, Jean. Look at it this way – it's good for Charity that she's made friends with Joanne. A sensible girl like Joanne will be good for her."

"Yes, but will she be good for Joanne?"

I scraped back my chair and scrunched the fish and chip papers into a ball. "She's a great friend," I said. "The best I've ever had. Don't you dare try to split us up."

"All I meant," said Mum, hand to her forehead, "is that you shouldn't get too close. Don't neglect your other friends for her. I don't want to see you let down."

"She won't let me down."

"And don't let her draw you into all this crazy Holy Spirit stuff. I've heard what goes on at the church meetings these days, from Mrs Pinderfield. I don't know why Tom allows it. I always thought he had his head screwed on."

"He does."

"Then why is he encouraging all this yelling and shrieking and prancing around in the middle of a service?"

"He's not. It's not him – it's more Alan who's into all that stuff."

"But Tom's letting him do it?"

"I don't think he's too keen."

"He should put a stop to it once and for all."

"Don't fret, Jean, it'll all work itself out," said Aunt Daisy. "I really think you should take a paracetamol and lie down. Go and watch *Coronation Street*."

My mother got herself a glass of water and took it through to the living room. Aunt Daisy began washing plates and I picked up the tea towel to dry them.

Once the TV was blaring, Aunt Daisy said, "You know, I think Charity is a really nice girl."

"Of course she is. It's just Mum – you know what she's like."

"She worries about you." Aunt Daisy stopped in the middle of scrubbing a plate, holding it vertically on the edge of the washing up bowl, watching the suds run down.

"She doesn't need to.

"She's your mother, it's natural. And she's a bit – well, traditional, in her views."

"You mean she's a snob?"

Aunt Daisy resumed activity, placing the plate in the drying rack. I left it there to drain for a few moments before picking it up to dry.

"No, I don't mean that. I mean she doesn't like change. Changes in the way people worship, or the way they live their lives."

"How do you mean?"

She turned to look at me. She was eight years older than my mother and her hair was almost fully grey. It had once been auburn and a few reddish streaks remained. She had never been married – had never even had a boyfriend, as far as I knew. When I asked her for details she had always refused to say. I'd decided she had a sad secret in her past – perhaps a long-ago fiancé who had died.

"Your mother will only be happy if you live a conventional life. Or she thinks she will. You may have to prove her wrong."

I froze, plate clasped to my chest, suddenly afraid that Aunt Daisy had guessed something about me.

"Whatever happens, you must live your life as you want to. Don't let anyone, least of all your mother, stop you."

"I won't." I felt as though I was making a promise.

"Good. But your mother is right in one respect. You must learn to take care. And you must learn to decide for yourself what's good and bad. What's worth pursuing and what isn't. The Crabbies, for example. Only you can decide."

"You mean I shouldn't go to Crabbies?"

Aunt Daisy sighed as she slid another plate into the sink. "No, I don't mean that. I mean, don't just accept what people say. You're an intelligent girl – think it through for yourself. All this Spirit business – is it really what you want?"

"I think it is. It gives me a good feeling. I feel closer to God and to… other people."

"Which other people?"

"The other Crabbies."

"Do you want to feel closer to them? Most of them are twice your age."

"That's the whole idea – Christian fellowship. And going to Crabbies makes me feel less, you know – ashamed."

"What would you be ashamed of?"

"Oh, just in general. Of being a sinner and all that."

Her lips pursed, she shook her head. "You're no sinner. Who's been putting those ideas into your head? Not that I need to ask…"

"We're all sinners, Auntie."

She shook her head again as she pulled the plug out of the sink and forced the debris down the plughole with her fingers. "I never believed any of that. My experience is that nine people out of ten do their best to live decent lives. Those that go wrong, it's usually their parents to blame. Of course there are always a few bad eggs."

"I can't explain it as well as Tom. Or Charity – you should talk to her. Jesus had to die, to blot out our sins and reconcile us with God."

"Well, it's your choice, what you believe. All I'm saying is, don't leave that brain of yours – the one you use for your schoolwork – at the door of the church hall. Charity may be a lovely girl but she's as gullible as the next person. And as for Alan – I'm in agreement with your mother on him. He may be one of the bad eggs I was talking about."

I dried the last plate and hung the tea towel on its hook. "He just gets a bit carried away. Tom trusts him, so he must be all right."

"I feel sorry for his wife – what's her name?"

"Louise."

"I've seen her pushing the pram up the High Street, meeting the little girl from school. She hasn't looked right for a while – Louise, I mean. I don't know what she sees in Alan."

"I like Louise."

"But not as much as you like Charity?"

Was she trying to catch me out? "Of course not. Charity is my own age. More or less."

"Joanne – remember what your mother said. Be careful. You could get hurt here."

"Charity's not going to hurt me."

"I'm not saying she will. Not deliberately."

"Aunt Daisy?"

"What?"

"I just wondered if you…?"

"If I what?" She turned from rinsing her hands and gave me a long thoughtful stare, her grey eyes unblinking.

"Nothing."

"Remember, too, what I just said. You must find your own way through life. No-one else can tell you what to do."

"Did you?"

"Did I what?" Her eyes flickered with what could have been amusement.

"Do what you just said. Find your own way."

She sighed, looked down at her slippers. "Not exactly. I tried, got bitten, gave up. Perhaps it was harder in those days. But that's no excuse. Maybe I was just a coward."

I waited for her to tell me more, but she looked up to the window, her eyes following the raindrops as they scurried down.

"I'd been thinking I might give up on Crabbies. Before Charity came. A lot of it didn't make sense any more."

"But Charity changed your mind?"

"She brings it all alive. When I'm with her I can almost see God. And the Holy Spirit."

"You don't think you're getting a bit confused? Between two kinds of love?"

"No. Of course not. Anyway, with Charity and me it's not love, it's friendship."

"If you say so."

"They're different things."

"Perhaps. But you and I are not so different, Joanne. I may understand better than you think."

"I don't know what you mean."

"No? Well, that's fine. I'll show you some photos sometime, if you like. Photos of me and someone very special, when I was young. If you'd like that."

I made for the door, desperate to hide my red face. "Okay, that would be good. I've got to do my homework now." And I fled upstairs.

As I tried without success to focus on my maths, I wondered how I'd ever face Aunt Daisy again. What had or had not been said? I couldn't bear to think about it for the moment – it was all much too embarrassing and painful.

"What's that book in the fireplace?" I asked Louise as she placed a glass of cola on the coffee table beside me.

David was on my lap, playing a game that involved touching my nose with his finger and then touching his own, making his pudgy, serious little face open up into a chuckle. Alice sat by my feet, drawing with a felt tip pen on sheets of wallpaper, producing what she called 'Barbie ladies', to be cut out for one of her games.

It was Saturday afternoon and Louise had phoned to ask me round for tea. Alan was out all day on a patio construction and wouldn't be back until late. She was fed up, she said, with the company of young children. I was bored, too, since Charity had gone to Barnsley for the weekend to stay with some old friends, so I agreed with enthusiasm.

Louise followed my gaze to the paperback – or the remains of one – lying in the tiled hearth in front of the gas fire. Its cover had been ripped off and several pages lay beside it, detached. On the front cover was a twisted helical shape I'd seen before but couldn't place. Its title was *The Selfish Gene*.

"Just a book I've been reading." She put down her cup of tea and scooped it up, pushing the pages back inside the cover and placing it under the telephone on the sideboard.

"Didn't you like it?"

"It's very interesting. By someone called Richard Dawkins. It's about evolution – you know, how life on earth developed."

"Daddy tore it up and threw it at the fire," said Alice, looking up from her drawing. "Mummy and Daddy had a big row and Daddy said, 'How dare you read that rubbish?' Mummy shouted, 'How dare you tell me what I can read?' and she cried."

"Don't be silly, Alice," said Louise. She turned to me. "She's exaggerating. We had a bit of a dispute, Alan and I. He's not into science. He thinks the Bible is the last word on everything. He thinks God created the world in six days and rested on the seventh."

"If Daddy tears *my* books he'll be in big trouble," said Alice. "I'll bite him."

"Alice – don't say things like that."

"Do you mean six actual days?" I asked Louise. "Not where a day stands for a million years or something?"

"That's what Alan believes. Six actual days."

"That's quite hard to swallow."

"You're telling me." Louise glanced at her daughter. Satisfied that Alice was once more engrossed in her drawing, she said, "Alan thinks the theory of evolution is the work of the devil. He says that to be a true Christian you have to take every word of the Bible as absolute fact."

"But Tom always says that parts of it are stories – not literally true."

"Alan disagrees. He says if you ignore one bit of it you might as well ignore it all. Who are we to pick and choose, he says. I told him I'd rather throw away the whole Bible than believe that. He got really mad, snatched the book off me, ripped the cover off and threw it into the fireplace."

"Why can't he let you believe what you want? Why do you have to believe the same things as him?"

"I wish I knew. Up to now we've agreed to differ over a lot of things. But he's changed, the last few weeks. He says he's worried that I'm losing my faith."

I couldn't quite believe that Louise was telling me all this – taking me into her confidence like an adult. It was a delicious feeling. I wished I could think of a sensible and grown-up remark. I tried to imagine what Aunt Daisy would say, but nothing came to mind.

David, frustrated at losing my attention, flung out his arm and socked me in the mouth.

"Ouch."

"David, be careful. Say sorry to Joanne."

"It's okay." I smiled at him.

"David is too small to say sorry," said Alice. "I'll say it for him. Sorry, Joanne."

"Thanks, Alice. Shall I help you with cutting out your Barbies?" I passed David to Louise.

It was good to be distracted. Louise looked as though she was about to cry and I had no idea what to do or say. After a minute or so she put David in his bouncing chair, blew her nose on a tissue and knelt down beside Alice to help make clothes for the dolls.

"Don't mention any of what I said to anyone, will you?" said Louise, once all the Barbie ladies were clothed in paper outfits attached by tabs.

"Of course I won't."

"I shouldn't have told you really. It's private stuff between Alan and me. He'd be furious if he knew I'd said anything."

I glanced at Alice, who appeared to be engrossed in her dolls. "You can trust me, Louise. Who would I tell, anyway?"

"Well, Charity, perhaps. I know you're very close."

She was right: I probably would have told Charity. "I won't tell her. But even if I did, I don't think she'd pass it on."

"I wouldn't be so sure. She and Alan seem to have a secret hotline between them."

I wanted to tell Louise that Charity didn't like Alan much. But Alice was looking at me, trying to work out what we were talking about, and it seemed unwise to pursue it. Louise appeared to assume that her daughter understood nothing of our conversation, but I was young enough to remember picking up a lot more than adults realised.

The back door rattled and in came Alan, damp and dirty in his work overalls, spilling bits of soil over the carpet and glaring at me as though I was an intruder.

"Daddy!" cried Alice, and he picked her up and hugged her. He deposited her on the sofa and bent to kiss David, who was sucking his teething toy.

"You're back early," said Louise.

"Got the job finished earlier than expected." He raised his eyebrows and inclined his head towards me as though to ask what I was doing in his living room.

"Joanne is here to tea with us. She's been helping Alice make her paper dolls."

"I'd better go," I said. "My mum's expecting me home."

Louise shook her head at me. "No, Joanne. Please stay. You told your mother you were here for tea, didn't you?"

I didn't answer, not sure what to say. Finally acknowledging my presence, Alan said, "Well, Joanne. Where's Charity today?"

"In Barnsley with her dad. Visiting their old church."

"Sounds like an interesting fellowship. Might be worth going over there sometime. I'll mention it to Tom. We could learn a lot from them."

"They sound like a bunch of cranks to me," said Louise, heading for the kitchen.

When she had gone, Alan said, "Don't mind Louise. She hasn't had the Spirit yet, that's why she doesn't understand. The things of the Spirit can only be apprehended by the Spirit. Isn't that right?"

I had no idea what he meant but I gave a murmur of assent because it seemed polite and I was their guest, after all.

He continued. “Louise is resisting the Spirit in a way I don’t understand. It may be the memory of her university studies that is getting in the way. All that astronomy and physics – it corrupts a simple faith. I was glad when she gave it up, but it seems to have left its mark.”

I was on surer ground now. “If science and faith are both true, how can they get in each other’s way?”

Alan gave a little jump as though startled that I’d dared to question him. “Joanne, you’re rather young to be tackling such big issues. I’d recommend you spend more time in prayer. And don’t believe everything they teach you at school.”

I bristled at the reference to my age. “Are you saying science isn’t true?”

Alan, sitting down now, started to pull off his mud-caked boots. “Not as much of it is true as they seem to think. A lot of it is just theories. And where it comes into conflict with God’s word, it can’t be true, can it?”

“You mean like the theory of evolution?”

He gave me a quick glance, but I assumed a look of innocence as Louise came in with a mug of tea for him.

An hour or so later, as we munched sandwiches and cake on our laps in the living room, Alan said, “While I was working today I had a brilliant idea. I’d like to know what Joanne thinks of it. It’s a pity Charity’s not here to give her opinion.”

“What is it?” asked Louise, mopping David’s chin with a facecloth.

“Is it to get a pony?” asked Alice.

Ignoring his daughter, Alan said, “I was thinking about how the Lord asks us to share our possessions with the poor and needy. How we should be willing to give up anything He asks of us – even our homes.”

“What are you talking about?” said Louise.

“Nothing we have is truly our own. It’s all on trust from God. It all belongs to Him and He can ask us to use it in His service at any time.” He looked at me. “Isn’t that right, Joanne?”

I made a sound that could have meant anything, and almost choked on a piece of ham. Louise tapped me on the back and David started to cry.

"Go on, then, what's your idea?" said Louise, once I had recovered and David was settled with his rusk. She didn't sound at all enthusiastic.

"To explain it properly, I need to go back to the Book of Acts," said Alan, looking at Louise and me in turn to make sure he had his audience. "You'll remember, I'm sure, that when the Spirit came down on the waiting believers, not only did they receive gifts and praise the Lord in tongues, but they shared everything they had. They held all their possessions in common."

He gazed in turn at us again, his face lit up with the idea. He paused as though expecting us to applaud. "Don't you see? That's what He wants from us. He wants the Crabbies to be a Spirit-filled community, sharing everything, to the glory of God. To show the people of Castlehaven what Christian love is all about."

Louise's face was blank, as though she hadn't heard him. Alice had stopped munching her egg sandwich and looked confused, her brow knitted in a little frown. David gave a high-pitched wail, to which Louise responded with the offer of half a biscuit.

I felt it was up to me to say something. "Wow." My voice lacked conviction. I tried again. "Gosh. You mean share our houses and cars and everything?" I tried, without much success, to imagine my mother and Aunt Daisy sharing Sea View Guest House. What could I share, I wondered – my cassette player, my collection of Agatha Christies?

"That's exactly what I mean," said Alan, giving me a toothy grin. "You see, Louise – Joanne understands, because she is filled with the Spirit."

"But would it work?" I asked. "Would people give up their stuff? Tony and Ray, for instance – do you think they'd be willing to share their motorbikes?"

Alan chuckled in a normal, non-spiritual way that reminded me for a moment of what he used to be like. "Perhaps not – or not straightaway. But it's amazing what a touch of the Holy Spirit can do. He opens up the hardest of hearts."

He turned to his wife. "Louise, I believe God is calling us to lead the way here – to show our fellow Crabbies what sharing is all about."

"How do you mean?" Louise's voice was low.

"I mean open up our home. Make this house available as a place of refuge for our brothers and sisters."

"You mean homeless people?"

"I mean anyone in our fellowship – or even perhaps outside it – who has a particular need."

"But is there anyone like that?" asked Louise. "Everyone in Crabbies has a home, don't they? Even in Castlehaven as a whole – we don't have many homeless people."

"Even one homeless person is too many for the Lord," said Alan. "But I was specifically thinking of our fellow Crabbies, at least at first. There are all sorts of problems in opening up your home to unbelievers."

"So who are you thinking of?"

"There was that family a year or so back. They couldn't afford their rent, remember? Had to leave the town."

"But we wouldn't have room for four people. Where would they sleep?"

"If the Lord wants us to do it, then He will provide."

"They can't have my bedroom," said Alice.

"I was thinking more along the lines of just one person," said Alan. "A single young man or woman, perhaps, living away from home. Perhaps a student."

"The nearest college is ten miles away. And anyway – we don't have the space even for one person. Unless we moved Alice back in with David."

"No!" said Alice.

"We may all have to make sacrifices," said Alan. "That's the nature of the Christian life."

"It's not fair to ask Alice to give up her room," said Louise.

Alice began to cry.

I tried to comfort her by saying, "Alice, don't worry, that won't happen." Alan glared at me and I wished I hadn't.

"Hush, Alice," said Louise. "Alan – it's the stupidest idea I've ever heard. And that's something, coming from you."

There was a stunned silence. Even Alice went quiet.

After what seemed liked ten minutes, during which no-one moved or spoke, Alan looked at Louise. I wasn't sure, but I thought I saw tears in his eyes.

"I can't believe you just said that." His voice had disappointment in it but also a touch of menace – enough to set off Alice's sobs again. I wasn't far from tears myself.

Alan continued. "All I did was suggest that we obey God's word by opening up our home. And I'm accused by my own wife of stupidity."

Louise said nothing but sat still, her mouth set in a straight line.

"Mummy, *my* bedroom is *mine*," said Alice.

I replied, "Yes, of course it is," but Alice was not interested in my response.

"Mummy, tell Daddy my bedroom is mine."

"Of course it's yours. Alan, just stop and think for a minute. We do not have room here for anyone else. We don't have a spare adult-size bed. We don't have the money or the space for one. Our kitchen is tiny and we can only just fit four of us round the table. How on earth are we supposed to cope with an extra person? Or, should I say, how am I supposed to cope? – because I'm sure all the extra work would fall to me."

"You're missing the point, Louise. Serving the Lord is a privilege. Any sacrifices He asks us to make, we'll receive back a thousand-fold. Isn't that right, Joanne?"

I was feeling more uncomfortable by the second and wished I could get up and leave.

Alan shook his head at my lack of support. "I'd have thought you, as a Spirit-filled believer, would get the point. I'm sure Charity would understand. Now there's someone who overflows with the love of the Lord."

"It's asking a lot, for Alice to give up her bedroom," I said with all the courage I could muster.

"Children are never too young to learn to put God first. Alice, stop that noise this minute."

"Perhaps *you* should give something up before you ask her to," said Louise. "Like some of the time you spend at church meetings.

You could spend a bit more of it at home with us." Her cheeks were flushed, her eyes sparking. I realised I'd never seen Louise angry before.

Alan paid her no attention. He turned back to me and said, "Joanne, I'm getting a bit worried about your so-called Special Blessing."

"Why?"

"I'm concerned it may not be genuine. No, no, shush, Louise. This isn't meant as a criticism. We can all be taken in by the powers of darkness. The devil sometimes does a remarkable imitation of God's work."

"Alan – you're not seriously suggesting that Joanne's blessing was the work of the devil?"

"I want to go home," I heard myself say, like a seven-year-old.

"Joanne – Alan doesn't mean it. Do you, Alan?"

"It's a possibility," said Alan. "I'm not saying Joanne is possessed by an evil spirit or anything like that. Just that she may have been the victim of some kind of spiritual hoax. The Bible warns us to beware of such things. The devil is constantly on the prowl, looking to see whom he may devour."

I couldn't swallow the ham sandwich in my mouth but felt I had to either spit it out or choke. I slid from my seat, meaning to head for the bathroom.

"I don't want the devil to come and live with us," wailed Alice.

"Joanne, don't go," said Louise. "Alice, stop crying. The devil isn't real – and he's certainly not coming here."

Somehow, the bread went down my throat and I stayed where I was.

Alan said, "Louise, don't fill our children's heads with lies. You know full well that the devil *is* real. Alice, he won't hurt you as long as you pray to Jesus. There's no need to be upset."

"There's every need," said Louise. "Filling their heads with that nonsense. And daring to suggest that Joanne's blessing wasn't genuine."

"Don't worry," I said. '*I'm* sure it was real."

Did I believe in the devil? I'd never thought about it until now. I wished Tom were there to tell us what he thought. Tom usually managed to make sense of the most puzzling questions.

Alan sat still, not eating, looking down at the half-wrecked sandwich on his plate. I could almost see fumes coming from his nostrils. After a minute or two, during which Louise managed to calm Alice, he said, "Well, something has come out of all this. At least I know where you stand, Louise, as regards your faith."

"And where do I stand?" Louise's voice was light and pleasant now, as though she was asking him to pass the cake.

"Well, it's obvious to me that you stand well outside God's grace."

"Meaning?"

"Meaning, if I need to spell it out, that you are well and truly backslidden. That you have allowed yourself to leave the protection of God's forgiveness and love, and slithered away into some region of doubt and unbelief where He cannot, at least for the time being, reach you. I can only hope and pray that you will become aware of your state and ask for His mercy."

"I *do* still have faith," said Louise, barely audible.

"It doesn't sound like it to me."

"Just because I don't believe all the impossible, ridiculous things you do – it doesn't mean I'm no longer a Christian."

"I didn't say you weren't. I said that you have temporarily fallen from grace. God will forgive you, if you ask Him."

"Why should I need forgiving, just because I don't believe in the devil?"

"Isn't it enough to believe in evil?" I asked. Something Tom had said in a sermon was coming back to me now. "Doesn't the devil stand for the force of evil? He doesn't need to be an actual person."

"Exactly," said Louise. "See – Joanne is fourteen and she understands it. Why can't you?"

"Because it's a lie, spread by the devil himself. One of his best ways of attack is to make us believe he doesn't exist. That way, he can do his work unhindered."

David was fretting so I took his cup to the kitchen and refilled it with juice. "Alice, have you finished?" I asked as I returned. "Would you like some cake? Or shall we make some more clothes for the Barbies?"

Alice came over and took my hand. Hers was hot and sticky. "Mummy and Daddy are having another fight," she observed.

"Never mind. Let's just ignore them. Shall we make this lady a dress?"

As we started drawing and cutting, I heard Alan say to Louise, "You need help. Real, serious, spiritual advice. I suggest we start by speaking to Tom."

Chapter 5

"Wow! You look amazing."

Charity gave a twirl and the green silky material of her dress fell in soft folds around her. Slits up the side seams revealed stretches of brown thigh, but she managed, as always, to avoid any hint of sluttiness.

"I got it from the Oxfam shop," she boasted.

We were in my bedroom, getting ready for the Crabbies' Christmas Party, which was always held on Boxing Day. I'd helped her apply a subtle shade of grey eye-shadow she had brought along. It emphasised the hint of green in her eyes, which in turn caught the hue of her dress.

"Let's do your face now," she said.

The spots that often broke out on my chin were temporarily in hiding and it didn't take Charity too long to make me presentable. The make-up added at least a couple of years to my appearance. I'd chosen to wear a grey velveteen sleeveless top with a high neck (my Christmas present from Aunt Daisy), a long string of chunky fuchsia beads and my new black jeans. My hair, blow-dried by Charity, had more life in it than usual and I felt an unusual sense of pride in my appearance.

She put her head on one side to survey me. "You look great. Mark will go crazy for you."

"Don't be silly."

"I'm not. Mark really likes you – you know he does."

"Well, I don't like him. Not in that way."

"He's not bad-looking."

"I know he's not, but I don't fancy him."

"Why not?"

"I just don't."

Why didn't Charity understand? What were all those kisses between us supposed to mean?

"Anyway, who's going to look at me when *you're* around?" I asked.

"Mark's not interested in me."

He must, I reflected, be almost the only man who wasn't.

I took another glance at Charity's legs, wishing her dress didn't reveal so much, surprised by a tightening in my chest that felt almost like anger.

"All the blokes will fancy you in that."

She stopped parading and stared at me. "Joanne – for goodness' sake. You're not usually like this."

"I'm not being like anything."

"Yes, you are. I thought we were best friends."

"We are."

"Don't you want me to look good? I'm not going to move in on Mark, don't worry about that. He's all yours."

The evening was bitterly cold. All day, banks of yellow-tinged grey cloud had threatened snow. It was only a ten-minute walk to the meeting hall, but I was glad to be wearing thick socks and trainers rather than high-heeled, strappy sandals like Charity's. She turned her heel a couple of times and fell against me. The second time, she giggled and said, "Don't know what I'd do without you, Joanne."

Alan jumped about two feet in the air when he saw Charity. I'd been expecting this but it still made my skin prickle. Ignoring me, he gave her a huge grin and provided more help than necessary in removing her coat. I followed him to the cloakroom to hang mine up.

"Hi, Joanne – you look lovely," called Louise, spotting me from the food table and hurrying over. She appeared unusually pretty in a deep crimson velvet dress with a big white collar and a full skirt. I hoped for her sake that Alan wasn't going to make a fool of himself that evening.

Charity and I took a glass of cherryade each and started chatting to Mark and Tony. Tony's eyes never left Charity. Mark cast frequent shy glances in my direction. Perhaps Charity was right and he did fancy me.

After a few minutes Steve picked up his guitar and struck a few chords. Charity started to sing and they began a silly version of *Karma Chameleon*. Mark and I, getting bored, decided to investigate the refreshments. Mark was a wheelchair-user and had a substantial tray attached to his chair, which we piled up with sausage rolls and chicken legs.

"Don't you want to go back to the others?" I asked. "We could give them some of this food."

Mark glanced across at Charity and Tony, who had been joined by Tony's twin, Ray. "No, I'm sure we can get through it between us. Sit down here." He passed me a sausage roll and when I had taken a bite, said, "You look really nice, you know."

I spluttered. "Me?"

"Yes, you. Who do you think I mean?"

The compliment pleased me but not enough to stop me looking across the hall to Charity and the others. She was now flapping her dress in a way that exposed even more thigh. Alan had attached himself to the edge of the group and was chatting to Ray while stealing frequent glances at Charity. Louise was nowhere to be seen.

"You want to dance, later on?" asked Mark.

"Okay."

"You'll be amazed what I can do with this chair."

I laughed. Tom had just joined us, looking rather fetching in a kind of cowboy outfit. I wasn't sure whether it was his standard party gear or an attempt at fancy dress.

"Having fun?" he asked.

"It's great," I said.

"Good to see you enjoying yourselves. I can't believe this is shy little Joanne."

"I've grown up a bit recently."

"You're telling me."

Tom watched the performers for a few minutes with a slight frown, as though he was trying to work something out. Then he said, "I'd better get some games going."

He stole a sausage roll from Mark's tray and hurried away. Patting the toy gun in his holster, he yelled, "Okay, folks – how about a Crabbie-style game of musical chairs? Everyone know the rules? If you lose your seat, you can buy yourself back in with a forfeit."

There was a mad scramble as two long rows of chairs were set up and Tom attempted to match their number to the number of Crabbies. The rules were vague and underspecified, but the fact that no-one knew what they were doing added to the fun. The high point came when the forfeit for a particular chair was declared by Steve –

who had somehow got himself in charge – to be a pair of lady's knickers.

The three contestants just eliminated were Charity, old Mr Sweeting and Mrs Pinderfield. Presumably Steve was hoping that Charity would be the one to supply the requested item.

Tom gave a little cough and stepped forward to intervene. But before he could speak, Charity had pulled off her flowery knickers and was waving them in the air.

Most people were laughing but a few, including Mr Sweeting, were puce with embarrassment.

When the commotion died down, Tom said, "Okay, everyone – time for a new rule, I think. No items of clothing to be demanded from now on except for shoes and socks."

I abandoned my chair and ran from the hall, down the corridor and into the toilets. Sitting down in there, I replayed the whole scene – Steve shouting, "Knickers, please!", the audience becoming hysterical and Charity waving her underwear in triumph. An image formed in my mind of Alan grinning, of the look exchanged between them. I couldn't tell whether it was a replayed memory or the product of my imagination – all I knew was that it hurt like hell.

I longed to run home, but Charity was staying overnight with us and I couldn't leave her. Sooner or later I would have to go back into the hall and try to pretend nothing was wrong.

I put off the ordeal by heading first to the kitchen for a drink of water.

Louise was sitting there with her head on the table, turned to one side so I could see her eyes were red and teary. I hurried out without my water and collided with Tom in the doorway.

"Something's wrong with Louise," I whispered.

"She stormed out a few minutes ago, didn't you see?"

"I was in the loo. What happened?"

"I'm not quite sure. Alan and Charity were – oh, never mind."

"What were they doing?"

"Oh, just acting silly. They got a bit carried away. You go back to the games, Joanne – I'll talk to Louise."

Louise feels like I do, I thought, making my way back to the hall. She hates whatever is going on between Alan and Charity.

A sense of cold fury towards Charity was massing up inside me. I wanted to drag her out outside and ask her what she was playing at.

Someone tapped my arm and I jumped. At my side was Mark.

"You okay, Joanne?"

"More or less. Bit of a headache."

"Not much of a party, is it?"

"Aren't you enjoying it?"

"Not much. If we could get some music going, start up the dancing…"

"Why don't you try?"

"They're all too busy with their silly games. Do you think Charity's put her pants back on yet?"

"I don't know and I don't care."

After a pause, Mark said, "Joanne, do you want to go out with me sometime? To a film or something?"

He'd made the question sound casual but I knew it was important to him. "I don't know. Sorry, Mark – I mean I'd love to go to a film with you. But just as friends."

There was another pause in which I could sense his disappointment. It was flattering but uncomfortable.

"Okay. If that's what you want, we'll go as friends."

"I'm a bit confused at the moment," I said.

"There's someone else, isn't there?"

"There might be. I'm not sure."

"I understand."

"Do you?" I wanted to tell him about Charity, but it didn't seem possible.

"Is it Tony?" A pause. "You don't have to tell me."

"No, it's not Tony."

"Okay. Well, good luck."

"Thanks, Mark."

"I'm always here, if you need to talk."

If only, I thought. Why is life not simple – why am I not a normal, straightforward person? I could be Charity's friend and Mark's girlfriend and everyone would be happy.

"You're all right, you know," he added.

"Am I?"

"Don't let them get to you, these Crabbies. They're a bunch of nutcases." He looked around the room and sighed. "I don't know why I don't leave."

"Me neither."

"Don't let them try to make you into one of them."

"No. I won't." For the first time, I regretted my Special Blessing – if that's what it had been.

"Look – they're clearing the chairs back for dancing. Want a go?"

The party fizzled out shortly before midnight. The last dance was a smoochy old-fashioned waltz which Mark and I sat out. Charity was nowhere to be seen. Alan and Louise were in each other's arms, but Louise gave the impression of trying to pull away from him, and neither looked happy.

After some time I tracked Charity down in the toilets, splashing water over her face.

"Are you all right?" I asked.

"Of course I am. I got too hot and my mascara ran." She raised her head from the washbasin – pink-cheeked and looking much younger without her make-up.

"Haven't seen much of you tonight," I said.

She pulled out a paper towel and dabbed her face. "No. I didn't want to interrupt you. You were getting on so well with Mark."

I turned on the cold tap and ran water over my fingers. "You seemed to be having a good time yourself."

"Yes, it was better than I expected."

"Did you get your knickers back?"

She screwed up the paper towel and tossed it towards the bin. "What's that supposed to mean?"

"Just what I said. Did you get them back? Or did Alan keep them as a souvenir?"

Her face was red now. "Joanne, what is the matter with you? That was just a bit of fun. Since when have you been such a prude?"

"I'm not. I just didn't like the way he looked at you. And you at him. And I want to know what happened after I left – what the two of you did to upset Louise."

"What the two of us did? Are you mad? Do you really think there's something going on between me and Alan?" She shook her head. "And what's all this about Louise?"

"She was upset. I found her in the kitchen."

"That's got nothing to do with me. I haven't spoken to her all evening."

"Charity, I don't like the way you flirt with Alan."

"*Flirt*? What a stupid word. You sound like something out of *Pride and Prejudice*."

"You know what I mean."

"No, I do not." She lifted a foot to the basin and examined a small hole in the knee of her stocking. "I don't know what's got into you."

"The way Alan looks at you, it's horrible. As though he's going to eat you. You must have seen."

She laughed. "It's those big teeth of his, that's all. You're thinking of *Red Riding Hood*. This is real life, Joanne, not a fairy tale. Don't worry."

"But you encourage him."

"Of course I don't. Men are *like* that, Joanne. You'll have to get used to it."

"I don't trust Alan. I know we're supposed to love and forgive each other but I can't stand him. He makes my skin crawl. And when I see him touching you..."

"Well, don't worry – he's not going to touch me again. Not till next year's party, anyway."

'Be careful, Char. And not just of him."

"Of course I will. Don't worry – I can look after myself. You haven't learned how to handle men yet, that's your trouble."

"I don't want to learn."

"No?"

"You know I don't. I don't like men – not that way."

She raised her eyebrows. "I thought maybe you and Mark..."

"No. I like Mark as a friend, that's all." I took a deep breath. "Charity – I think I'm gay."

In the silence that followed, Charity turned on the warm air dryer and twisted her hands under it. I sat down on the cold lino, staring at the worn toes of my trainers.

Eventually she said, "Are you sure?"

"Almost. I get more sure every day. Tonight, watching you, I was completely sure."

"Oh, my God."

I took another breath and felt the adrenalin first in my thighs, then my stomach. "I thought you might be, too."

"What, gay?"

"You seem it sometimes." I sensed that all was lost now – things couldn't get any worse. I might as well say it. "When we touch – when we kiss. When I brush your hair. I thought you liked it."

She stared hard at the taps. "I do."

"Well, then?"

"I don't know if it means that."

"But if you like it…?"

"I like it because… we're friends. That doesn't mean…"

"Are you sure?"

"We're not allowed to be gay, are we? It goes against God's natural order. So my dad says, and the people in my old church."

"They might be wrong. Tom says it's okay."

"Does he? When did he say that?"

I tried to remember. "A while back. Before you came, in a meeting once. He said he thought God made us the way we are and that we should accept ourselves."

"There are some verses in the New Testament about how homosexuality is evil."

"That's how they thought in those days. Lots of things were different then."

"But we can't pick and choose which bits of God's Word we believe. It doesn't work like that."

I thought of Alan and Louise's argument. "But we do it all the time! We don't stone people to death any more –"

"That's different," she said.

"Why is it?"

"I don't know. You should talk to my dad – he knows all the verses."

I ran cold water over my other hand. "Can we get back to *us*?"

"Us?"

"You and me."

Charity gave another sigh. "Joanne – I don't know what to say. You're my best friend and I love you."

"Do you?"

"As a friend, I mean. As my sister in the Lord. But all that other stuff…"

"When we touch, don't you feel something special?"

"Maybe. But I've sometimes felt that way with boys, too."

I was silent, trying to take this in. "Are you sure?"

"Yes."

I took another deep breath. "Have you ever done it with a boy?"

"You mean had sex?"

"Yes." I felt sick, waiting for her to reply. I bit my lip and studied the grey swirly pattern of the floor tiles.

"No. Only kissing. And a little bit more."

"But you felt…?"

"Yes, a bit. I don't know." She scraped hard at her thumbnail, removing flakes of pink varnish. "I might be bi."

"Bi?"

"Bisexual. You must have heard of that."

"Of course I've heard of it."

"Well, that's what I am – maybe. I'm not sure. Sometimes I think it's the devil tempting me."

"I don't believe in the devil." I gazed at the floor again.

"You should. He's dangerous."

"I bet Tom doesn't believe in him, either."

"I bet he does." Charity looked at her watch. "We should get back to the party. It's gone quiet out there. Do you think they've all gone home?"

We emerged to find the place almost empty. Tom and Louise were clearing food off the tables and piling up plates. Louise's make-up had run, as though she'd been crying. Both jumped when they saw us.

"I thought everyone had left," said Tom.

"We were just in the toilets," I said.

"Good thing you appeared when you did – we might have locked you in." Louise gave us a closer look. "Are you okay?"

"We're fine – we were just tidying ourselves up a bit," said Charity. "Where's Alan?"

"He had to go," said Louise. "My mother was babysitting and she doesn't like being kept up too late."

"Can I give you girls a lift home?" asked Tom.

"I'm staying at Joanne's," said Charity.

"And Mum gave me the money for a taxi," I added.

But Tom insisted. In view of the lateness of the hour and the shock of cold that hit us as we left the building, I was relieved.

I assembled our ancient camp-bed in my bedroom for Charity. It took up most of the floor-space and did not look at all inviting, even when piled up with blankets, rugs and a duvet. Charity glanced at it and then at my bed, which was almost a double. I imagined us curled up there together.

"I'll have the camp bed," I said. "I've slept on it before – I know where the bumpy bits are in the mattress."

"Are you sure?"

"Of course I am."

The image of Charity and I together in my bed dissolved, leaving disappointment.

Sometime in the early hours, I woke to the sound of sobbing.

"What's wrong?"

There was no reply. Charity appeared to be fast asleep, wrapped tightly in the duvet, her face hidden. The sobs stopped for a few minutes, then resumed. I abandoned my warm cocoon and sat up on the bed beside her, chilled immediately by the icy air. My mother did not believe in heated bedrooms – she said we could not afford it and it was bad for the health. The guests, of course, had heaters in theirs and I knew Aunt Daisy kept a small fan heater hidden under her bed.

Charity raised her head for a second and subsided with a little cry. I stroked her hair and accidentally brushed her cheek, which was warm and moist.

"Charity, what's the matter? It's all right – I'm here."

"Go away," she groaned.

I pulled back my hand. "Sorry."

"Make it go away."

"Make what go away? There's nothing here. Only me. You're having a nightmare."

She gave a little sigh and turned to face me. "Don't let it come back."

"It won't come back." I manoeuvred myself under the duvet so that our pyjama-clad bodies made contact. She didn't object or squirm away.

I waited a few minutes, until her breathing became calm and slow. Then I huddled up to her, going over our conversation in the toilets, trying to rewrite the bit where she said she fancied boys. Torturing myself, replaying her dancing, her charged looks at Alan and the way his eyes followed her.

Long after she had fallen asleep I lay there thinking. Lying as she was now, relaxed in my arms, she no longer seemed a threat. She was mine, and under my breath I said, "Charity, I love you. I'll always be here."

She stirred a little and I wondered if I'd woken her. But her eyes stayed shut as she murmured, "Love you too," and my pain, for the time being, subsided.

Tom's journal, Monday 26th December 1983

My poor, dear Louise.

Father – forgive me. I should not have written that. But I can't get her out of my head – her face bent over the table in the Crabbies kitchen, tears splashing out of her eyes like a little girl.

And Alan 'carrying on', as I heard someone describe it, with Charity.

I try to tell myself it's harmless. Alan is a responsible member of the fellowship – a married man with children. He would never touch a girl of – how old is Charity? Sixteen now? Still fifteen?

Louise clearly thinks there's cause for alarm. She's a sensible young woman, not given to fits of jealousy as far as I know. If she thinks there's something going on, I'm right to be worried.

There's no doubt that Alan is besotted, infatuated. And that Charity, whether she means to or not – plays up to him. But is there any more to it than that?

I must talk to him again, without delay.

And I must sort out this business in my head with Louise. Admit that I like her – that I'm attracted. I must confess the thoughts I've taken too far. Ask God's forgiveness and put them behind me. It wouldn't be the first time – I'm only human. Then try to get on with the job He has given me to do.

"Joanne – please can I stay for a few days? Just till my dad gets back?"

It was three days after Christmas and my mother and Aunt Daisy were both down with flu. I'd become their dogsbody – rushing round in my embarrassingly healthy state, refilling hot water bottles, making lemon drinks, boiled eggs with bread fingers and whatever else their fevered minds saw fit to demand. I was bored, weary and irritated and the idea of Charity's company appealed even more than usual.

"Of course you can," I said.

"You'd better check with your mum."

"She's too ill to make a fuss."

Unfortunately, however, this proved not to be the case. My mother croaked, "Of course you can't bring her here among all these germs. And the house is a complete mess – I bet you haven't hoovered the carpets since I took to my bed."

I admitted I hadn't. "But Charity won't mind about that. Her dad's away on a business trip and she's lonely and fed-up. She could help me look after you. She could even help me do some hoovering."

My mother gave a contemptuous sneeze. "No, Joanne. I'm sorry. She can come to stay sometime when I'm back on my feet. You'll probably go down with this bug yourself in a couple of days and then where will we be? We can't have Charity racing round after the three of us." She paused for a cough and a swig of tea.

"Mum – I can't say no. I've already told her..."

"I hope you didn't tell her she could stay, without asking me first?"

"No – not exactly…"

"Well, tell her I'm sorry, but it's not a good time." She broke into another bout of coughing and I went back to the phone to give the bad news to Charity.

"Never mind." I could hear the disappointment in her voice. "I'll be fine. My dad should be back in a couple of days."

"I'll come round and see you tomorrow." My mother and Aunt Daisy would have to spare me for a few hours.

But next morning I woke with a sore throat and headache that proclaimed the onset of my own attack of flu. By lunch-time I had been sick three times and was confined to my bed. Aunt Daisy, who had turned the corner to recovery, hovered over me with offers of hot drinks and various forms of egg.

It was a short but severe bout and I spent the next two or three days feeling sorry for myself, with few thoughts to spare for Charity or anyone else. On the evening of New Year's Day, just when I had started to feel better, the phone rang and I jumped at the sound of Charity's voice.

"Hi, Joanne. I'm at Alan and Louise's."

"What, for a meal?"

"No, to stay. I phoned them earlier on. The heating has gone wrong at home and it's freezing. My dad's not coming back till the weekend. I was a bit upset and Alan said he'd come and get me."

"Why didn't you phone me?"

"I did, yesterday. Your mum wouldn't let me speak to you. She said you were too ill. Are you feeling better?"

"I'm fine now. It was just a stupid cold. She should have let me speak to you."

"She said you kept throwing up."

'Well, I'm better now. We all are. You can come and stay with us as long as you like."

"But I'm settled here. Louise is making all my favourite meals. I'm getting on ever so well with Alice and David – they're sweet. Alice moved out of her room for me without making any fuss. Alan says they've been thinking for a while about opening up their home to other people so it's good practice for them, having me."

I remembered the conversation at their house. "What does Louise say about that?"

"As I said – she's really kind. It's like having a mother again."

"What about Alan? How's he?"

"He's nicer than I expected. He's great with the kids. Makes up all these silly games. I sometimes join in. But he's very religious at other times. He makes us say grace before every meal. We have to take it in turns, even little Alice. When he prays it goes on for half an hour. And we have a family time every night, where we share what God has said to us during the day and then pray about it."

"I thought you liked that sort of thing."

"With Alan it's a bit too much. I think if lived with him all the time I'd rebel."

"Is he – you know – all right in other ways?"

"What kind of other ways?"

"The way he looks at you, that sort of thing."

"Joanne – don't be stupid. He doesn't look at me in any way. It's all in your imagination."

"Don't egg him on."

"Egg him on? What do you think I am? I sometimes wish we'd never had that conversation about sex. You've been funny ever since. I shouldn't have said about being bi. Look, Joanne – get this into your head. I do *not* fancy Alan. And if he fancies me that's because he's a lecherous old fool and it's his problem."

"I just want you to be careful."

"Let me tell you something to make you feel better. I heard Alan and Louise last night, hammering away at it through the wall."

I made a gulping sound of disgust. Charity laughed. "There – so you've nothing to worry about. They were at it like a couple of pigs."

"Pigs?"

"You know – snorting and harrumphing. Well, he was, anyway. Grotesque. I jammed my fingers in my ears but those walls are so thin. But the point is, you don't need to worry. They've obviously got a great sex life."

The thought of the snorting and harrumphing reduced us both to giggles for a few minutes. When I had recovered, I asked, "How about your nightmares? Have you had any?"

"No, not a single one. Louise put a little nightlight, in the shape of a rabbit, by my bed. It used to belong to Alice. And she said to just bang on their door if I'm scared. But I haven't been. I've been remembering to pray my prayer."

"You were going to make me a copy, so I can pray it for you, too."

"I keep forgetting."

"I'd like to."

"Okay, I will. I'll write it out for you tonight. And, by the way…"

My body tensed at her change of tone. "What?"

"What I said after the party."

"What did you say?" I remembered every word, of course – I was playing for time.

"About not knowing if I was gay, and thinking it might be wrong."

My heart was thumping fast. "Yes? What?"

"I've decided. I am gay."

"You are? That's great. I'm really glad."

"Though I like boys as well. So I suppose I must be bi."

I swallowed hard, unable to speak for a moment.

"Joanne?"

"I don't know what to say."

"What's the problem? Have I upset you?"

"The thought of you being bi…"

"Oh, you silly thing. You needn't worry, because you're the one I love. I've been thinking about it, since the night in your bed. I really do love you." She paused. "If that's all right with you?"

All the tension inside me collapsed. I felt sunshine break into my voice. "Of course it's all right. It's magic. It's brilliant."

"Good. So we're together – you and me?"

"You bet we are."

"Will we tell people?"

I thought of my mother. "Let's see how it goes. Take it slowly."

Charity gave a relieved laugh and I guessed she was thinking of her dad.

Chapter 6

Two months passed where little happened on the surface – just the usual run of school and Crabbies and chores.

Except that Charity and I were now together and spent every moment of our spare time in each other's company. We giggled, we prayed, we played tapes and we tried on clothes. We kissed and I brushed her hair. She asked the Spirit to give me more gifts. He didn't, but I didn't care. Hearing her ask was gift enough for me.

At Crabbies, Alan continued to fawn over Charity, but she pushed him aside as politely as she could. Surely, I thought, he would get the message soon.

A few more Crabbies received the Special Blessing and there were some heated discussions about whether or not it was a good thing. Tom looked more strained every time I saw him, and Louise didn't look very happy either. But I was too taken up in my own pleasure to pay them much attention.

Then came the shocking Saturday when Charity and I did the pregnancy test.

Next day, she missed the Crabbies' Sunday service for the first time ever. Tom asked if I knew why and I told him she wasn't well. I phoned her in the afternoon and again in the evening, but no-one answered.

I was relieved to see her at school on Monday. As we emerged for morning break she was beside the snacks table, her hair hanging in unwashed strands, her tie loose and a coffee stain on her shirt.

She acknowledged me with a brightening of her countenance that wasn't quite a smile. Her features seemed to stick in their new position as though she couldn't summon the effort to release them. Her skin was pale apart from a pink blotch on each cheek. She looked, as much as anything, exhausted.

I wanted to hug her but it wasn't usual at our school to embrace your friends at break-time. I put my hand on her arm and said, "Are you okay?"

"Let's walk across the field."

It was a day of furious wind blustering off the sea, throwing gritty sand into our faces and making it almost impossible to talk. After a few minutes we took shelter by the disused bike-sheds. No-one else was around, the weather being too unpleasant for even the keenest smokers.

From where we sat on a pile of paving slabs, we could see the waves lashing and curling, hurling themselves at the harbour wall. A few seagulls squawked, but most appeared to have gone inland for shelter. The sky was leaden grey, with even darker clouds crossing it at speed like whorls of smoke. Neither of us had coats and we were both shivering. But it seemed right to stay where we were for this conversation.

I waited, and after a few minutes she said, "I went to the doctor's first thing today. She did a test."

Another wait.

"She says I *am*. I'm pregnant."

"Oh God. Charity…"

"I know."

A gust of wind swung round behind our backs and caught our clothing as though trying to pull us into the sea. Charity gave a gasp. I put my arm round her shoulders and she clutched my other arm with both her hands, so hard it hurt.

"I'm really scared, Joanne."

I squeezed tighter. "Don't be. I'm here. You've got me."

I'd had the weekend to adjust to the probability of Charity's being pregnant. I had tried to tell myself, at first, that the test could be mistaken, but I never believed it. My initial pain had lessened, at least for the time being, to the point of being able to focus on her, rather than on my own jealousy.

"You don't seem surprised," she said.

"Well, no. Not after the test we did. Are you?"

"No. I knew I was pregnant."

After a few moments, during which I stamped my feet to try to get some warmth into them, I said, "Are you going to tell me who?"

"Who?"

"Who it is. The father."

She shook her head and gazed out to sea.

"Is it Alan?"

Her voice was flat. "Of course it's not."

"Are you sure?"

With a little more vigour, she said, “Yes, I’m sure. How could it be Alan? Do you really think I’d have sex with *him*?” A note of scorn, her bow-shaped lip curling.

“Well, it has to be someone.”

“It *isn’t.*”

“What do you mean, it isn’t?”

“It isn’t anyone. I haven’t had sex.” She looked down at her shabby, frayed trainers.

I tried to look her in the eyes, but she avoided my gaze.

“Look, I know this is hard, Char, but there’s no point denying it, is there? It’s obvious that if you’re pregnant that you must have done it with someone.”

“I haven’t. Honestly, Joanne – I haven’t.” She made eye contact for the first time since we’d sat down. Her irises showed little of their usual brilliance – they were a dull metallic grey like the sea. The wind had dropped briefly and as long as I stayed completely still I could almost believe I was warm.

Her denial re-stoked my hurt. Was she trying to protect me from the truth, from the fact that she had betrayed me?

“Charity, I’m not stupid. I do know the facts of life.”

“I never said you were stupid.”

“You must think I am, if you expect me to believe you became pregnant by a miracle.”

“I don’t understand it either.”

“Think back. Around Christmas time.” I had a sudden thought. “The day you went to Barnsley, with your dad. Did you…?”

“Did I what?”

“You know. Meet anyone. From your old church? You said you used to have a boyfriend there.”

“That was years ago. Of course I didn’t – are you suggesting I took up with an old boyfriend and had sex with him?” Her eyes turned back to the horizon.

“I just thought it was a possibility.”

“Well it’s not.”

‘Someone at school? One of the boys in your class?’

“No!”

“One of the boys from Crabbies? Not Steve?”

‘No, no, no!’

"It has to be someone."

She looked at her watch. "The bell must have gone. We'll be late for our lessons."

"I don't care. I just want to know who you slept with." I paused while a wave of anger swamped my brain. "I've a right to know. We're supposed to be best friends. I tell you everything."

"I *would* tell you, Joanne, if I knew."

"When you told me you were bi, I never thought…"

"You never thought what?" Her voice had taken on a note of hostility – her words pinched tight as though she'd been falsely accused.

"That you were going to go and have sex with a man."

She stood up. "Let's walk back. I've got English."

"I don't care what you've got." Instead of heading back to the school, I started walking towards the sea. The wind had turned and was knocking me sideways now. She followed.

"Joanne – slow down a minute. Listen. This is going to sound weird."

"What is?"

She stopped walking and grabbed my arm at the elbow. "Something happened, a while back. I'd almost forgotten. But it makes sense now. It all hangs together."

"What does?"

"My vision, or whatever it was. I had a sort of experience." She spoke in a low, barely audible voice.

"What sort of experience?"

"A bit like the Special Blessing but a sort of extra one. I was saying my prayer – the one about the Terror – when it happened. I suddenly felt God's presence, really close. As though He was saying, 'Don't be afraid. I'll protect you.'"

"That's nice." I wasn't sure whether my words were sarcastic or not.

"It was. It was wonderful. I had a very strong sense of – well, like being visited by God. Taken over. Flooded."

"What's that got to do with your pregnancy?"

"I don't know. I'm just beginning to see. Yes! Of course."

"What?"

She paused, breathing quickly. "Yes, that's it. It must be. It was God visiting me. Alan's prophecy has come true."

"What prophecy?"

She was almost jumping on the spot. "Don't you remember, at the prayer meeting a couple of weeks ago? Alan spoke in tongues and someone interpreted what he said. Tony, I think it was. God told us He was going to send a very special new visitor to our fellowship, one who would bring great change."

I didn't remember. Events like this were two-a-penny at Crabbies meetings in recent days.

"You *must* remember, Joanne. God's message to us was, 'Be faithful, be obedient, stand strong in your faith,' – and He promised to reward us with a new visitation from on high. This must be it."

"I still don't understand."

"My baby! It's God's visitor, His messenger to us. He's made me pregnant by the Holy Spirit, just like Mary. It all makes perfect sense now."

We'd reached the fence that marked the end of the school grounds, not far from the cliff edge. Below us the sea churned and frothed. I was stunned into silence.

Eventually I managed to mouth some words. "You're not trying to say…?"

Charity seemed to be talking to herself. "Yes, I get it now. God's been trying to tell me for weeks. Why didn't I listen? Asking if I was ready to take this on. Telling me it wouldn't be easy, that I'd get lots of opposition, lots of unbelief."

"You're telling me! You can't really expect anyone to believe that the father of your baby is God?"

"*Please* believe me, Joanne. If you don't, no-one will."

"Well, I don't. I'm sorry, but this is too much."

"You've heard of miracles, haven't you?"

"Of course I have. But they don't happen nowadays – not ones like this."

"I expect Mary thought that, too. Until it happened to her."

"But that was Jesus. You can't mean God has put another Jesus inside you?"

"I don't know, yet. Perhaps not quite. This baby… I think it might be a girl."

"How can you tell?"

"Just a feeling. Quite a strong one, though. Yes, I'm sure. God has given me a little girl. His daughter. He is doing something new among the Crabbies that will spread to the whole world. Alan's been saying that for weeks. I can't wait to tell him – and everyone else."

"Even Alan won't believe this – let alone the others."

"Perhaps not at first. We'll have to give them time. But you believe me, now, don't you, Joanne?"

"I don't know." My head was reeling, my thoughts all over the place. "I don't know what to think. You seem so sure, but…"

"Joanne, I truly, truly have not had sex with anyone. You must believe that."

I had a new thought. "Charity – you're not trying to protect anyone, are you? Did someone attack you? Have they threatened to hurt you if you tell?"

"Do you think I'd let someone do that?"

"Well, if they were stronger than you…?"

"No-one has done anything to me. And I wouldn't let them blackmail me even if they had. Stop doubting, Joanne, and accept the truth – this baby is God's own daughter. I've been chosen, just like Mary was. It's a huge honour. I can't believe He thinks I'm worthy to be the mother of His child…"

Charity collapsed into sobs and I tried to comfort her, my own exploding brain put to one side while I held her until she finally stopped shaking.

Far away, I heard the bell ring. We'd missed a whole lesson.

"Charity, do you want to go home? Shall I come with you?"

"No. My dad's there. I don't want to see him.'

"What does he say about the baby?"

"I haven't told him yet."

"Are you going to tell him what you've just told me?"

"What else can I say? I'll have to tell him."

"Will he believe you?"

"I don't know. If you don't, I don't expect he will."

I waited a moment or two. "It's not that I don't believe you. Not exactly. It's just so hard to take in."

"It's hard for me, too. I don't know why God chose me. In some ways I wish He hadn't."

"Come on, Charity. If He has chosen you for this, He'll help you cope. That's what Tom always says. If God asks you to do something difficult, He'll give you the strength you need."

"I hope you're right."

"Speaking of Tom, why don't you talk to him? He's a great person in a crisis. We could go and see him together if you like."

"You think he'll believe me?"

"I don't know. But he'll be able to advise you what to do."

"I know you like Tom, but what I need here is proper spiritual wisdom. Someone who understands the mind of God. Tom isn't like that. He's so sceptical, I sometimes wonder if he's a true believer at all."

"How can you say that?"

"Look at the way he is over the Special Blessing. He's always trying to quell the Spirit."

"He doesn't want people getting carried away. He's worried the Crabbies will split down the middle, like your church in Barnsley."

"He should have more faith."

"He's the person *I'd* want to talk to."

"I'd rather talk to Alan."

"Alan? Are you completely mad?"

"You still think it's him, don't you? You think I slept with Alan?"

"No. Not if you say you didn't. I don't know what to think."

"For the millionth time, Joanne – I am a virgin. I have not had sex with anyone."

"Okay." My resolve to make sense of the situation crumbled to dust. All I felt able to do now was stay beside Charity and try to comfort her.

"So you do believe me?" Her voice lightened with so much hope I hadn't the heart to voice my confusion. I stroked her hair smooth against her damp cheek and said nothing.

"Tom – can I talk to you? Something's happened to Charity."

I was in a phone box a little way along the road from Charity's flat. It was the day after our conversation on the school field. Charity had not appeared at break-time and her classmates told me she was not at school. I'd spent the day worrying. There wasn't time to get to her flat and back over lunchtime, but I'd hurried out of school at three pm, skipping my last lesson, which was games. I'd no doubt be in trouble, but I was too concerned about Charity to care.

No-one answered the doorbell. An elderly man, clipping a bush in the narrow strip of garden along the front of the flats, called out to me. "You looking for t' young lass? Her and her dad went off first thing this morning. It were before seven – woke me up. The car piled up with luggage – wouldn't surprise me if they were away for good."

I stood and stared, unable to speak, aware of my mouth dropping open with shock.

The neighbour studied me more closely. "You're the lassie that used to come and see her. I've seen you round here a few times."

"I'm Charity's best friend," I said, finding my voice, though it had a shake in it. "Have you any idea where they've gone?" My heart was pumping hard and I had a sick feeling in my stomach.

"Haven't a clue. As I say, though, I'm not surprised. Never thought they'd stay here long. One of them fly-by-night business types, that Mr Baker. Here today and gone tomorrow. Wouldn't surprise me if he were up to no good."

"But I saw Charity yesterday and she never said anything."

"I'm sorry, love – I can see you're upset. Wish I could help." He leaned towards me and tapped his nose. "Between you and me, lass, there was a bit of a scene. A lot of shouting and crying. The walls in these flats are like cardboard – you can hear every sound. The young lass was in a right state – yelling and screaming like there's no tomorrow." After a pause, he said, "Can I make you a cup of tea, love? Do you want to come in and sit down for a minute?"

It was a kind offer but I'd been well drilled not to accept such invitations. Besides, I needed to be alone to get my thoughts together.

"No, thanks. I'd better be on my way."

"All right – take care, then."

I trudged along Charity's street, which was damp after a heavy shower and almost deserted. Heading towards town and spotting the telephone kiosk, I had an idea. Tom would know what to do.

"Joanne, what is it? What's happened?"

I took a deep breath. "Charity's gone. She wasn't at school and their neighbour says they left early this morning in a car. It was piled up with luggage."

I felt so much better that Tom now knew at least this much. Though he didn't know about Charity's pregnancy – I'd have to break that news next.

There was a short pause. Then he asked, "Did she say anything about going away? Could her father have taken her on one of his business trips? Or to stay with someone they knew in Barnsley?"

"Not in term-time. And she would have told me. I saw her yesterday at school."

"It does sound rather odd," said Tom. "But there's probably a simple explanation. Perhaps her mother has been taken ill."

"Charity would have phoned me before they went. The neighbour said he heard her crying. Screaming. Last night."

"My goodness."

"She was kind of upset yesterday at school. And there's something else I haven't told you yet."

Tom's voice was more serious. "Go on. Tell me."

I took another deep breath, trying to focus on the wet pavement outside the phone box, a toddler in yellow boots skipping beside her mother. I felt a wave of claustrophobia and longed to escape. There seemed to be no air in the kiosk and it reeked of urine and disinfectant.

I was aware of breaking Charity's confidence but I had to say it. "She had a test done yesterday at the doctor's. She's pregnant."

Tom seemed to take forever to process my words. When he spoke it came out as a croak and I couldn't make out what he said. Then the pips started to go and I scrabbled in my purse for another five-pence piece, but I was too late and we were cut off.

I dialled Tom's number again and he picked up his phone at the first ring. He sounded more composed now. "Joanne – why don't you come round to my place, where it's easier to talk? Where are you? I can come to your house if it's easier."

I thought of Tom turning up at home and my having to explain everything to my mother and Aunt Daisy. "No, I'll come to you." I checked my purse. "I'll get the bus."

"Okay. See you soon, then."

Standing at the bus stop, I began to feel better. It was good to have a plan, to be on the way somewhere. Tom, I told myself, would know how to find Charity and bring her home. As the crimson shape of the double-decker appeared out of the misty drizzle, it occurred to me that Charity's elderly neighbour might be mistaken about their leaving being permanent. Maybe Tom was right and they were on a quick visit to Barnsley. Charity's father might be returning some furniture he'd borrowed. Or some of the slot machines he'd bought for his casino. That would be it. It was faulty and he was taking it back. In the half-light, I could believe the neighbour had got it wrong. Perhaps Charity had woken up feeling unwell and that was why she hadn't gone to school.

As I dropped my fare in the driver's box I felt a flare of hope. By the time the bus pulled up outside Tom and Pattie's bungalow I had convinced myself there was nothing much to worry about. Perhaps my visit to Tom was unnecessary – but I was still glad to be seeing him.

He opened the door to me, gave his usual wide grin and said, "Gosh – you're soaked. Let's get your wet coat off and make a cup of tea."

I hung my sodden jacket on the newel post and followed him into the warmth of the kitchen. He moved a pile of books and papers off a chair to let me sit down. Damp washing seemed to be draped everywhere. It struck me that we were lucky to have a laundry room. Perhaps there were some advantages to living in a guest house, after all.

A few minutes later, my hands round an enormous mug of tea and a plate of biscuits on the table in front of me, I found myself in tears.

Tom sat opposite, his long legs stretched out. His workaday jeans were stained and tatty, with a gaping hole in one knee which he covered with his hand, embarrassed.

"Sorry about the state of me. Been doing a bit of housework." He passed me a box of tissues. "Just take your time." Then he waited in silence, his eyes on the rain running down the window, until I had calmed down.

"Just had a thought," he said. "Before we start talking – does your mum know where you are? Should you give her a ring?"

I looked at the clock on the wall. Four pm. "I'm only just due out of school. I skived off early."

I expected some kind of disapproval but he said, "Okay. You were obviously very upset. But if you need to call your mother, you're welcome to use our phone."

"She'll think I've gone to Charity's." The thought made me want to cry again. I cleared my throat to remove the rising sob. "I often do, after school."

I dipped a chocolate biscuit in my tea and took a bite, relishing the smooth sweetness. Then I remembered it wasn't good manners to dip biscuits as a guest, and felt the colour rush to my cheeks. My mother would have slated me.

Tom didn't appear to notice. "Now, do you want to tell me some more? Did I hear you rightly, about Charity being pregnant?"

"Yes. She is." My biscuit was finished and I felt lost without it. Would it be rude to take another one?

Tom propped his chin on one hand, his elbow on the pine table. He looked through the window at the dripping garden, then back at me. "Wow. Well. That's quite a shock. Is she absolutely sure?"

"She went to the doctor's for a test. Before that, on Saturday, I helped her do a test herself. One of the ones you get from Boots. It came out positive."

Tom let out a sigh. "And you last saw her at school yesterday?"

"Yes. We had a long talk on the playing field. She was going to tell her dad in the evening."

"And the neighbour you mentioned – he heard her crying, later on?"

"That must be when she told her dad. The neighbour said she was screaming, too."

"The pregnancy must have come as a shock to Mr Baker."

Another lump formed in my throat. "Where do you think he's taken her, Tom?"

"I don't know, Joanne. But we'll find out. Try not to worry." He pointed to the biscuits. "Have another."

I took one and fiddled with its wrapper without opening it.

"And no-one at school knows anything about it?"

"No. I asked some people in her class and they didn't know where she was. One of her teachers even asked me if I knew why she was off."

Tom looked surprised.

I explained. "Even though she's in the year above me, we spend all our breaks and lunchtimes together. Everyone knows we're best friends."

"I see. Look, Joanne..." He took a gulp of tea. "I must admit, I'm quite concerned myself. Especially because of the pregnancy. I'm going to give your head-teacher a call."

"Miss Dodd? Do you know her?"

"She's a good friend. We've worked together on various committees. If she knows anything about Charity, she may be willing to tell me, though she probably shouldn't." He got up from his chair, scraping it back over the tiled floor. "I'll phone her from the living room. You stay here and finish your tea. Have as many biscuits as you like."

I looked down at the empty wrapper in my hand. I didn't remember removing it and eating the biscuit. I took another one.

Unconstrained in Tom's absence, I dipped my third biscuit in the cool remainder of my tea.

Tom and Pattie's children, Juliette and Craig, would be home soon from school. They were eleven and eight. Pattie would not arrive, I guessed, until after five.

As soon as Tom left the room, Fred, the family dog, padded over to me, his eyes pleading. I held out the remainder of my biscuit and he took it delicately from my palm. He was a red setter, rather old and lacking energy. When he saw there were to be no more biscuits he lay down on my feet, his weight and warmth giving comfort.

Tom came back after a few minutes and I could see in his face there was some news. "I've just spoken to Margaret – Miss Dodd, I mean."

My heart began to thud. "What did she say?"

Fred shifted his position as though disturbed by my panic.

Tom said, “It’s okay, Joanne. Charity’s fine. Her father called Miss Dodd this morning. He’s taken Charity to France to be with her mother.”

“But why?”

“Because of the pregnancy, I suppose. He told Miss Dodd about that, too.”

“Is she angry with Charity?”

“Not so much angry as shocked. Like the rest of us. But she said she was sure there was no cause for alarm. Mr Baker explained he thought Charity needed her mother at this time, and it seemed the best thing to do.”

“But Charity and her mother don’t get on at all.”

“I’m sure they’ll overcome their differences, in these circumstances.”

“But they won’t – it’ll make things worse. Why couldn’t she stay here, with her friends?”

“I got the impression Mr Baker wanted to get her away from Castlehaven. You can see why, in a way. Look, Joanne – I shouldn’t really have told you what Miss Dodd said. Don’t say anything at school, will you?”

“Of course I won’t.”

“I expect it will get out. Have you told your mum?”

I gave a little shudder. “No.”

“I’m not saying don’t tell her – just advising you not to say too much. Nor to the other Crabbies.”

“Don’t worry, I won’t say a word.”

Tom drained his cool tea. “Joanne – I perhaps shouldn’t ask you this. But have you any idea who the father of the baby might be?”

I shook my head.

“Are you sure? Does Charity have a boyfriend?”

“No!” This came out with more force than I’d intended. I wanted to tell Tom about the relationship between Charity and me – that of course she didn’t have a boyfriend because we were both gay and we were together, sort of. But it was too complicated to explain.

Tom picked up his empty mug and frowned at it as though wondering where the tea had gone. "I thought maybe it was someone from school?"

"She would have told me. She tells me everything." I wriggled my feet, which were developing pins and needles under Fred's weight. Fred grunted and shifted his position.

Tom said, "It has to be someone."

Now or never, I thought. "Charity thinks it isn't."

"It isn't what?"

"It isn't anyone. The baby's father."

"How can it not be anyone? I don't understand."

My cheeks warmed with another blush. "You know – like Mary."

"Mary?" Tom's face creased in bewilderment.

I had expected him to catch on more quickly. "Mary – Jesus' mother. She got pregnant by the Holy Spirit, didn't she?"

The colour drained from Tom's face, leaving it greyish-white.

"She thinks it's like that," I continued. "She says it must be like that, because she hasn't – well, you know…"

The tone of Tom's reply was short and clipped. He sounded like an angry teacher and I began to feel this was all my fault. "Joanne – are you telling me that Charity denies having had sex with anyone?"

"Yes."

Tom raised a hand and banged it down on the table, making the mugs and biscuit plate jump. Fred gave a yelp and scrambled to his feet.

"Bloody hell!"

I'd never heard Tom swear. None of the Crabbies swore – not in my hearing, at least. We were taught that it was wrong to take the Lord's name in vain. Even Charity only did it occasionally, when trying to impress me.

I wanted to giggle, but managed to stifle it. "She told me God visited her, a couple of months ago. She thought it was a new Special Blessing. She was flooded by the Spirit."

"Flooded?"

"Yes. She says she realises now that it was the Spirit making her pregnant."

Tom stared at me.

"She keeps saying how it's a great privilege – being chosen by God to be the mother of a new Jesus."

"A new..." His voice tailed off. Some colour had returned to his cheeks but his face looked hollow, years older.

"Sort of. Not exactly. She knows it can't be Jesus again. We don't need another Saviour. She thinks this baby will have a different job to do, but we don't know, just yet, what it will be. She thinks it's going to be a girl."

"A girl?" All Tom could do, it seemed, was echo my words.

"The baby. She's going to call her Rosie."

Juliette and Craig burst into the kitchen at that moment, fair-haired, ruddy-cheeked, noisy and damp. Fred leapt up and licked them. They raced over to Tom and embraced him, ignoring me. They were, I guessed, used to visitors.

Then Juliette noticed me and smiled.

"Hi," I said.

"Where's Charity?" she asked.

Tom listened to their news about school for a few minutes, then sent them with their glasses of milk and snacks into the living room, explaining that he needed to talk to me. I felt embarrassed in my adult role and wished I could go and watch TV with them.

When they'd gone, Tom said, 'Can you stay a bit longer, Joanne? Or should you be on your way?'

"I can stay another ten minutes."

"When Pattie gets back I'll drive you home, if you like."

'Okay. Thanks'

I had a sense that Tom and I had exchanged places. He'd gone from being the one in control, assuring me that Charity was fine and I didn't need to worry, to a shaky, trembling figure who needed me to stay.

"Has she ever said this kind of thing before?" he asked. "You know – weird stuff?"

"Not really. She always talks a lot about the Holy Spirit and the Special Blessing, but never like this."

"And you've absolutely no idea – hand on heart – who the father of the baby might be?"

"No. No idea."

Tom wasn't giving up easily. "You must have thought about it, since she told you she was pregnant?"

"I… I sort of believed her. Not at first, but after a while, when she told me about being visited by the Spirit. She seemed so sure."

"You mean you believed her about the baby's father being the Holy Spirit?"

"Yes." I felt ashamed, now, to admit it. "She was so amazed at being pregnant. Said she couldn't possibly be."

"Do you know how many weeks she is?"

I didn't know much about these things. "No. I think it's quite early on."

Tom was looking at the calendar on the sideboard behind me, counting under his breath. "Around Christmas time or early January. What happened then?"

"Nothing much. The Christmas party, I suppose."

Tom drew a sharp breath. "Did she go straight home after the party?"

"She stayed the night with me. At our house."

"Right. Did anyone else stay? Any of the boys?"

"No way! My mum would never allow that."

'Sorry. I'm just trying to work things out."

"Tom – you don't think it could be true?" I looked hard into his eyes, which I suddenly noticed were deep blue, like the delphiniums Aunt Daisy grew in summer. "The Holy Spirit thing?"

His eyes seemed to fill up with sadness, as though he was disappointed in me. I felt I'd let him down.

"What do *you* think, Joanne?"

Something deflated inside me. "I suppose it can't be."

"You're a sensible girl. You know such things don't happen."

"They did once."

After a pause, he said, "Only once. And even then…"

"Even then – what do you mean?"

"Nothing. Joanne – this baby has a human father. She – it – must have. We know that, don't we?"

"I suppose so."

"Charity may have all sorts of reasons for saying what she says."

"She believes it. I could tell. And she would never lie to me."

Tom sighed. "We have to bear in mind that she's going through a very difficult time."

"I know. I want to help her. That's one reason I'm so upset she's gone. She needs me."

"I know. I want to help her, too. Perhaps all we can do for the moment is pray."

"I do that already. I pray for her every night. I pray that she won't get her nightmare."

"What nightmare is that?"

I felt embarrassed for Charity and wished I hadn't mentioned it. "Oh, she gets bad dreams sometimes. She has a special prayer she prays, to stop herself getting them. She was going to write it out for me but she never got round to it. I had to make one up of my own."

"You're very close, you two, aren't you?"

"Yes, we are. We..." I wanted once again to tell him, but was unable to begin.

"She's lucky to have such a good friend. Let's hope she writes to you soon, with her new address. And perhaps you'll be able to phone her."

"How much does it cost to phone France?" I imagined my mother's face when she saw the telephone bill.

"I'm not sure offhand. Perhaps, say, once a week, you'd like to phone her from here?"

"Thank you. That's really kind of you."

"Not at all. You can tell me how she's getting on."

"I will."

The door opened and in came Pattie, carrying two big shopping bags. She looked tired – her face drawn into lines and her hair blown about by the wind. Tom got up to kiss her and put the kettle on.

"Hello, Joanne," she said. "Everything all right?"

"I'll tell you soon," said Tom. "Joanne has some news about Charity. I'm just about to take her home."

"Right you are." Pattie, now sitting at the table beside me, looked around the kitchen. "Weren't you getting the dinner tonight, Tom?"

"Oh gosh. Sorry. I clean forgot. Tell you what – I'll pick up fish and chips on the way back from Joanne's."

Pattie's mouth formed a tight line before she said, "We can't afford another takeaway meal. I'll put some potatoes in the oven to bake."

"Sorry I stopped you cooking," I said as I got into the car.

Tom gave a guilty-sounding laugh. "Not your fault. I'd have probably forgotten anyway. I'm afraid I often do."

"Pattie looked really tired."

"She works too hard. They're understaffed in the Housing Office."

He drew up a couple of blocks before Sea View and pulled away as soon as I had thanked him and got out. I was relieved not to have to explain anything to my mother.

Aunt Daisy was in the kitchen, her face bright with news. "I've just seen Eileen Pinderfield in the Spar. She tells me Charity is pregnant."

Chapter 7

I never found out how Mrs Pinderfield got hold of the news about Charity's pregnancy. I had spoken to no-one but Tom. It was unlikely that Charity would have told anyone besides me. Perhaps her father had said something to an acquaintance before he left, or someone at school had overheard Miss Dodd's phone conversation with Tom and passed on the gossip. Whatever had happened, the worst of it as far as I was concerned was that my mother now knew.

Aunt Daisy, once she saw how upset I was, told me not to worry. These things happened, she said, and she was sure Charity would be all right, that her parents would know what to do. Although I wasn't convinced by this, Aunt Daisy's kindness was comforting. She came from an age where an unmarried pregnancy, at any age, was a scandal, and I could see she was doing her best to hide her shock.

My mother's reaction was a different matter. "I never trusted that girl," she said as we ate our toad-in-the-hole.

"Mum, that's not fair. What did Charity ever do to make you not trust her?" I glanced at Aunt Daisy, hoping for support. She turned raised eyebrows to my mother, looking for an answer, too.

"A certain look in her eye," said my mother. "A knowing look. You understand me, don't you, Daisy?"

"I know the kind of look you mean," said Aunt Daisy, "but I'm not sure that Charity had it. She came across to me as an innocent kind of girl with a sort of artless enthusiasm."

I nodded, though I wasn't sure about this last phrase.

My mother replied, "Artless? Innocent – with all that mascara? And those short skirts? The way she carried on at the Christmas party? Eileen Pinderfield told me all about that. Flirting with every man she laid eyes on. Especially that awful Alan…" She stopped mid-sentence as though a thought had struck her.

"That was just a bit of fun," I said, trying to stop my voice from going up high.

"I'm sure she meant nothing by it," said Aunt Daisy, giving me a look I couldn't fathom.

My mother seemed distracted for a few moments, as though working something out. Then she gave a little shake of the head.

"Well, she's gone and got herself pregnant. What more proof do you need?"

"She's not like that," I said. "She's not some kind of tart."

I wished I could tell them about Charity's conviction that God was the father of her baby. But I could anticipate their scepticism – Mum would give her cynical cough and Aunt Daisy's face would take on an expression of disappointment in me, rather like Tom.

"I expect she got a bit carried away," said Aunt Daisy. "She's such a pretty girl – no doubt the boys are always milling round. She probably let one of them go a bit too far and there you are – too late…"

"No –" I began.

At the same time, my mother said, "Well, it's good riddance as far as I'm concerned. She was a bad influence on you, Joanne. And she caused nothing but trouble in the Crabbie meetings, from what I've heard."

"Mum – Charity was my best friend. She still is. Stop saying horrible things about her."

"Let's hope she writes to you once she's settled in France," said Aunt Daisy.

I felt a dart of hope. "I wonder if she'll have her baby there and then they'll come home?"

My mother and Aunt Daisy exchanged glances. In the air between them I could read the words 'get rid of it', like a speech-bubble in a cartoon. My hope was replaced by a shot of panic, knotting up my stomach.

The conversation died and we left the table.

Just before I went to bed, my mother said, "Joanne, I've been thinking. I don't want you having any more to do with those Crabbies. It's not just Charity – the whole lot of them are a bad influence on you."

Aunt Daisy wasn't there to help me this time. She wasn't keen on the Crabbies but she would probably have stepped in to defend them.

"But Mum – they're my friends. And you like some of them – what about Tom and Pattie? And Louise? And Mrs Pinderfield?"

"Eileen is thinking of leaving, herself. She says this Holy Spirit business has got completely out of hand. She blames Tom for not taking a firmer line. He's a nice man, I'll give you that. He was good to us when your father died. But I've always thought he was a bit weak and this proves it. He should have clamped down from the start. He's let it go too far and now look what's happened." She paused and added, "And I've never liked Alan."

"You don't really know him."

"I know him as well as I want to. Him *and* his family – a dreadful crowd. He was always in trouble at school. And let's not forget that he's been in prison."

"That was ages ago – before he became a Christian. He left all that behind."

My mother snorted. "Only if you believe all that palaver. Leopards don't change their spots, in my experience. Once a troublemaker, always one."

"That's so unfair." I squeezed my fingernails into my palms. How had I got cornered into defending Alan?

"Wait till you've lived as long as I have." My mother picked up our empty cocoa mugs and turned towards the kitchen.

"I'll never be as horrible as you, however long I live…" I began, my face burning.

She turned back at the door. "Joanne." She said my name in the way she reserved for those times she was most angry with me – with a gap between the syllables almost long enough to draw breath.

"What?"

"Do you remember where Charity stayed, just after Christmas? When she wanted to come here and we all had flu?"

"With Louise." I could hardly get the words out.

"With Louise *and Alan*." She paused, still standing in the doorway. "Now put that alongside the way she and Alan carried on at the party."

I said nothing.

"Do you really need me to put two and two together for you, Joanne? You're supposed to be the mathematician. If I can make four, I'm sure you can."

"I don't know what you mean."

"Yes, you do."

I looked at her glinting eyes and wondered what my father would have thought. I remembered him as a fair-minded man, slow to judge, always keen to discover the full facts before reaching an opinion. I longed so much to speak to him.

I imagined myself inside his skin, facing my mother with courage. "It wasn't Alan. He is *not* the father."

"And how would you know, madam?"

"Charity would have told me, if there was anything going on between them. We tell each other everything."

"Hmm. It sounds as though she's got up to a few things she hasn't told you about."

"And she wouldn't have done it. Not with Alan. Not with anyone."

"I wouldn't put it past him to have attacked her. Under provocation, of course."

"Mum – this is Alan you're talking about. He's a Crabbie. A Christian."

"That man has a history of violence."

"He hit someone outside a pub. That's not the same thing as…" I couldn't say the word 'rape' in front of my mother.

My mother gave her head a slow shake, lips pursed. "Well, I'm sure it will all come out, in time. Of you go to bed, now. And remember what I said – I want you to have nothing more to do with the Crabbies. If you see Alan or Louise or any of the others in town, don't speak. Turn your head away. They'll know why."

"I can't do that. Louise is my friend. So is Tom."

"They are not your friends. Apart from anything else, they are adults and you are a child."

I got up from the sofa, picking up my library book. Avoiding her gaze, I pushed past my mother and left the room, biting my lip to hold back tears.

I woke at ten past five next morning to the sound of heavy rain on the window. I felt as though an alarm had gone off in my head, calling me to action, yet there was nothing I could do. It was impossible to go back to sleep so I turned on my lamp and opened the Bible I kept on the bedside cabinet. The dust made me sneeze, reminding me that I hadn't opened it for some time.

I read the part where the angel appears to Mary to tell her she will give birth to God's child, and tried to imagine how Mary must have felt. How old was she? The same age as Charity or even younger? Women married early in Biblical times. What had her parents said about it? Joseph, her fiancé, had believed her story, we were told – but how long did it take him? Was I meant to be some kind of Joseph figure to Charity in all this?

I got up, opened the window and stuck my head out into the icy rain. After a few minutes, my face frozen, I withdrew and rubbed it dry with my dressing gown. The shoulders of my nightdress were damp, too.

I crept downstairs and shut the kitchen door behind me before filling the kettle and turning it on. The last thing I wanted was to wake my mother. I made a mug of tea, with a vague desire to recapture the comfort I'd drawn from the one Tom had made me yesterday afternoon. There were no chocolate biscuits in the tin so I took a couple of digestives, wishing I could talk to Tom again. It was still only five to six – much too early to phone him.

Drinking my tea scalding hot, unable to wait for it to cool and half-enjoying the burning in my throat, I made a decision.

I dived into the supermarket opposite the school and found enough change in my purse to buy a packet of crisps. I'd had no breakfast because the early-morning digestives had left me feeling sick. A can of cola would have been good, too, but there wasn't enough money for that.

When I emerged, the rain had almost stopped. I'd spent my bus fare on the crisps so I jogged to Louise's house, stopping occasionally to regain my breath or cross a road.

As I reached Louise's she was just arriving home with David in his buggy.

"Joanne! Is everything all right? Why aren't you at school?"

"Can I come in? Just for a minute?"

"Of course you can." She unlocked the door and I helped her hoist the buggy up the step.

I was still hungry and consumed several of the pink wafers Louise offered me, apologising that she had nothing more grown-up in the way of biscuits.

"Alan and I are trying to give them up," she said. "He's decided that biscuits are an unnecessary luxury."

She lifted David out of the buggy, removed his outdoor playsuit and put him in a high chair at the table next to me, where he waved his arms and copied the faces I made at him. Louise gave him his plastic training cup of juice and a pink biscuit.

"I keep these hidden from Alan, just for David," she said. "I probably shouldn't, but he loves them."

"What about Alice?"

"I can't let her see them – she would tell."

I reflected that being married to Alan must be rather like living with my mother, if not worse.

Louise gave me a glass of milk and sat down with her mug of coffee. I'd forgotten to tell her that, in my new adult state, I now preferred tea.

"Now, tell me, Joanne. I can see something's wrong."

I felt tears welling. I nodded and said, "Have you heard about Charity?"

She looked puzzled and then concerned. "No. What's happened to her?"

"I'm surprised no-one has told you. She's…" I started sobbing.

"She's what? Joanne, tell me."

"She's pregnant."

"What?"

David dropped his cup and started to cry.

"And she's gone away. Her dad has taken her to France."

In the silence, a blast of rain hit the window like a handful of pebbles.

"Are you sure?"

"Of course I'm sure."

"About the pregnancy, I mean."

"Yes. We did the test together on Saturday. Then she went to the doctor's. It's definite."

I told Louise the rest of the story, including Tom's phone-call to Miss Dodd.

"I can't take it in," said Louise, who now had David on her knee. His eyes were beginning to close and he made rhythmic sucking sounds on his dummy.

"Neither can I."

"You and Charity are very close, aren't you?"

That was what Tom had said. "She's my best friend. The best I've ever had. And I've got a horrible feeling I'll never see her again."

"I'm sure that's not true." Louise's voice was soothing, but I could hear the panic beneath.

"My mother thinks they might make her have an abortion. She didn't actually say so but I saw her think it."

"Oh gosh. Though I suppose…"

"What?"

"Nothing. I'm just thinking what might be best for Charity. She's so young."

"Charity would never have an abortion."

Louise rocked the now-sleeping David from side to side. "Have you any idea who the father is?"

"No."

"Is Charity seeing anyone?"

"No. No-one."

"She doesn't have a boyfriend from school? Or at Crabbies?"

"No." This time I couldn't keep the sharpness out of my voice. David stirred and gave a little moan.

"All right. Sorry. But it must be someone."

I looked at David as I spoke, watched his eyelids slowly shut until only a sliver of white was visible. "I thought maybe you'd noticed – Charity and me…" I turned to Louise.

She met my gaze without understanding at first. But as I waited, something flickered in her dark brown eyes. "What – you two?" She looked uncertain, as though afraid she had jumped to the wrong conclusion.

"Yes. Me and her. We're a couple." It was the first time I'd used those words, even to myself. I liked the sound of them, the feel of the word 'couple' in my mouth.

"I'd no idea."

"We're lesbians."

"Wow. Well. Good for you."

It was a funny thing to say, but I knew what she meant. She was expressing approval and support – assuring me she wasn't homophobic like some of the Crabbies. I'd known that anyway.

I didn't mention Charity's claim to be bisexual. It was too much of a complication and I didn't want to think about it.

"Don't tell any of the Crabbies, will you? Not yet."

"Of course I won't."

"I'll tell them when I'm ready."

"I understand." She paused. "Gosh. So what's happened is all rather… unexpected? Sorry, I'm floundering a bit here. I'm just wondering how it could have come about."

"Charity doesn't understand it, either. She hasn't been with a boy. She's completely sure. You can't make a mistake about a thing like that."

"Well, no." Louise thought for a few moments, stroking David's sleeping head. "How long has Charity known she's gay?"

"Ages. Since before she came here."

"So it couldn't be someone from before the two of you got together?"

"No."

"So how does Charity explain it?"

"She doesn't – she can't. Not in the usual way. She says there's only one thing it can be."

"What's that?"

I paused for effect, then said, "She thinks God made her pregnant. By the Holy Spirit – like with Mary."

Louise almost dropped David from her lap. "She can't possibly believe that."

"She does believe it. I'm sure she does. She wouldn't pretend to, if she didn't."

"I know she's a bit of a fanatic – sorry, but you know what I mean. But even Charity can't think the Holy Spirit got her pregnant."

Louise's disbelief was not what I wanted. "So you don't think she could be right?"

"Of course I don't."

"Tom doesn't, either."

"That doesn't surprise me. I'd be worried if he did."

"But while she was saying it, I kind of believed her. She sounded so sure."

"She's protecting someone – that must be it."

David, awake again and fretting, pulled a strand of Louise's long dark hair.

"He's ready for a proper nap," she said. 'I'll put him down in his cot – just a minute."

While she was gone, I watched the rain streaming down the window onto Alan and Louise's tiny garden, bouncing off the wooden boxes and plastic tubs. I wondered if Louise could possibly be right. Was it possible that Charity was lying – refusing to say who the father was, perhaps from fear of what he might do to her? Could such a thing happen in Castlehaven, among people we knew? If it had she would have told me – I was sure of that.

The pots outside would be full of daffodils and tulips in a couple of months' time. Louise always complained that being married to a professional gardener meant she had to do all the gardening at home because Alan got enough of it at work.

I suddenly longed for it to be spring.

"Let's move to the living room – I'll put the gas fire on," said Louise on her return. "We've a couple of hours before I need to pick up Alice."

"Will Alan be home for lunch?"

"No – he's out on a job all day. They've got an indoor contract for a garden centre. Just as well or he'd be stuck at home now, moaning about the weather."

"What you just said – about Charity protecting someone. She's not, I'm sure."

I thought of what my mother had said – about Alan being the father. Here in his and Louise's home, it was impossible even to contemplate the idea. But I felt ashamed, as though the thought might somehow show on my face.

"It must be someone at school, or someone she met at a disco, perhaps," said Louise. "Her father's away such a lot. She could have asked someone back to the flat. She's probably too embarrassed to say."

"Don't you believe me, about her being gay?"

"Of course I believe you. Joanne, I'm sorry – I know it sounds as though I'm accusing her of being unfaithful to you. I'm sure Charity wouldn't want to hurt you. But sometimes, when you're young, it can take a while to be sure. Some people need to experiment a bit."

"She's already done that. She had a boyfriend in Barnsley, before she came here."

"That must be it, then." Louise's face cleared with relief, as though the mystery was solved. "She must have seen him. That day she went back with her dad, to visit."

Was it possible? Could Charity have done this, and kept it from me? A plug of misery formed in my throat.

Then Alan's face, with his strong jaw and big white teeth, appeared inside my head. I struggled to push it away, without success. The thought of him was in the room with us, as strong as his actual presence.

Something made me say it, though I hated myself as the words came out. "Charity stayed with you and Alan, didn't she, just before Christmas?"

Louise's face froze. She must have been thinking it, too, or trying desperately hard not to, because she knew instantly what I meant. Her voice was icy. "Joanne – are you suggesting what I think you are?"

"I'm not suggesting anything."

Her eyes sent out cold waves. "I think you might be. Come on, out with it."

"No. I didn't mean it like that."

"You think it's Alan, don't you? You think my husband got Charity pregnant?"

"No, I don't. Truly, I don't." I was frightened, my voice shaking.

Louise was on fire. "I bet that's what your mother thinks, too. And Tom. You *all* think it's Alan. That's why you came round here, I bet. Did Tom send you round to see me, to accuse Alan?"

"Of course not. I came because I wanted to see you. To talk to you. I felt so upset." I was crying hard, now, with full-on sobs, fumbling for a tissue.

Louise passed me a box. Her face had thawed a little and she looked close to tears herself. "I think you'd better go. You should be at school, anyway."

"I can't face school. Or home. It's all so horrible…"

"I still can't take it in." Louise took a tissue from the box and blew her nose hard.

I scraped back my chair and got up ready to go, but she said, "No, Joanne. Stay, if you want. Have some lunch with us. Stay all day if you like. I'm sorry for what I said."

"I'm sorry, too. I shouldn't have said that thing about her staying here. I don't know why I did."

"We're both in a bit of a state. You don't really think it was Alan, do you?"

"Of course I don't." I didn't tell her what my mother had said.

Louise picked her tissue to pieces, laying the tiny strands on the chair arm beside her, while I ate another biscuit. Then she said, "Did Charity say anything to you about that night?"

"About what night?"

"She hasn't told you, then? About the night I found Alan in her room?"

My heart gave an enormous bump. "No."

"It was the last night she stayed here. Oh God, I shouldn't be telling you this. If you didn't suspect Alan before, you will now."

"What happened?"

Louise looked at the ceiling, up into the corner where a stray cobweb strand hung down, slowly wafting from side to side, caught by the light from the corner lamp.

"I heard a sound in the night. I got up and checked the children but they were both asleep. Then I thought it might be Charity, because she'd told me she sometimes had nightmares. I opened the door and saw that Alice's pink nightlight was on. Charity was sitting up in bed in her white pyjamas. Alan was on the bed, beside her… just sitting there." She paused, took a breath. "Holding her hand."

I breathed out and in again, hard and slow, before I made myself say, "He probably heard her cry and went in. She gets very upset when she has her nightmares. I've heard her myself. I bet that's why Alan took hold of her hand, to comfort her." Relief washed through me as I heard my own words.

After a long pause, Louise said, "Yes. That would make sense, wouldn't it? It's what I thought at the time."

"Did you ask them about it next day?"

"No. I don't think Alan saw me there – he had his back half-turned. I'm not sure about Charity. She didn't mention it. Perhaps she never properly woke up."

I still felt odd – perhaps because I'd held my breath so long. It seemed an effort, now, to breathe at all. I counted up to seven before Louise said, "You won't mention this to anyone, will you?"

"Of course not. Who would I mention it to, anyway?"

"Your mother. Or Tom."

I shuddered at the thought of my mother's response to any of this. "I won't say a word."

"Good. I shouldn't have told you. I keep forgetting how young you are."

"That makes a change. Most people still treat me as if I was ten."

"You're unusually sensible and mature for your age. But this is all very hard for you. Especially as you and Charity are… together. Does Tom know, by the way?"

"No. He doesn't even know I'm gay. Unless he's guessed."

"I don't suppose he has."

"I was going to tell him yesterday but I couldn't get started, somehow."

"You should tell him. He'll be fine. Does your mother know?"

"No. She's the hardest person to tell."

"What about your aunt?"

"Aunt Daisy might have worked it out. She gives me funny looks sometimes, and says strange things to me."

"That's interesting. Of course, she's never been married, has she?"

"Are you thinking the same thing as me?"

"It's a possibility."

"She's quite good at understanding me. Better than Mum."

"Perhaps you should broach the subject, sometime?"

"It's not easy. If she takes it the wrong way and gets mad at me, she might tell Mum."

"It's a risk, I suppose. All you can do is look for opportunities."

"She sticks up for gays when Mum goes off on one of her homophobic rants. But that might just be because she's a nicer person. I'm glad she lives with us. I hated it at first, when Dad died and she came to stay and never went home. But now it's more like having a big sister, even though she's so old. She doesn't always take my side against Mum, but at least she dilutes her a bit, if you know what I mean."

Louise laughed. "I like your Aunt Daisy."

"She's good fun, especially when she gets away from Mum. It's hard to believe they're sisters."

"Your mother's had a hard time, though, losing your dad."

"Sometimes I wonder if Dad crashed that bus on purpose, just to get away from her."

"Joanne – that's a terrible thing to say."

"But then he must have wanted to get away from me, too." I couldn't believe my own words. I'd never admitted these fears, even to myself, before.

"Of course he didn't! He loved you both very much, I'm sure of that. I remember your dad – a lovely, kind man. It was a terrible accident. You know that, really."

"I suppose I do. But first my dad gets taken away and now Charity. Perhaps God's punishing me."

"What on earth for?"

"I don't know. Everything."

"The God I believe in wouldn't do that. Even if you had done something bad, which I'm sure you haven't."

"Some of my feelings are horrible. I felt so jealous of Charity at the party."

"Did you? Why?"

As she asked me, I realised, from the depths of my self-absorption, what I'd said. "Oh – you know. Just the way she flirted with the boys…"

"You mean with Alan?"

"Not just him. All the men and boys."

"But it was mostly Alan, wasn't it? And he lapped it up. I'd begun to wonder if it was my imagination. No-one else seems to have noticed."

"I suppose it didn't matter so much to them."

"Exactly. Whereas for us, it was our other halves making exhibitions of themselves with each other. Oh God – I shouldn't be saying this to you…"

"It's all right." I straightened my back, drawing myself up into my new status as an adult. "But I still don't think it was Alan."

Louise's voice was high with panic. "I'm beginning to think it was. Oh my God. Joanne – I don't know what to do."

"Talk to Tom." It was all I could think of. Louise's wild eyes frightened me. I wished Tom was with us – solid, slow-spoken and unflappable.

"I daren't."

"Why not? If it *is* Alan, Tom will know what to do."

"What can he do? Charity is underage. Alan will go to prison."

"Can anyone prove it?"

"Possibly. They can sometimes use blood tests."

"But it *wasn't* him. This is your Alan we're talking about. It can't have been him. The tests will show it wasn't." I had a sense of role-reversal again, as though I was trying to reassure Louise. An odd but not unpleasant feeling.

Louise dug both sets of fingernails into her cheeks. "I can't get the thought out of my head. The memory of what I saw that night. Him sitting on her bed…"

"Try not to think about it."

"I can't help it."

"For the millionth time – Charity would have told me."

"What if Alan is threatening to hurt her if she speaks out? Maybe she told that to her dad, and that's why he's taken her away?"

"But if Mr Baker thought that, he'd have been round to see Alan. Probably to beat him up."

"He might have contacted Alan without my knowing. Alan was in a funny mood at breakfast time. What if he'd had a phone call from Mr Baker? He wouldn't necessarily tell me."

My head was starting to go into a fuzz with all these possibilities. "Shall I phone Tom for you? Ask him to come round?"

"No. Not yet. I want to think."

"Shall I go away and let you talk to him on your own?"

"No, please don't go. Stay for lunch. I'll need to nip out and get Alice. Perhaps you could stay here with David?"

"Okay. My mother thinks I'm at school."

"You'll be in trouble with your teachers. And your mother, if she finds out."

"I don't care."

"That's not like you."

"Nothing matters, compared to this. I don't care if I fail all my exams, including maths."

"You won't do that. But I'm afraid I've made things worse for you, getting into this state."

"It's okay."

"No, it's not. You've had an awful shock, Charity getting pregnant and disappearing, and all I've done is go on and on about Alan."

"I'm not a child any more. I can cope."

Louise looked at me in silence – trying to decide if it was true?

After a minute or so, I said, "If only this baby *could* be God's child."

"I know what you mean. It would make things simpler, wouldn't it? In a way."

"You don't think it possibly could be?"

"No, Joanne, I don't."

Chapter 8

Received Thursday 8th March 1984:

Dear Joanne,

I'm sorry I left without letting you know. I wanted to phone you that night but Dad wouldn't let me. He went completely mad when I told him I was pregnant. He didn't let me get a word in edgeways about it being the Holy Spirit's baby. You'd think he'd never heard about Jesus, the way he went on

He thinks it's a boy from school or Crabbies. I wanted to tell him about you and me but I didn't dare. He was in such a mood. He started throwing things round the kitchen and yelling at me. He said he was going to get me out of Castlehaven as soon as possible. I dialled your number but he snatched the phone out of my hand.

Anyway we are in France. See the address above, though I'm not sure if I have got it right. I don't know the postcode or whatever they have here. We are staying with my mother and Aunt Stella. They share a house. Aunt Stella is weird. To be honest, she is horrible. Very thin and witch-like. I keep well out of her way. Dad goes off all day. I don't know where he goes. I mainly stay in my room. It's quite nice but I miss my things.

I feel sick all day until about 4 o'clock. Then I start feeling better and very hungry. I eat lots of French bread and pastries. That's the best thing about being here. The only nice thing, really. No, there is one other good thing, that my mother doesn't seem to be drinking.

I miss you ever so much, Joanne. Do you miss me? Give my love to everyone at Crabbies. Tell them I'm okay. Tell Tony I'm sorry the tape he lent me is still back at the flat I think.

I hope you are telling everyone that the Holy Spirit made me pregnant and I am going to give birth to God's daughter. I hope He will let me call her Rosie and not choose a stupid Bible name for her. Some of the Crabbies will probably not believe you, specially the ones who are resistant to the Spirit. But keep working on them. They will have to believe in the end.

Can you tell people at school where I am, please? Don't tell them I'm pregnant. Dad said he would phone Miss Dodd but I don't know if he did. Tell Mr Adams I'm sorry I can't be in the play. Jane Bowen can be Joan of Arc instead. She wanted the part, anyway. I bet she's pleased I've gone.

Mum is taking me shopping tomorrow to buy some maternity clothes. I still can't believe there is a baby inside me and it will start to show soon. I hate going in shops here. No-one understands my French and I don't understand theirs. It's too fast without any gaps between the words. Tell Mrs Ford she is teaching it all wrong!

I have written out my prayer for you. Please pray it for me every single night. Don't miss out any of the words. If you make a mistake it's best to start again, just in case. God seems very fussy about getting it exactly right.

I start crying when I think of you and the Crabbies and Castlehaven. But I'll be all right. God will protect me and Rosie. We are part of His perfect plan. So are you. I hope your mum is not being difficult. How is your Aunt Daisy?

Lots of love and hugs from Charity xxxx

After reading Charity's letter I felt almost convinced again. Her certainty that God was the baby's father was difficult to resist. I had let her down by not arguing her case hard enough with Louise and Tom – by giving in too easily to their scepticism – to what Charity would describe as their 'resistance to the Spirit.'

The letter arrived two days after my visit to Louise. I'd gone back to school next day, armed with a note I'd written, complete with my mother's forged signature. I felt only a moderate twinge of guilt. Events had taken such a turn that the old rules seemed irrelevant.

On Friday, the day after Charity's letter came, I got home from school to find my mother in a state and Aunt Daisy nowhere to be seen.

"I've just heard the latest in the Charity saga," Mum said, her voice grim, verging on sinister. She didn't know I'd had the letter, since I'd managed to beat her to pick up the post.

I hardly dared ask. "What have you heard?"

She waited a moment or so to maximise the effect. "Alan has left home. Mrs Elliot from the pet shop saw him first thing this morning, while it was still dark. Walking in the direction of the station with a suitcase in each hand." She looked at me with a triumphant, I-told-you-so expression. "So does that prove he's the father or doesn't it?"

I was too stunned to answer. My mother's lip curled with pleasure. She continued, "Anne Skidmore, in the bank, told me told me she saw Louise later on, on her way to pick up Alice from school. Her face was all red and puffed up with crying. Louise, that is, not Alice."

Feeling my legs about to give way, I sank onto a kitchen chair.

"What have you got to say now about your beloved Crabbies?"

I found my voice at last. "Nothing. I don't know…"

"No, I don't know, either, and nor does anyone else. Castlehaven has never known such a scandal. It's worthy of the Sunday papers. 'Assistant pastor knocks up fifteen-year-old girl.'"

"Mum. We still don't know for sure it was Alan. And Charity's sixteen, anyway."

"She was only fifteen when he knocked her up."

I'd never heard my mother use such language. "Don't jump to conclusions," I said. "He might have gone away for some other reason."

"What – gone off on his holidays, all on his own, at the beginning of March? Leaving his wife in tears?"

"It could be a work trip."

"Since when does a jobbing gardener go on a work trip? You'll be telling me next he's at a summit conference. Representing Castlehaven at the United Nations."

"Don't be silly, Mum."

She snorted. "I don't know why you're so keen to defend Alan, after what he's done to your friend."

"I'm not. But we don't know all the facts yet."

"I know quite enough facts to satisfy me. So do Anne Skidmore and Mrs Elliot and Eileen Pinderfield. All I can say is I hope Mr Baker reports him to the police. He could get ten years in prison for this, and that's the least he deserves. Taking advantage of a vulnerable young woman..."

"A few days ago you were saying it was Charity's fault – that she asked for it."

"I'm not saying she didn't. But he still shouldn't have taken advantage. If it turns out to be rape, he could be in for life." My mother suddenly seemed to remember she was speaking to her fifteen-year-old-daughter, who, she fondly believed, knew next-to-nothing about sex. "Anyway, that's enough of that kind of talk. It's none of our business, any of it. Why don't you start your homework and I'll make you some hot chocolate?"

"Can I have tea instead?"

"We *are* getting grown up. Very well, madam – your wish is my command."

"Where's Aunt Daisy?"

"It's her theatre club night. They've gone to see a play in Leeds."

"Wish I could go."

"Well you can't – you have to be eighteen."

"That's silly. Fifteen is old enough to go to the theatre."

"You have to be eighteen to join the theatre club. Anyway, you've got homework to do."

"A couple of weeks ago you were telling me off for being a swot."

"You're getting rather cheeky and unpleasant of late. I think it's the influence of Charity Baker. Thank goodness she's gone."

As soon as I got the chance, when Mum was glued to the TV screen watching Coronation Street, I got on the hall phone to Louise. It rang for ages and I was about to give up when she picked up and said, "Alan, is that you?"

"No, it's me, Joanne."

"Oh. Hello." Her voice was flat.

"Mum told me about Alan. Is it true he's left home?"

I heard her swallow. "When I woke up this morning he'd gone. Not that I slept much – we were arguing half the night. He left a note on the kitchen table."

"But why? Why's he gone?"

"He went to see Tom yesterday evening. Tom kind of summoned him there and more or less accused him of fathering Charity's child. Not in so many words – but Alan said it was obvious that's what Tom thought."

"But Tom doesn't think that."

"It appears he does. Anyway, whatever he said, it got Alan really mad. He came home in an awful mood. When the kids were in bed I tried to talk to him, to calm him down. That went on for hours. Then he asked me what I thought."

"What did you say?"

"I told him the truth. That I trusted him. That I didn't think he was the father."

"So why – ?"

"He didn't believe me. Said he could see the suspicion glinting in my eyes. That was the phrase he used. Accused me of being in league with Tom. I said I wasn't. Then he asked if I trusted him a hundred percent."

"And?"

"I made the mistake of hesitating – just for a second or two – then I said, 'Yes, of course.' But it was too late. He said the fact I'd had to think about it meant I wasn't sure. He said he couldn't live with a woman who didn't trust him completely. We went round in circles for hours. Whatever I said made things worse. He said he would sleep on the sofa. When I woke at six, he'd gone."

"What did the note say?"

"There was more about my not trusting him. The horrible thing is…"

"What?"

"That it's kind of true, now. He's made it true. Before he went, I did trust him. Almost. But now he's gone I keep asking myself why. Why would he leave, if it wasn't guilty conscience? Or fear of getting found out."

"Do you know where he's gone?"

"No idea. I haven't heard from him. That's why I thought it might be him, when you rang just now."

"I'm sorry." I paused. "I don't know what to say."

"Of course you don't. No-one does. There's nothing *to* say. Alice keeps asking where her Daddy's gone. David won't stop crying. I'm going slowly mad."

"Shall I come round?" I began planning how I might sneak out of the house.

"No, it's all right. Tom's coming to talk to me this evening. I've got a few things to say to him, I can tell you."

"I can't believe he thinks it's Alan."

"Perhaps he knows something we don't. Perhaps Alan told him something. Or maybe Charity has been in touch."

"I got a letter from her this morning. She still thinks it's the Holy Spirit."

"The poor child. God – how do we get out of this mess?"

I heard footsteps behind the living room door. "Mum's coming – I'll have to go."

I put the phone down as my mother appeared in the hall, giving me a suspicious look. "Who were you speaking to?"

It was becoming all too easy to lie to her. "Claire from school. It was about her project."

"It's good to see you making some new friends. But go and do your homework now, there's a good girl."

"I've finished it."

"Have you? Well, come and watch TV with me. It's lonely without Daisy."

"I've got things to do upstairs."

"Give your room a tidy while you're at it." The signature tune announced the second half of Coronation Street. "See you at suppertime, then."

Sprawled on my bed, I wrote a long letter to Charity. I didn't mention the father of her child or Alan's departure. I had doubts whether my letter would reach her – the address she'd given me looked suspiciously incomplete.

Tom's journal, Thursday 8th March 1984

Charity Baker – pregnant and in France. Don't know where to begin. Such a terrible shock. I feel so sorry for the poor girl. Guilty, too, for it's clear that we, the Crabbies, and I in particular as her pastor, have let her down.

I suppose I must be naïve, but I somehow assumed that a young woman so steeped in the Word of God, burning with such enthusiasm for His work, so full of yearning for His Spirit, would not, to put it crudely, be having sex. Yes, I'm naïve – I see that now.

Perhaps we failed to set out the Lord's teachings with sufficient clarity. We assumed our young folk knew what was

right and wrong. Or perhaps Charity knew, but simply fell to temptation, as we are all prone to do from time to time. Perhaps – heaven forbid – someone took advantage of her warm, generous, loving nature.

I can't get this last thought out of my mind. Someone older – someone in authority – someone she respects? Someone she is afraid of? Otherwise, why would she deny it? If the baby's father is a boy from school, why not say so? If she is reluctant to name him for some reason, why not simply say it's someone like that? Instead of denying that she ever had a sexual relationship with anyone. Does she really expect us to believe her? Even young Joanne, who seemed inclined to believe her story at first, saw sense when we discussed it.

What is Charity trying to do – kid herself it never happened?

If only I could speak to her. I'm sure, given time, she would tell me the truth.

Later:

I can't stop myself wondering whether it could be someone in our fellowship.

Forgive me, Father – I can't stop thinking of one person. I hardly dare write his name.

Alan.

I feel so bad to have even thought it. To suspect him – one of my closest friends, my confidant, my faithful assistant. Dear Alan, so enthusiastic and hard-working, so good with the youngsters and the elderly, so quick to welcome Charity to Crabbies and recognise her gifts.

Such a transformed man since his conversion seven years ago. A fine example of a 'man made new' by God's grace. His past forgiven and wiped out – a whole new course ahead of him. His devotion to Louise and the children. His unswerving loyalty to me.

I feel ill when I try to suppress my fears, even worse when I give vent to them. I keep seeing Alan with Charity at the Christmas party. I see Louise in tears. She has told me since, in the counselling sessions we've had, how unhappy he has made her with his attentions to Charity. She says he is infatuated with the girl and I can't help thinking she is right.

Yet Louise's kind-heartedness led her to ask Charity to stay with them just after Christmas when her father was away. Which, by my reckoning, would be just about right...

Oh God, my Father – help me do the right thing here. If Alan has transgressed with Charity, it's far worse than 'just' marital infidelity. It's sex with an under-age girl. Whether or not she encouraged him, he has broken the law. If he did it, that is. I mustn't slide into making assumptions. If he did it against her wishes... no, I mustn't think that way. I can't think such things of my brother-in-the-Lord.

Yet I have a responsibility to Charity and the rest of the fellowship. Perhaps, even, to protect others from him.

God help me. Help all of us.

Tom's journal, Friday 9th March 1983

I've done it now. Challenged Alan outright. Asked whether he is the father of Charity's child.

Never seen him so angry. Don't think I've ever seen anyone so angry. He thought I was accusing him of rape – the rape of an under-age child. I tried to explain I was just asking – giving him the chance to confess. If he had anything to confess. He said he couldn't understand how I needed to ask. I'm his friend – couldn't I trust him? I said I wanted to, more than anything, but I needed to be sure.

Thought he was going to hit me. Eyes blazing, fist raised. But he stormed out, slammed the door. When he'd gone I thought I had my answer – it couldn't possibly be him. But then I thought about it. If it was him, he'd be terrified. Ashamed, deep down, but terrified on top. Of course he would deny it, even to me.

So I'm no nearer the truth.

Later:

Just had a call from Louise. Alan has left home. He accused her of not trusting him either.

That worries me. If Louise thinks it might be him – well, she's his wife. Knows him better than anyone. And she's a sensible woman – I'd trust her intuitions any day.

What can I do? I just rang Margaret Dodd again, voicing some of my fears. I didn't mention Alan by name, of course. She says do nothing for the moment. She will try to make some enquiries in France.

Now I must go and visit poor Louise.

Received Saturday 17th March 1984:

Dear Joanne,

I got your letter! It was lovely to hear from you. It made me feel so homesick for Castlehaven. I'm glad you miss me as much as I miss you.

I'm really bored. I never thought I'd miss school, but I do. I can't watch TV because it's all in French. I haven't got any cassettes with me and Mum's tapes are all crap. There is no-one my age. A horrible doctor examined me and gave me yucky medicine for my morning sickness. It made it even worse.

They are starting to get to know me in the village shops. Some of them are friendly and speak some English. I have learnt a few things to say in French. I asked Dad if I could go to church but he said no. He says it's a bad influence. I can't believe how much he's changed since we lived in Barnsley. He was a really strong Christian in those days.

I am doing my best to keep my faith strong. I read my Bible all the time – partly because there is nothing else to do. God keeps reminding me that He will be with me whatever happens. It's a great comfort.

Who did they get to play Joan of Arc? I hope whoever it is doesn't make a mess of it. I was looking forward to being in that play. I would love to be an actress. Maybe one day I will be, if it's what God wants for me.

I'm so bored I'm starting to notice stupid nature things like buds coming out on the trees. It's a very pretty village. Is it still raining in Castlehaven? I keep asking Dad when we can go home but he says he wants me here for the next few months. He must mean until Rosie is born.

Are you saying my prayer every night? I think you must be, because I sometimes forget, and I haven't had a single nightmare. Thanks.

I was worried at first that Dad and Mum might make me have an abortion. But they haven't said anything and Mum has bought me lots of maternity clothes so it must be all right. There are some nice shops in the town a few miles away. Mum seems to have loads of money. We are getting on a bit better now. She told me how sick she was when she was expecting me. And she showed me some baby photos I hadn't seen before. I was a weird-looking baby!

I can't wait to have Rosie. I suppose she will look a bit like me – but who else? What does God look like? Will she take after him? I hope she doesn't have a long white beard, ha-ha. But seriously, I was thinking about genes and DNA. You know more about these things than me. How would it all work?

Will Rosie be like ordinary children and be able to live at home with me? Jesus lived with his parents, didn't he? I suppose he went to school, if they had them in those days. I hope Rosie can have a normal life. Maybe when we are a bit older you and I can live together, Joanne. Would you like that? Then Rosie would have two parents. Forget what I said about being bi. I am sure now that I am gay. You can be Rosie's second mother, if you like, and we will be a family together. I can't wait.

Give my love to everyone.

Love you lots,

Charity xxxxx

Received Friday 30th March 1984:

Dear Joanne,

Sorry to take so long to answer your letter. I have been quite ill with a virus but I am better now. The horrible doctor came to see me and prodded my stomach. I was afraid he might hurt Rosie. He said I would have to go to hospital if I kept on throwing up. But then I started to feel better.

It is lovely here now with all the leaves coming out and lots of flowers. Mum got a book to help me learn some French. I'm getting quite good at it. I can watch TV now and understand some of it. When I come back to school Mrs Ford will think I'm a genius.

What is happening in Crabbies? You don't say much about them. Please tell me all the news. I hope they believe by now about Rosie being God's child. Keep working on them until they do. Even Tom will have to admit it in the end. He is like Doubting Thomas in the Bible.

Every day I feel more full of God's Spirit. I suppose that's because His child is growing inside me. When I feel a bit down I remind myself how lucky I am to be chosen. I wonder why God chose me? It is a great honour and I will try and live up to it.

Are you still getting top marks in maths, you swotty thing?

What you said about chromosomes and Rosie made a bit of sense. Though not a lot. I am no good at science. But I am sure God knows what He's doing.

I miss the way you used to brush my hair. It makes me tingle to think about it. Sometimes I have lovely dreams about you, then I wake up and feel sad. But God will reunite us in His own good time.

Keep praying my prayer. No nightmares yet!

Love you,

Charity xxx

Tom's journal, Saturday 31st March 1984

Perhaps I have been too hasty in condemning Alan. I simply don't know. Speaking to Louise and seeing how much she <u>wants</u> to believe him innocent has brought me to my senses. That young woman's generosity of spirit is phenomenal. Yes, she is his wife – but with things as they stand, would Pattie still trust me? Would I trust her, if it's possible to imagine such a reversed set of circumstances?

Louise is showing herself to have immense strength of character. Here she is, struggling on alone, caring for her children. Her parents are helping, of course. What must they make of it all? She is getting support from a number of the Crabbies. But there is so much gossip. I'm doing my best to quell it, but it's a losing battle.

I've seen nothing of Joanne since she called to see me that afternoon. I tried to ring, but Jean told me she was asleep. At eight in the evening? I have a feeling I'm being kept away. Louise tells me she has seen Joanne and that the girl seems to be coping. It's very hard for her – she and Charity were very close friends.

I hope to speak this afternoon to my old friend, Jack. The best mentor anyone could have. He'll have good advice, I'm sure. There's no-one in Castlehaven I can turn to.

Meanwhile, what's wrong between Pattie and me? She seems so cool all the time. We never get down to talking properly. Even when we get the chance she says she is too tired. We haven't made love for weeks. She is working much too hard, that's part of the problem.

Does she blame me for this awful situation with the Crabbies? I blame myself, that's for sure. I hope Jack can help me.

Received Wednesday 2nd May 1984:

Dear Joanne,

This is only a short letter. We are moving to a different place. I don't know where. I'm quite sad, because I've got used to being here. I have even made a friend, a girl who works in the baker's. She has taught me lots of French words – some of them rude. She's called Annelise and she's a Christian. She wants the Special Blessing and we have been praying for it but no success yet. I hope she does not give up when I go away.

I will miss her but not as much as I miss you. Nowhere near as much. Don't worry, I don't fancy her or anything. Don't you go looking at any other girls while I'm away! Only joking – I know you won't.

I have no idea where we are going except that it is still in France. Dad says it's time to move on. Perhaps it's because of his work. I will send you a letter with my new address.

My morning sickness is a lot better. Mum says I will feel Rosie kicking before too long. I can't wait! I talk to her before I go to sleep at night (Rosie, not Mum). I have told her all about you.

I'm glad you like the idea of living together when we are older. I know you will probably want to go to university first. It would be a shame to waste your genius at maths. I don't think I am clever enough to do a degree. Maybe I can go to drama college, if they have a crèche for babies.

Rosie will be so lucky, won't she, to have two mothers – you and me? My parents will not be happy and I don't expect your mum will be, either, but who cares what they think? If we are doing God's will, that's all that matters.

I have to stop now and do some packing.

Lots of love,

Charity xxxx

Tom's journal, Thursday 4th May 1984

I have such admiration for Louise. She is continuing to cope superbly well, in a situation that would test anyone. Each time I visit her I come away feeling better. She is an inspiration and she's helping me keep going. She's very concerned about the effect all this is having on me. She really cares, I can tell. That's the sort of person she is.

Alan is such a lucky man – how could he throw all that away?

He is staying with his cousin, Louise tells me, in a village fifteen miles or so inland. I don't much like the sound of this cousin – Rob, I think he's called. I know that several of Alan's family have been in trouble with the law.

Alan comes to Castlehaven every Saturday to see the children. He and Louise only exchange a few words. She keeps

trying to talk to him, but he refuses. She tries to tell him she doesn't think he is the father, but he won't listen.

I managed to speak to Joanne a week or so ago, when I bumped into her in town. She was very furtive. I think her mother has told her not to speak to me. She has had a number of letters from Charity, but nothing now for about three weeks. Charity's address has changed and she doesn't know the new one. I tried writing to the old address but it was returned to me. The same thing happened to Joanne's letter.

Margaret Dodd hasn't managed to find anything out. Nothing from the Barnsley church, either. No-one there seems to have heard from Mr Baker since he and Charity went away.

I'm beginning to wonder if we'll ever hear from Charity again.

Louise told me something interesting. I knew Charity and Joanne were close, but I hadn't realised they were, as she puts it, 'a couple'. I was gob-smacked. Mainly, I suppose, because of the way Charity flirts with the men and boys. What's all that about? Louise asked me to keep it confidential, and of course I will. There are people in the Crabbies, sadly, who will not 'approve'.

All I can do is to keep supporting Louise as best I can. I would like to speak to Alan, but she says he won't meet me. I still have a deep fear that he is the father. I only wish I didn't. But I expressed myself badly when I saw him and I want to apologise.

I would be delighted to discover that it wasn't him.

I wish I could get out of my head the expression on his face when he used to look at Charity.

Pattie went off to work this morning looking dreadful. I wonder if she is sickening for something. She won't go to the doctor – says she is just tired.

All this is taking its toll on her and on Juliette and Craig, too. I can't help wishing, sometimes, I was in a different job.

Give me the strength, Father, to cope.

Tom's journal, Monday 8th June 1984

I'm going to pour out all my feelings here, as I can no longer pray.

I have this frenetic excitement, this charge in my veins. The glorious, glowing feeling I've had for the last few weeks – the calm, delightful joy I've felt in Louise's presence – has turned into this frantic, desperate longing – this gut-tightening sickness – this sense that any moment I'm not with her is wasted time.

I'm finally admitting it – I'm in love.

In love with Louise – the wife of the man who may be the father of Charity's child. What a mouthful. What a mess.

I feel so guilty towards Pattie. Not that I've done anything wrong, not outwardly. Not that Louise returns my feelings or even suspects how I feel. I'm struggling to keep it from her. Knowing I'm in love with her would only make her situation worse. She relies on me for support, strength, counsel. I can't withdraw those things. There's no-one else can help her the way I do. I don't say that with pride, but I know it's true. She trusts me the way she can trust no-one else these days. I can't betray that trust.

God help me. If it's any fault of my own that I've developed these feelings, I'm truly sorry. I try not to indulge them. When Pattie and I made love the other night – first time in ages – I struggled so hard not to think of Louise. But her face kept forming in my mind.

My children look at me, as always, with such love, and I hate the way I'm betraying them, if only in my heart. What can I do? Jack says pray, pray, pray. But I can't pray. All thoughts of God are obscured by Louise. Jack is a wise man but he's forgotten what it's like.

Louise, Louise, Louise. It's summer and the blossom's out, the sea is brilliant blue. Children are playing on the sands. I want to take your hand and walk for miles along the cliff-top, lie down with you in the soft grass, take you in my arms and pour out all my love. You are intelligent, resourceful and kind. You have a sense of humour I never suspected when I saw you with Alan. A desire to see the best in people. Unswerving loyalty to those you love. You are all I ever wanted to be and all I ever wanted.

My dear Pattie – was it ever like this with you? It must have been once, I suppose, but I can barely remember it now. Forgive me, my wife of so many years, mother of my dear

children. Forgive me, Juliette and Craig. You deserve a better father than me.

I wash carefully, all over, before I visit Louise. I change my underwear, as though I'm planning to strip naked and make love. Yet I know this is impossible. Even if she wanted it, and I've no indication that she does, I would never let it happen. I'd be betraying my family, my vocation and my God.

Yet every atom in me yearns to join with her. Louise, Louise. Most beautiful name, most beautiful woman. Loveliest of eyes. Dark, rich, abundant hair that is rarely tidy and all the better for it. Roundness of figure. She tells me she has put on weight since Alan left, because she comfort-eats. In my view, her face and figure have filled out to a more womanly shape. To me, she is perfect. With a smile to light up heaven.

I love her Lord. I'm sorry, but I do. I sing my favourite hymns, not to You, but to her. I'm sinking fast. Help me, before I lose all desire to be helped.

"Tom! Louise!" My voice merged with the cries of the seagulls. It was one of those midsummer evenings where the sea is a flat swathe of blue silk. An occasional wave summoned the energy to rise and then topple, exhausted by the effort, into a line of foam. It was just after nine and salmon streaks were appearing in the sky.

The sand-wrinkles left by the outgoing tide dug into the soles of my feet as I ran, stabbing my toes on pebbles and broken shells. Tom and Louise stood together at the edge of the sea. As I approached the shoreline, I caught a whiff of seaweed mixed with decaying fish, replacing the scent of wild roses wafting down from the cliff path.

As they saw me they jumped apart. Not that they'd been touching, not exactly. But they'd been standing close in that way that couples sometimes do, aware like ballet dancers of the space between them, as though at any moment they might embrace.

It was a shock to see them like that. Tom, after all, was married to Pattie, as well as being the Crabbies' pastor. Louise was still Alan's wife, though they no longer lived together. But I couldn't help admire the beauty of their pose. I envied them, too. It should have been Charity and I meeting there. The thought made my throat ache.

"Joanne – hi!" Tom's deep voice carried up the beach.

I noted a look of exaggerated innocence on both their faces. They were like children almost caught out doing something forbidden, but confident they had escaped detection.

As I reached them, Louise said, "Lovely evening, isn't it?" Without letting me reply, she added, "Tom and I are having one of our counselling sessions. It was too nice to stay indoors, so we decided to come down here."

Tom said nothing. His cheeks had a faint blush.

"I'll let you get on with it," I said.

"Oh no – don't go. We've nearly finished," said Louise. "Why don't we all sit on the rocks for a while?"

"Good idea," said Tom.

"Okay," I said, and followed them.

When we had settled ourselves, Tom asked, "Have you heard any more from Charity?"

"Not for nearly a month now. She still hasn't sent me her new address."

Tom looked out to sea and sighed. "It's a long time."

"I'm really worried about her," I said.

"I'm sure she's okay." Louise's voice was weak, as though she wasn't sure at all. "Perhaps her letter got lost in the post."

I drew a wide arc in the sand with my big toe. "She would have written again by now."

Neither of them replied. A seagull gave a loud squawk above our heads.

"What if her parents have made her have an abortion?" I asked. "What if it went wrong and she bled to death?"

Louise reached over and rested her hand on mine. "Joanne, that sort of thing doesn't happen nowadays. And her parents wouldn't do that, I'm sure. She must be well on with her pregnancy now."

"Rosie is due in October."

"Rosie?" asked Tom.

"That's what she's calling her baby. She's sure it's a girl."

"I knew what both mine were going to be," said Louise. "I could just tell."

"Where are Alice and David?" I asked.

"Staying the night with my parents, as a special treat."

There was a pause.

"We've missed you at Crabbies," Tom said.

"I don't feel like going at the moment."

"That's fine – I understand. Just wanted you to know we're thinking of you. You're not forgotten."

I tried to imagine a Crabbies meeting without Charity or Alan. It was difficult. "Thanks."

"I wish there was something we could do," said Tom.

"I just want her to come back. Or even to know she's okay, that would be something."

He sighed again. "I'm sure she's fine. She's with her parents – we know she's safe."

"We don't know that for sure," I said. "She doesn't get on too well with her mum. She might have run away."

"She's got too much sense for that," said Louise. But once again, she didn't sound convinced.

There was a long pause while we all gazed out to sea. The tide had turned and each wave crept a little further up the sand. I wanted to believe these adults, to lean on their experience and wisdom. But their uncertainty was obvious and they seemed at least as vulnerable as me. Growing up, I saw, wasn't all about gaining. You lost something, too – the security of believing that grown-ups understood the world better than you.

Louise broke the silence. "Have you tried the school again?" she asked Tom.

"Several times. Margaret has promised to tell me if she hears anything."

Tom and Louise exchanged a glance. I'd no idea what it meant and felt excluded. I wanted, suddenly, to be at home, away from them.

PART 2

Chapter 9

December 1984

"Joanne, you'll never guess what – Charity's here! Do you want to come round?"

It was a damp, foggy December day with little light. I'd been home from school about ten minutes and had just got myself a plate of biscuits and a glass of milk to take to my room. My mother and Aunt Daisy were both out. If my mother had answered the phone I would not have been allowed to speak to Louise.

I hardly dared ask. "Has she got Rosie with her?"

"She certainly has. You never saw such a gorgeous baby."

"Okay – I'm on my way."

As I put the phone down I managed to dislodge a porcelain horse from the hallstand. It shattered as it hit the floor tiles and I pushed the pieces down the back of the shoe cupboard. My dad's photo also fell but was undamaged.

Heart thumping, I scribbled a note on the telephone pad to say I'd gone to my friend Nicola's and would be there all evening. I'd tell my mother the truth later. It would hardly be possible to keep Charity's return a secret for long.

I'd heard nothing from Charity since that letter in May announcing that she was about to move. Nor, to my knowledge, had anyone else. My mother had continued to forbid any contact with the Crabbies but I managed to see Louise from time to time. Alan was still staying with his brother and visiting his children at weekends. Nothing had changed.

The mist was thickening and it was almost dark. I had a strange, dislocated sense of awareness of all that I should be feeling but somehow wasn't. It was as though the fog in the streets had got into my brain, blocking out the thrill and anticipation. Charity, after all, was back and I would see her in less than ten minutes. As my feet thudded over the slippery pavements, my shoulder bag bumping against my back, I told myself over and over, "Charity's here!" But all I felt was a slight foreboding that things were not quite right.

She came to the door behind Louise and I could see straightaway she was different. Her face was pale and she had her hair tied back so there seemed to be much less of it. When she smiled, it was far below her normal standard. I could half-believe she'd forgotten me.

But, I told myself, she was preoccupied with the screaming Rosie. I tried without much success to hug them both at once, and then stood back to look at the howling white-clad bundle with the red face.

"She's lovely."

Charity managed a bigger smile this time as she wrestled with Rosie's flailing arms.

Louise was fiddling about with a sterilising unit and bottles. "Charity hasn't brought much stuff with her," she said. "She came by train and couldn't carry most of Rosie's things. The poor little thing is starving. Luckily I've still got David's feeding stuff and the right kind of milk powder."

"Aren't you breastfeeding?" I asked Charity.

She looked startled. "No."

"It's supposed to be better, isn't it?"

I don't know why I said this. I was hardly an expert on babies and my first question had clearly made Charity uncomfortable. She now looked as though she was about to cry. I noticed she had patches of dry skin on her cheeks and a few spots on her chin.

Louise said, "It's not always easy to breast feed, especially with a first baby. Bottle feeding is almost as good, as long as you take care."

Charity watched Louise closely as she prepared Rosie's milk. Perhaps, I thought, her mother had always done it when they were in France. Or Louise's equipment might have been different. It all looked rather complicated and I was struck by how big a responsibility a baby was.

"How old is Rosie now?" I asked Charity.

"About two months. I mean, she's two months exactly."

"So she was born on October 6th?" said Louise.

"Yes. That's right."

"How much did she weigh?" I asked.

Charity frowned. "I can't remember."

"Never mind," said Louise. "Joanne, could you do us a favour?" She raised her voice above Rosie's wail. "We need some disposable nappies. Could you nip over to the Spar and get some? The next-to-smallest size."

I didn't want to leave the three of them and the warm house, but I pushed my feet into my boots and fastened up my damp jacket. Louise gave me a ten-pound note from a jar on the kitchen shelf.

The shop, which was only five minutes away, had a large collection of baby paraphernalia. I'd never paid attention to such things before. In addition to the nappies, I bought some nappy cream and a small pink rabbit I planned to pay for myself. My first gift to Rosie.

When I got back, Charity was lying in an awkward position on the sofa, with Rosie on her lap feeding from a bottle. Alice, beside them, nursed one of her dolls with a toy bottle to its mouth, mimicking Charity's every move. David was pushing his yellow tractor across the carpet, pausing every few seconds to stare at Charity and Rosie, then at his mother, who sat nearby. I felt unnecessary and out of things so I went into the kitchen to tidy up a bit.

There was an oddness in the atmosphere I couldn't define. Something brittle that might snap if I said or did the wrong thing.

As I put the lid on the milk powder and wiped the work surfaces it struck me that Louise was offering a surprising degree of welcome to the person she suspected of being her husband's lover. Of course, it would have been difficult to turn away a girl who turned up at the door with a crying baby, but Louise's welcome seemed more than dutiful – it was warm and genuine. Had she decided that Alan wasn't the father after all?

Surely, I pondered as I washed the sink clean, Louise hadn't come round to believing Charity's story about her virgin birth? Was Charity sticking to that? There was so much to ask them both, but it seemed impossible to start.

Over the past few months, hearing nothing from Charity, I had begun to accept that her claim couldn't be true. I still found it difficult to believe that she would have lied to me, but it had begun to feel like the only explanation. I'd never believed that Alan was the baby's father and had come to think that it must be a boy from school.

I returned to the living room. Rosie had stopped sucking and her eyes were half-closed. Charity looked as though she was not far from sleep herself.

"Can I hold Rosie?" I asked.

Charity didn't seem to hear me. Louise said, "She needs to be burped first. That's it, Charity, hold her up against your shoulder."

Even when Rosie had been burped, Charity didn't want to relinquish her. She slouched on the sofa with Rosie snuggled against her, now fast asleep. I felt another pang of exclusion. I reminded myself what Charity had said in her letters, about the two of us living together, being parents to Rosie. But this didn't stop the clawing discomfort in my stomach.

"Alice and I have got Rosie's cot ready," said Louise. "Perhaps Joanne can carry her to bed?"

Charity didn't move. To be fair, she looked exhausted.

I crouched down beside Charity and with one finger stroked Rosie's forehead, now flushed a gentle pink. Her eyes opened for a moment and she gave a little gurgle. Charity opened her eyes, too, and gave me a smile which made me feel better.

"It's lovely to have you back," I whispered. "And to see Rosie. She's beautiful."

"Mmm. She is, isn't she?"

"Are you here to stay?" I asked.

"I hope so."

"Are you back in your old flat?"

Charity looked surprised. "No – my dad put the flat up for sale. I think someone else has moved in."

"So where are you living now?"

"Nowhere. I mean…" She glanced at Louise.

Louise said, "Sorry, Joanne – we should have explained. Charity is back here on her own."

"What – without your dad?"

"He's staying in France. He and Mum are trying to get back together, now she's off the booze."

"So you came all the way from France on your own – you and Rosie?"

"It wasn't that hard. I got a train, then a ferry, then three more trains."

"Wow."

"That's why Charity didn't bring any clothes for Rosie," said Louise. "She couldn't carry any more. She had Rosie in a baby sling and a bag for her own things – that was quite enough."

"Rosie must have gone a long time without a feed," I said.

"I filled up a couple of bottles for her before I left," said Charity.

"But still, she must have been starving…"

"It doesn't bear thinking about," said Louise. "But never mind, she's fine now. And remember what I said, Charity – you and Rosie can stay as long as you like."

"If you're sure…" said Charity.

"Of course I am. It's a pleasure to have you both. Alice has really taken to Rosie, haven't you, Alice? And David will get used to her soon. You can come here to see them whenever you like, Joanne."

"Thank you. I'll have to get round Mum, somehow."

"Why, what's the problem?" asked Charity.

I felt awkward. Charity, it appeared, had no idea of the trouble her pregnancy and departure had caused. I wondered how Louise had explained Alan's absence to her.

"You know what my mum's like," I said. "She thinks I should stay in to do my homework."

"Homework." Charity shook her head. "It seems so long ago."

"You've missed a lot of school. Are you planning to go back?"

It was obvious she hadn't thought about this. "I don't know. Will they let me? Will I be able to take Rosie with me?"

"Maybe we can sort something out," said Louise. "Don't worry about it for the moment."

A few minutes later, Louise took Rosie from Charity and put her in the cot they'd prepared. I tucked the pink rabbit I'd bought beside her and kissed her goodnight. I still hadn't held her, but there was always tomorrow.

Relieved of her baby, Charity stood up, straightened her loose grey woollen dress and pulled the rubber band from her hair. It cascaded down, falling over her face in the way it used to, restoring some of her prettiness. I thought of paintings of Mary and the baby Jesus and wondered whether Charity still believed, in her heart of hearts, that Rosie's father was God.

Later, after we'd eaten one of Louise's substantial vegetable soups and Alice and David were in bed, Charity fell asleep again.

"It must have been a hell of a journey," said Louise.

"I can't believe her parents let her come back on her own."

"Let's talk in the kitchen, so we don't wake her up. I'll make some hot chocolate."

We went through and she pulled out a chair for me. "I was a bit worried at first that she might have run away," she continued. "But Charity assures me that her parents know where she is."

"But where do they think she's staying?"

"She told them I'd invited her to stay with me."

"But you didn't know she was coming, did you?"

"I'd no idea, until she arrived on my doorstep at half past four."

"That was a bit cheeky of her, turning up like that."

"Not really. I think she was planning to ask a few different people if she could stay, until she found someone willing. She was going to ask you and then Tom and Pattie, if need be."

I thought of what my mother's reaction would have been. "Charity doesn't know any of the trouble she caused, does she?"

"Not yet. She'll find out before long. I'll have to try to break it to her gently. She couldn't believe it when I told her Alan had gone."

"You didn't tell her why?"

"No – I just said we'd had some rows, That we were having a temporary separation."

"If she goes to Crabbies, she'll soon hear everything."

"I know. I'm worried what kind of reaction she'll get there."

"Does Tom know she's back?"

"Not yet. I suppose I should ring him."

"Does he still think – you know…?" I couldn't say it.

"About the baby? That Rosie's father is Alan?" Louise, stirring milk in the pan, let out a sigh. "I'm not sure what he thinks."

"But you don't?"

She shook her head. "No. I haven't thought so for quite a while. I'm not sure I ever did – not really. But as soon as I saw Rosie I was absolutely sure. There's no way that baby is Alan's daughter."

"How can you tell?"

"The way she looks. The feel of her. Everything about her."

"I don't understand."

"I can't explain it properly – all can say is, I'm sure."

"Will you tell Alan?"

"I've already told him I don't believe he's the father. Several times."

"So why hasn't he come home?"

"He can't forgive me for doubting him, even for a short time." She stirred chocolate powder into the hot milk and poured me a mug full.

I took a sip. "Has Charity said anything about who the father is?"

Louise brought her mug across to the table and sat down beside me. I noticed for the first time how tired and strained she looked, with fine lines on her face as though she'd aged ten years.

"She's still talking about the Holy Spirit," she said.

"She still thinks God is Rosie's father?"

"That's what she says."

I took another sip of chocolate, unable to think of a reply. Then something else occurred to me. "Did Charity bring any money with her?" I knew Louise was poor since Alan left. "Will you be able to afford to look after her and Rosie?"

Louise gave a grimace of a smile. "I'll have to do my best. Maybe her father will send some money, once he knows she's living here."

I remembered Louise's change and retrieved it from my pocket. "I'll pay you back for the pink rabbit. And perhaps I can give you some of my pocket money, to help out. It won't be much…"

Louise smiled. "That's very sweet of you, but there's no need. We'll manage somehow."

"I'd better go soon. My mother will be making a fuss."

"Okay. I'll phone Tom when you've gone."

"Louise..." I stood in the hall shortly after with my coat and boots on. "Do you think there's something the matter with Charity? She seems so different."

"No, I think she's okay. Just very tired after the long journey. And having a baby is a big strain, especially at her age. I think she's doing really well. She'll be right as rain soon, don't worry."

"She hardly seemed to know me."

"She was strange with me when she first arrived. She thrust Rosie at me, sat down at the table and cried for about twenty minutes."

"Gosh."

"It's sheer exhaustion. She'll be fine after a good night's sleep. Off you go home now. Come back after school tomorrow if you like."

"Of course I will."

Despite Louise's reassuring words, I couldn't get rid of the sense of being rejected, or rather ignored, by Charity – as though I was no longer relevant to her, no longer a part of her life. After all the months of waiting and worrying about her and the baby, it was almost too much too bear.

What had I done, or failed to do, to deserve such treatment? What had become of all the plans we had made to live together and be parents to Rosie?

The fog was closing in around me thicker than ever as I turned the corner and approached Sea View.

"Get the door, would you, Joanne?" asked Louise.

It was Friday evening, the day after Charity's return. We were in Louise's living room, surrounded by the remains of the tea party we'd held in honour of Charity and Rosie. The carpet was strewn with biscuit crumbs and Alice was still munching a piece of the special cake made by Louise and decorated with green icing and cherries.

David had loaded his toy truck with left-over cake and was pushing it around our feet with a noisy vocal accompaniment. Charity sat in Alan's big armchair, feeding Rosie from her bottle.

I got up to answer the door, afraid that my mother might have discovered I wasn't at Claire's house as I'd pretended, and come to track me down.

In the porch-light stood two uniformed police officers, one male and balding, the other tall, dark, female and much younger. The male officer held out a document, which I suppose was identification, and reeled off some names.

I yelled, "Louise!" Then my jaw began to quiver and I found myself in floods of tears.

A little later, sitting on the sofa with Louise's arm around me, I had recovered enough to explain. The sight of the police officers at the door, turning up as they had on a dark winter evening, had taken me back to the day my father died. The police had come to the house on that occasion – two of them, as now – to tell us about the coach crash.

"We're very sorry to have alarmed you," said the female officer. "No-one is dead, let me assure you of that."

The tightness in my chest gave way to relief. For some reason I had feared an accident involving Aunt Daisy – though why I thought the police would come to Louise's house, I have no idea.

"We are just here to ask a few questions," said the male officer, whose name turned out to be Inspector Hunter.

"What sort of questions?" asked Louise, a shake in her voice. Her face was white and I saw that she was frightened, too.

It occurred to me that Alan might be in some kind of trouble.

"It's the young lady with the baby we would like to speak to," said Inspector Hunter, turning to Charity. "Can you confirm your name for me, please?"

"Charity Baker." Her voice was low and sullen and she barely raised her eyes from Rosie.

"Miss Baker, could you tell me the identity of the baby you are holding?"

Charity still didn't look at him. "She's my daughter. Her name's Rosie Baker."

The female officer, WPC Jones, scribbled something in her notebook. "Is there any possibility, Miss Baker, that you might be mistaken?"

"Mistaken? Of course not."

"Are you absolutely sure of that?" asked Inspector Hunter. "There's no chance you might have made some kind of mistake?"

Charity spoke up louder now, her tone indignant. "I'm hardly likely to make a mistake with my own baby, am I?" She looked across at Louise, appealing for help.

Louise said, "I can assure you that this baby is Rosie Baker, Charity's daughter."

WPC Jones turned to Louise and said in a sharp voice. "Did you say you were a relative of Miss Baker's?"

"No, I'm a friend," said Louise. "Charity and Rosie are staying at my house. Could you please tell me what all this is about?"

"We are doing some routine checks," said WPC Jones. "We won't keep you any longer than we have to." Her eyes, which were deep blue, darted round the room as she spoke, fixing on each adult in turn and finally on Rosie. Her lip curled as though she was disgusted at something – perhaps the mess of crumbs on the floor.

Charity removed the bottle from Rosie, who was almost asleep. Louise took it through to the kitchen and hurried back, a frown on her face.

Alice had finished her cake and was watching everyone, eyes wide. David, after gazing open-mouthed at the visitors for several minutes, went back to his truck and began to manoeuvre it around Inspector Hunter's boots. The inspector moved his feet apart so David could park the truck between them.

WPC Jones pushed her long red fringe back off her face and said, "Miss Baker, we would like to take your baby to the police station to examine her."

Charity's chin jerked up and she looked WPC Jones full in the face for the first time. "No! You can't do that."

"We have the required authority to do so," said Inspector Hunter. "We would value your cooperation, Miss Baker."

"If you could just explain why?" Louise's voice was shakier than ever.

WPC Jones said, "We really are sorry to have to do this. Especially to disturb Rosie when she's just gone to sleep. But we'll need you, Miss Baker, and your baby, to come with us to the station.

We'll try not to take too long. Hopefully, when we've had a look, we can bring you both back home."

Charity sat in silence, looking down at her shabby maroon slippers, lent by Louise.

Inspector Hunter addressed Louise. "Mrs Watson, you say you are a friend of Miss Baker's. How long have you known her?"

"Over a year."

"And how did you meet?"

"We both belong to a group called the Crabapple Christian Fellowship. That's how we met. Charity started coming to meetings a year or so ago."

"And how long has Miss Baker been staying with you?"

"Since yesterday, when she and Rosie arrived from France."

"She was staying with her parents there," I put in, feeling a sudden urge to say something.

Charity glared at me and I wished I hadn't spoken.

Rosie opened her eyes for a second, gave a little grunt and closed them again. I was struck once more by what a beautiful baby she was, and resolved to do anything, anything at all, for her. And, of course, for her mother.

I'd been, I decided, far too hard on Charity. Giving birth at sixteen was not an easy thing to do – nor was taking a ferry and several trains from France to Castlehaven with a two-month-old. No wonder she was worn out and in a strange mood. As soon as these busybodies had gone I would double my efforts to be kind to her and reawaken her affection.

"Could you get me some outdoor clothing for the baby, please?" asked WPC Jones, looking at Louise, who got to her feet, her face now bewildered.

My heart began to pound again, though I had no idea what was going on.

WPC Jones turned at Charity. "I'll dress Rosie, if you'll kindly pass her to me."

Charity was biting her lip again, her face white. "No, you can't have my baby!"

"Could you explain?" Louise's voice now had a touch of ice in it. "We've been very patient up to now. Please tell us what's going on."

"I'm sorry, we can't say any more for the time being," said WPC Jones. "Miss Baker, perhaps you would like to pack a bag with the baby's things? You may be some time at the station. You'll need a bottle for her."

Charity pulled herself slowly to her feet. She gave Rosie, who had gone back to sleep, to WPC Jones, then sat back down, staring at her slippers once again.

Inspector Hunter uncrossed his legs ready to stand up. "Miss Baker, we really need one or both of your parents to be present. Is it possible to contact them?"

"They're in France," muttered Charity. "Joanne told you – weren't you listening?"

Louise reappeared with Rosie's red snowsuit – one of many purchases they'd made that morning – and handed it to WPC Jones, who rather inexpertly bundled Rosie into it, turning her into a mini-Santa.

Inspector Hunter turned to Louise. "Mrs Watson, would you be willing to accompany Miss Baker to the station in lieu of a parent?"

"Yes, of course," said Louise. "But what about my own children? Joanne, is there any chance you…?"

I said, "I'll look after them. But why do Charity and Rosie have to go to the police station?"

"I don't know," said Louise. "I'll phone you as soon as I can. We may be late – can you stay over?"

"Yes, no problem." This wasn't strictly true. My mother would be furious but there wasn't much she could do.

"Don't forget to phone your mum. Tell her it's an emergency. Tell her I'm very sorry."

My mother knew – I'd told her at breakfast – that Charity was home. She had tutted some more about her bad character and said she hoped I would have no more to do with her. There hadn't been time to argue – that's why I had told her I was going to Claire's.

WPC Jones was standing up now, with Rosie nestled comfortably against her white blouse. Charity hadn't moved – her eyes were still on her slippers. She refused to look at me.

Louise bustled around, putting things in bags. "David will need his bath, Joanne. Alice can skip hers for once, but make sure she uses the flannel and brushes her teeth. Don't let them stay up too late and only read them one story each, however much they beg for more."

She kissed Alice and David, explaining that I was going to stay with them overnight, "As a special treat."

Alice yelled, "Yippee!" while David remained unmoved. He would cry, I knew, as soon as Louise had gone.

When everyone was ready to leave, Charity heaved herself, still in slow motion, from the armchair and put her arms in the jacket Louise held out to her. I tried to give her a reassuring smile but she refused to look at me. My heart seemed to catch on something inside my chest and stop for a moment.

"Take care," said Louise. "I hope we won't be too long."

Inspector Hunter banged the door behind them, and David started to wail.

I woke next morning with a crick in my neck from sleeping on the sofa and Rosie's pink rabbit clasped to my chest. I'd lain awake most of the night worrying about Charity and trying to imagine what was happening at the police station. It was ten past eight now and the phone was ringing.

"Joanne – it's me, Louise. Are the children awake yet?"

Alice had persuaded me to let her sleep in her own bedroom – the one Charity had been using. I put down the phone and, pulling on my wool jumper, opened her door a crack.

"Alice is still fast asleep," I whispered down the line to Louise. "Hang on – I'll take a look at David."

I peeped in David's door and returned to the phone. "He's asleep, too."

"Good. Hush, don't wake him. I've got something to tell you while they're not around." She paused. "It's not good news, I'm afraid."

My stomach dropped. "What is it? What's happened?"

I heard Louise swallow before saying, "Oh, Joanne. It's awful. Sit down before I tell you."

"I'm all right. Just get on with it." My heart was thudding nineteen to the dozen.

"The police have been questioning Charity all night. They've charged her with kidnapping Rosie."

"Kidnapping?" Images of armed robbers flashed through my mind – of ransom demands and shoot-outs. "But you can't kidnap your own baby."

Another pause. "Joanne, I'm afraid that Rosie isn't… she isn't Charity's baby."

"What?"

Louise's words came faster now, tumbling over each other, unreal as pantomime snow. "Charity stole her from a pram outside Barnsley railway station on Thursday lunchtime. Then she brought her here."

I was stunned into silence while I tried to take it in. After a few moments, I said, "But why? Why would she do that? And where's her own baby?"

"We don't know. There are lots of things we don't know. It took hours and hours to get Charity even to admit to taking the baby."

"I don't understand."

"Neither do I. Listen, Joanne – I'm sorry, but I may have to go any minute. Are you all right?"

"Not really. Not since you told me – that…"

"I know. I'm sorry. I can't believe it myself."

"Can I come and see Charity?"

"No, I'm afraid not."

"She's not in a cell, is she?" I pictured Charity handcuffed in a dim little room with dripping stone walls.

"She's in an interview room at the moment, answering more questions. The police are trying to find out where her parents are. Either she doesn't know or she's not saying."

"Please let me come. I'm sure she'll talk to me."

"The police wouldn't let you. Perhaps later – I don't know."

"What will happen next? Will she go to prison?"

"She's too young for prison. They seem to think her mental balance is disturbed. That she didn't know what she was doing."

"They think she's mad?"

"Well, not mad exactly – but sort of temporarily insane. They're supposed to be getting a psychiatrist to come and talk to her."

"She must have made a mistake. Charity would never steal a baby. She must have picked up the wrong one."

"No. It seems there wasn't another one. She didn't bring a baby from France. She bought a baby carrier in a department store, just after taking the baby. Then she caught a train to York and another one to Castlehaven. Lots of people saw her."

I felt dizzy and faint and had to slide to the floor, where I sat against the wall, my bare legs sticking out. It was cold but it didn't seem to matter. I tried very hard to take deep breaths.

Louise continued. "Charity has been saying some very strange things. I wondered if she'd said anything to you?"

"What kind of things?"

"When she finally admitted to taking the baby from its pram – she said God had told her to do it. That He told her to leave France and go to Barnsley – that she would find Rosie there, in a pram outside the station, waiting for her. Did she say anything like that to you?"

"Of course she didn't. She hardly said anything to me."

I still couldn't get my head round the fact that Rosie – the baby Charity had brought to Castlehaven – wasn't her baby at all. That she wasn't Rosie, but was some other woman's child and belonged to a family of her own.

"That's why they think Charity is deluded," Louise went on. "They've decided she's a religious fanatic – that's she's having hallucinations or something."

I remembered that my mother had described Charity as a religious fanatic – for nothing more than being interested in the Special Blessing. "This is like a nightmare, Louise."

"I know it is." Louise's voice dropped – she sounded suddenly exhausted.

"It doesn't make any sense. Where's the real Rosie?"

"Charity started crying – screaming, really – saying that her father stole Rosie when she was born. Took her away without letting Charity see her."

I tried to make my brain work. "But why would he do that?"

Louise gave a deep sigh. "One possibility is that Charity's baby was born dead. Perhaps her parents thought it would upset Charity too much to see her."

"But..."

"We just don't know. Charity says her father told her he was giving the baby to another woman – because Charity was too evil to be a mother, or something. She's obviously very confused."

"I *must* see her."

"You can't. Not yet. I'm sorry. Look – I've got to go. Are you all right with the children for another couple of hours?"

"Yes, I'm fine." My mother's anger had started to bubble up when I phoned to tell her where I was. She'd made me promise to be home by ten. She would just have to boil over.

"Did Alice and David get off to sleep all right?"

"Yes, no trouble at all."

"Any waking in the night?"

"No." This was a fib. Alice had woken twice – calling the first time for her mother and the second time for her father. Her calling "Daddy" made me sad and set me off wondering whether Alan would ever come home. David had cried out once but settled quickly after I gave him a drink.

"I'm so grateful to you for looking after them."

"Not at all." I didn't tell Louise that I had read Alice six stories in succession. "Louise – are the police really sure that Rosie isn't Charity's baby? Maybe she got confused with all the questions?"

"The baby matches perfectly the description of a baby girl who went missing from her pram outside Barnsley station on Thursday. Her parents have come to pick her up. They've already left with her, I think."

"Did you see them?"

"Just briefly, in passing. They were both crying with relief."

"They must have been so worried."

"I can't bear to think about it. All the time we were cuddling Rosie – feeding her, playing with her – her real parents were in agony – not knowing if she was alive or dead."

I couldn't speak.

"I feel so guilty." Louise's voice cracked.

"It's not your fault, Louise."

“I should have seen that something was wrong. How could I be so stupid? Charity didn’t know how to make up Rosie’s feed. She held her awkwardly. I put it down to tiredness…”

“I should have realised too.” I had known there was something wrong with Charity but I’d taken it personally – I’d thought she’d turned against me for some reason.

“I really have to go now, Joanne. Tell Alice and David I’ll be home for lunchtime. Don’t forget to let your mum know what’s going on.”

Shuddering at the thought of my mother learning this latest news, I put the phone down and drifted into the living room. Rosie’s pink rabbit lay on the sofa. I picked it up and held it to my face, smelling her faint, milky baby smell. It was impossible to believe she was not Rosie at all – not Charity’s child, not the little girl we had planned to bring up together. That the real Rosie, perhaps, was dead.

I held the soft pink fur to my face and began to cry.

Chapter 10

"Just try a couple of spoonfuls, Joanne." Aunt Daisy picked up the teaspoon and scooped out a little of the boiled egg from its cup on the tray beside my bed. "Come on, you must eat something."

"I can do it myself – I'm not a baby. I'll eat when I'm hungry."

Aunt Daisy's forehead was creased into a frown. It was Monday and I'd been sent home from school early after bursting into tears in a geography lesson. Gossip was all round the school about Charity and someone had just asked me whether it was true she'd been arrested for murdering a little girl. Following my outburst, the teacher summoned Miss Dodd, who drove me home herself. My mother was out when we arrived, to my great relief. She hadn't wanted me to go to school at all that day, but I'd insisted. Aunt Daisy took things calmly and, once Miss Dodd had driven off, made me a batch of my favourite ginger biscuits. I had only been able to manage a few crumbs.

"Have a soldier, then," she persisted, picking up a finger of buttered bread. "You used to love these when you were little."

"I'm not little any more and I'm not hungry."

"You hardly ate anything all weekend."

"Aunt Daisy, I'm sorry – I just can't." It was true – I couldn't bear the sensation of food in my mouth.

"But why? I don't understand."

I couldn't explain, not even to my sympathetic aunt. "It's all to do with Charity."

"But your not eating won't help her. You need to keep up your strength, so you can support her when she comes home."

I swallowed saliva, grateful for Aunt Daisy's optimism, whether it was assumed or real. I'd begun to wonder if I would ever see Charity again. My mother had gone berserk, as I'd predicted, when she heard about Charity's detention and questioning at the police station and the charge against her of abducting a baby. At the same time, she had managed to convey that she wasn't at all surprised, that it was no more than she would have expected of 'that girl'.

The doorbell rang and I hoped against hope it might be Charity, though I knew it couldn't be.

"You stay here – I'll see who it is," said Aunt Daisy.

When she'd gone I jumped out of bed, trying to ignore the buzzing in my head, and listened from the landing.

I heard my mother's voice. "No, I'm afraid she isn't in a fit state for visitors. No, not even for a few minutes." Her tone was high and sharp. I waited for the reply but it was too faint to make out. The door banged and my mother's footsteps sounded in the hall.

I jumped back into bed and pulled the covers up as Aunt Daisy returned.

"Who was it?" I asked.

"It was Louise. She came to see you."

"But Mum said no?"

Aunt Daisy sighed. "Your mother is worried about you. That's why she's the way she is."

"She doesn't need to worry. I'm not a child and I'm all right. I just want to see Charity, or at least to know what's happening to her. Why doesn't anyone understand?"

"I understand."

"Do you?"

Aunt Daisy gave me a long, searching look which suggested that perhaps she did. Or that she was at least prepared to try.

"Was Mum horrible to Louise?"

Aunt Daisy gave a wry smile. "Let's say she was rather short with her."

"I don't see why she's blaming Louise for what happened."

"She's not – not really. It's just that she mistrusts all the Crabbies at the moment. She was railing against Tom earlier on, saying that it was his fault for not keeping a tighter rein on them."

"It's not Tom's fault, either."

"I know. Your mother will calm down, in time. If you could only eat something and stop her worrying, that would help."

I looked at my plate with the egg and soldiers and shook my head. "I can't."

"A ginger biscuit?"

"No. Sorry."

What I hadn't managed to explain to Aunt Daisy, because I didn't properly understand it myself, was that my revulsion towards food had something to do with the image in my mind of Rosie with the bottle in her mouth, feeding contentedly when the police arrived. Although I had begun to love Rosie in the short time she had been with us, the idea of babies and feeding them sickened me now. Even taking a drink of water was difficult, though my thirst made me do it somehow.

I heard my mother's feet on the stairs. "Auntie – tell her I'm asleep. Please."

Aunt Daisy gave me a matey grin, picked up my tray and left the room, shutting the door with a gentle snick behind her. I heard her speak in a low voice on the landing.

"Good," my mother replied, and I was left alone with my worries and fears.

An hour or so later, Aunt Daisy came back. I was lying still, pretending to be asleep, in case it was my mother.

"I've had a word with Louise," she said, putting a mug of soup down on the small bookcase beside my bed.

'Did you go to her house?'

"No, I phoned. Your mother popped out to the shops so I took my chance. I told Louise you were sorry not to see her."

"What did she say?"

"She sent you her love and hopes you feel a bit better soon."

"What did she say about Charity?"

"I'm coming to that. She says Charity is in Scarborough hospital, having various tests and things. She's under sedation – you know, various drugs to calm her down. They've decided she has some kind of mental disorder – possibly schizophrenia. That's what gave her the delusions about the baby being her own child."

"So she *is* mad?"

"Not mad, just ill. Something they can treat."

"So does she still think Rosie – that baby – was her own baby?"

"I think so, by the sound of it."

I struggled to take this in. "But she must be so upset. She's had her baby taken away a second time now. Or she thinks she has. She must be in an awful state."

"The drugs will help."

"No, they won't! Poor Charity – I *must* go and see her. You have to let me. Will you help me get there, behind Mum's back? Please, Aunt Daisy?"

"I can't do that, my love. You really aren't well enough to go out. And I don't think Charity is allowed any visitors at the moment."

"Why are they being so horrible to her? Taking her baby away and giving her drugs to keep her quiet. Not letting her have visitors. It's like torture…"

"Of course it isn't. They could hardly let her keep the baby, could they, even if she does believe it's hers? Once the drugs start to work, she'll come to her senses. She'll get better and be able to come home."

"What if they never let her out?"

"Of course they will. I haven't finished, anyway – there's a bit more news. They are planning to move her, today or tomorrow, to a residential unit somewhere near York. A special place for adolescents with mental health problems. It sounds much better than hospital."

"Will I be able to go and see her there?"

"I expect so, when you're feeling better. Apparently they haven't managed to get hold of her parents yet, so they're letting Louise visit her instead."

"That's not fair – it should be me."

"I think it has to be an adult at this stage. At least Louise will be able to tell you how she is. Pass some messages between you, perhaps. She's going to see Charity tomorrow."

I wasn't sure how to feel about this. It was good to know what was happening to Charity and, I told myself, having Louise visit her was the next best thing to seeing her myself – as long as my mother would let Louise in to see me. But I couldn't help feeling a sharp tug of jealousy in my gut, that Louise, not me, was to be the one to visit Charity. Louise was great, but she didn't understand Charity the way I did. Charity was *mine*.

"I'm sorry, pet," said Aunt Daisy. "I know it's not the best news."

With what must have been hurtful ingratitude, I pulled the bedcovers over my head and refused to say another word.

That night, I had Charity's dream. I recognised it as soon as it started – the creaking open of my bedroom door, the sense of a hostile presence in the room. But the knowledge that I was dreaming didn't help at all – made it no less real. I lay there, frozen into immobility, filled with an overwhelming sense of powerlessness, aware that there was nothing I could do to protect myself from the malevolent intruder. Ice in my veins, my heart thumping fit to burst out of my chest. Sickness in my mouth that I could not swallow. The man, or monster – the Terror by Night – was drawing closer every second.

A hand touched me through the covers and I screamed – but no sound came. I smelt foul breath and opened my mouth to scream again. Suddenly the light was on, flooding the room like yellow paint.

My mother stood beside me in her white nightdress, her face as frightened as I felt. Her cheeks were pink and puffy with sleep but her eyes were wide open and glinting.

"Joanne – whatever is the matter?"

Then she took me in her arms while I sobbed myself back to sleep. Some of the words of Charity's prayer came into my head as I drifted off and I repeated them over and over. "Dear Lord, protect me from all evil." I thought of Charity and prayed it for us both.

"I'd like to strangle that girl for putting you through all this," were my mother's first words as she appeared next morning with my breakfast tray.

"It's not Charity's fault I had a bad dream."

"If it wasn't for her, you'd be at school today."

"That doesn't make it her fault."

"Of course it does. Now, I hope you're going to be sensible and start eating again."

"I'll try." But, looking at the bowl of Frosties and the slices of toast and marmalade, I knew I wouldn't be able to.

I took a mouthful of tea and willed it to go down my throat. Most of it stayed in my mouth, flooding it with a bitterness that made me want to retch.

My mother watched me. "I could put some sugar in it?"

Sweet tea – heaven help me! "No – please don't. I'll manage this if you leave me."

I pictured myself tearing up the toast into tiny pieces. Would it flush down the toilet? Anything to stop my mother plying me with more horrible stuff to tempt my appetite.

Disposing of my breakfast proved simpler than I had expected, though it took several flushes. If asked, I planned to say I had an upset stomach. I didn't dispose of everything, but left half a slice of toast on the plate and a few Frosties in the bottom of the bowl. I managed to swallow a couple of sips of tea and poured the rest away.

When my mother came to collect my tray I was sitting up in bed looking pleased with myself.

"Well done," she said. "You'll soon get your strength back now."

It was as easy as that to deceive her, and the guilt churned around in my stomach with the twenty millilitres or so of tea.

I scraped back the red and silver foil and bit the head off the chocolate Santa, relishing the sweet rich silkiness in my parched mouth. Suddenly I was desperate for water and drank a glassful before taking a second bite.

"Thanks," I mumbled to Louise.

She laughed. "That's okay."

I remembered my manners and offered her the remains of the Santa. "Would you like some?"

"No thanks. You enjoy it. It's good to see you eating something."

Louise had produced the Santa from her bag and I'd bitten into it without thinking. "This doesn't mean I'm eating again."

"Doesn't it?"

"I'm not sure." I thought of other foods and felt my throat constrict. "Probably not."

"Well, don't worry about that for now. Enjoy your chocolate. At least it'll give you some energy."

I'd been surprised, to put it mildly, when my mother showed Louise into my bedroom. It was Friday now and I had left my bed only to visit the bathroom in the four days since Louise had last called and been turned away. I'd eaten almost nothing in that time, but had managed to hide this from my mother and Aunt Daisy by some careful disposal down the toilet, both instead of and after swallowing it. Only Louise knew I wasn't eating, but I hadn't told her I was making myself throw up.

The doctor had been to see me that morning and pronounced me still 'in shock'. He recommended bed rest and no school until after Christmas.

"How come Mum let you in to see me?" I asked Louise.

"She's very worried about you. I think it was a case of being prepared to try anything – even me."

"I'm glad she did."

"Me too. It's good to see you."

"Where are Alice and David?"

"Alice is at school. David is with my mother."

"Will you bring them to see me sometime?"

"Of course – when you're a bit better."

"I'm fine, honestly."

"You don't look fine. You're very pale and your face is thinner."

"Do I smell?"

"A bit. In fact, I'll open your window, if you don't mind." Without waiting for a reply she got up and let in a blast of icy air. "That's better."

My smell hadn't, I reflected, stopped her from giving me a hug when she came in.

"Have you been to see Charity?"

"Yes, I have. Tom drove me to the unit yesterday afternoon."

"Tom? Has he seen her too?"

"No, they wouldn't let him in. I'm the only visitor she's allowed for the time being. In place of her parents. Tom waited for me in the car."

"How is she?"

Louise paused long enough for a knot of worry to tie itself in my stomach. "She's – not too bad. Very calm and quiet. I suppose that's partly the drugs."

"What did she say?"

"She sent you her love."

"Did she?"

"Yes – and a big hug."

I found it hard to believe this, somehow. But would Louise lie to me? I'd never doubted her word before – I generally believed what people told me – but it seemed too good to be true. Perhaps my recently-acquired habit of lying to others had eroded my trust in them, or recent events had made me cynical.

"How long will she have to stay there?"

"They don't know just yet. It's going to take a while for her to get back to normal."

"Did she say why she took the baby?"

"We didn't talk about it much. She was so sleepy – her mind kept wandering off. But she still seems to believe that the baby she took was her own and that God told her to take it."

"Is she upset?"

"Not exactly. I'd describe her as dazed, more than anything. But she kept saying that God would bring her baby back to her. Oh yes, she told me to remind you to keep saying her prayer for her. Do you know what she means?"

I nodded. "It's a special prayer she wrote out, one that stops her having nightmares."

"I remember now. She told me about it when she stayed with us."

As we both thought of those days and nights Charity had spent at the Watsons', almost a year ago now, it was as though Alan appeared in the room with us. I could see his thick black hair and white teeth. A little shudder went through me.

Louise got up and half-closed the window.

"Is it a nice place?" I asked.

"It seemed quite pleasant. Very spacious and clean. The nurses and assistants were all friendly."

"Has she got her own room?"

"For sleeping, yes – though I didn't see it. During the day the patients sit in a lounge. There are various activities they can take part in."

"Next time you visit her, can I come with you?"

Louise frowned. "I wish you could. I did ask, but they say she can only have one visitor and it has to be an adult."

"I *am* an adult."

"They have lots of silly rules. You have to be eighteen unless you're a relative."

"Louise – I *have* to see her. Can't we pretend I'm a relative?"

"Perhaps, as time goes on. When you're a bit better."

The sun, emerging from a cloud, flooded the room with sudden light. Louise peered at my face. "What are those marks on your cheeks?"

"Just little scratches. It was an accident."

"How can you accidentally scratch your own cheeks when you're lying in bed?"

"Not that kind of accident. I didn't mean to do it – it just happened."

She pulled the curtains back to let more light in, since the sun had disappeared again. "You've drawn blood. Has your mum seen it?"

"Yes – she was pretty angry. She went on about it for ages. Please don't you start."

She shook her head, sitting back down beside me. "I'm not angry – just worried about you. Why did you scratch yourself?"

"I don't know. It felt like the only thing I *could* do. I hate myself."

"Why?"

"Everything that's happened." I suddenly felt too tired to talk about it, and wished Louise would go.

"But none of it's your fault."

"I should have known something was wrong when Charity came back. She looked so different. I thought it was just because she had a baby."

"I feel bad about that, too. I should have realised, when she didn't know how to make up a bottle. But we can't blame ourselves, Joanne."

"If I can't see Charity, I want to die. There's no point in living."

"Don't say that."

"I mean it."

Louise touched my cheek with her finger. "Charity will get better and come home. She's being well looked after. The doctors and nurses know what to do."

"What if she never comes out of that place? Mum told me someone she went to school with has been in a mental hospital all her life."

"That won't happen to Charity. We must have faith. God will protect and heal her."

"I don't know if I have faith any more. I don't know if I even believe in God. He's the cause of all this mess."

"That's a strange bit of reasoning. If you don't believe in God, you can hardly hold him responsible."

"You know what I mean."

Louise sighed. "Yes, I suppose I do. My faith isn't in a very good state, either."

This cut through my anger and made me warm to her a little. "You don't think, do you, that it could possibly be true?"

"That what could be true?"

"What Charity says. About her baby being stolen. And God telling her to go to Barnsley to find it."

"Of course it's not true. We know that baby belonged to someone else."

"Maybe Charity got the wrong baby. God meant her to pick up another one. Her own baby – Rosie – is still waiting somewhere for her?"

Louise gave me a long look, her head on one side. I noticed for the first time that her eyes were as beautiful, in their own way, as Charity's. Dark brown in Louise's case, with long curling lashes. She looked very young at that moment – almost like a child, like Alice.

"No, Joanne. I'm sorry, but we have to accept that Charity is suffering from delusions. We don't know what happened to her own baby. I suppose there's a remote chance that she is still in France and they may be reunited. Perhaps she is in foster care or has even been adopted. But I'm inclined to think she may have died at birth. Tom and I were discussing it in the car. He thinks it may be the shock of losing her baby that started all this off for Charity."

"But she already thought God was the baby's father."

"That's true. I suppose that was a delusion in its way – if she really believed it."

"She did, I'm sure."

"Well, let's hope the people in the unit can help her. I'm sure they'll do their best."

"What did Tom say about it? Is he angry with Charity, for taking the baby?"

"No, of course not. He's worried, just as we are. He blames himself as well. Says he should have realised something was wrong."

"But what could he have done?"

"Perhaps suggested she spoke to someone, like a doctor or a psychiatrist?"

"She would never have done that."

"Well, he holds himself responsible, anyway, as pastor of the Crabbies."

"Will Charity go to court?"

"I don't know. Maybe she won't have to appear in person. Whatever happens, they'll take into account that she's ill. I'm sure it'll be a case of treatment rather than punishment."

We fell silent. I licked my finger and picked up crumbs of chocolate from my duvet cover, transferring them to my mouth. After a few minutes, Louise said, "I'll have to go and pick up Alice soon, from school."

Suddenly I didn't want her to leave. "Will you come back tomorrow?"

"Of course I will. If you like, we could go for a little walk. We could go to a café – how do you fancy an all-day breakfast in Brown's?"

"No."

"Just a walk, then, on the cliff-top, to give you a bit of fresh air?"

"You sound like Mum and Aunt Daisy now."

"Sorry."

"If I can't see Charity, I'm not going anywhere."

"All right then. I'll come and see you, anyway."

"Will you bring me another Santa? Please?"

"I'll see what I can do, if you promise not to scratch yourself again."

"Okay."

"And have a wash? A shower, even?"

"Maybe."

She kissed my cheek, got up and fastened her coat. The room felt cold and empty when she'd gone, but I consoled myself with the thought of my mother's leg razor, the one I'd found in the bathroom bin and hidden in my dressing-table drawer. I had no plans to use it for anything, but it was good to know it was there.

My mother came in and I tried to look cheerful, to prove that Louise's visit had done me good. That way, Mum would let her visit me again.

Later, after flushing the crumbled remains of a cheese sandwich down the toilet, I lay in bed and began to hatch a plan.

Next day, I riffled through Louise's handbag while she was in the bathroom and found a scrap of paper with the address of Charity's unit scrawled in Louise's handwriting. I retrieved Charity's prayer from under my pillow and used a biro, also from Louise's bag, to copy the address onto the back of it. Later, I would sneak into Aunt Daisy's bedroom and look up the whereabouts of the nearest village, Helmsall, in her atlas. Louise had told me that the unit itself was out in the countryside, but if I could get myself as far as Helmsall I was sure to think of something.

I planned to make my trip on Monday. Over the weekend, I pretended to feel a little better each day, and made a show of eating all the food that was brought to me. Most if it, once again, went down the toilet pan. On Sunday evening I went as far as having a shower and coming downstairs to watch TV. My mother and Aunt Daisy both clapped when I appeared. The effort, together with the guilt, exhausted me, but I tried not to show it.

"I feel well enough for school tomorrow," I said, knowing they wouldn't let me go.

"No, it's far too soon," said my mother. "Though I'm glad you're so much better. Perhaps you could visit one of your friends, instead, after school. Find out what you've been missing."

"I could go round to Claire's," I said. "I'll phone her now."

Claire promised to cover for me. I didn't tell her I was going to see Charity – just that I needed an alibi. She probably assumed I was going to meet a boy or something, but I didn't care.

"If my mother phones, tell her I've gone out for a few minutes," I said, and she promised she would.

My mother and Aunt Daisy always went shopping after lunch on Mondays, so I planned to leave the house shortly after them. I'd raided my piggy bank and found only seven pounds, so I decided to take a further twenty-pound note from my mother's kitchen jar. She would discover it at some stage, I knew, but that could be dealt with later. I'd pay it back by doing the washing up for the next three years, if necessary. All that mattered for the time being was to get myself to the unit to see Charity.

The village of Helmsall was about fourteen miles north of York. I hoped there might be a bus from York station, but I had enough money to cover my taxi fare in case there wasn't.

On Saturday, Louise brought me another chocolate Santa, as requested. On Sunday, she took from her bag, instead, some chocolate shapes she had made herself on greaseproof paper. The flavour wasn't as good but I pretended to be grateful. It didn't occur to me that she probably couldn't afford to buy me a chocolate Santa every day.

"You said you'd bring Alice and David to see me."

"I'll bring them when you're a bit better."

"I am better."

I knew the reason she hadn't brought them – she was afraid I'd become violent and start breaking things. I'd told her how I'd smashed all my ornaments a few days earlier by throwing them at the wall. I'd hidden the broken pieces in my dressing table drawer and swept up the remaining dust, so my mother and Aunt Daisy had no idea. I wasn't sure why I'd done it, except it gave me a good, clear reason to feel sad.

Louise told me that when Alan came to take the children out on Saturday, she had asked him to come home. Begged him, even. Told him, again, how sorry she was for allowing herself to suspect him of being the father of Charity's child.

He'd said no, he wasn't coming home. That he could never forget how she had doubted him – that he couldn't live with a wife who didn't trust him. That their marriage was over and he wanted a divorce.

I could see Louise trying to keep calm as she told me, but her voice cracked and her eyes filled with tears. I passed her a box of tissues and put my arm round her.

When she had recovered a little, she told me that Tom still believed that Alan was the baby's father. They'd spoken about it on their car journey to Helmsall. Tom told her he had phoned Alan at his brother's and tried to get him to confess. Alan got angry, told Tom that if he tried to contact him again he would get himself a lawyer, and slammed down the phone.

"Why does he still think it was Alan?"

"I don't really know. I think it's got something to do with the way Alan went overboard with the Special Blessing. Tom seemed to turn against him then."

"And maybe the way he was with Charity at the Christmas party." I winced at the memory.

"Well, yes. That's what made me suspect Alan, more than anything. But I can see now that he was just infatuated with her. He would never have done anything about it."

"What made you change your mind?" I asked her.

She gazed for a moment at my empty shelf where the ornaments had been. "I suppose it began to seem less likely over the summer, all the time that Charity was away. And as I told you before, as soon as I saw the baby I knew she wasn't Alan's child."

"But that baby wasn't Rosie, anyway."

"I know. But once I'd made my mind up, I couldn't go back on it. I was convinced by then."

"If I said something like that, you'd say it was faulty logic."

She gave a little smile. "Of course I would. It is. But the fact remains – I'm sure, now, that Alan didn't have an affair with Charity."

"So who do you think the father is?"

She hesitated. "I suppose it must be someone Charity met through school or at a dance or something. Or that boyfriend from her Barnsley church."

"No." I realised, in that moment, that I'd been hanging onto the twin hopes either that Charity's pregnancy was supernatural or that she'd been raped by Alan. Horrific as the latter notion was, I'd preferred it to the idea that she would willingly betray me. Now that both alternatives were fading, all I was left with was the betrayal. I was too choked to say anything more.

Louise spoke gently, putting out a hand to touch my forehead. "Joanne, I'm sorry. I know it hurts. But wouldn't you feel better to know it was a boy of her own age, rather than someone like Alan? Whoever it was, I'm sure it was a mistake on Charity's part. A spur of the moment thing that doesn't affect the way she feels about you."

Her words didn't comfort me at all. Something acidic welled up in my gullet as though I was going to be sick. My only hope was that when I saw Charity, she would tell me the truth.

Chapter 11

My stomach heaved, sending waves of nausea up into my head as I struggled to focus my attention on a line of wind-bent trees silhouetted against the horizon. The sky was darkening by the second, sickly clouds like yellow-stained sheep-fleece coalescing into a thick black mass broken only by a line of silver light.

My head swam and I knew I couldn't hold on. "Please stop," I begged the taxi driver. "I'm going to be sick."

By way of reply he gave a short grunt and accelerated sharply into the next bend.

"Please. Just stop for a minute – I need some fresh air."

This time he answered, barely audible above the engine roar. "Can't stop here – it's not safe. There's a lay-by in a mile or two."

I'd made the mistake of re-reading Charity's letters – the ones she'd sent me from France – while in the back seat of the taxi that was taking me from York to the unit where Charity was staying. I'd been fine for the first twenty minutes of the journey, then all at once the car-sickness familiar from childhood journeys with my parents had enveloped me. I'd forgotten how bad it was – the way it took over your senses, merging sight, sound and smell into a whirlpool of anguish – my body protesting that it couldn't stand another second of it.

"Look at the horizon – you'll feel better in a minute," my mother used to say. Occasionally this worked, and almost imperceptibly the nausea subsided into something manageable, followed by the relief of recovery. Sometimes it didn't work and the car was suddenly full of vomit and shame. I was terrified this would happen here.

I scanned the roadside for the lay-by. After what seemed more like five miles than one or two, the taxi driver slowed down and pulled in.

"Be quick, lass," he said. "I've another job after this. No time to hang about."

I opened the door and was engulfed in cold air. Stumbling, I managed to put a few feet between myself and the car before giving way to the irresistible contractions. The stuff that hit the grey moorland grass was thin and green-tinged, with little substance. It burned my tongue and the insides of my cheeks. I wanted to cry, both with relief and an acute sense of being alone and far from home.

I found a tissue in my bag and wiped my mouth and then my shoes. The taxi driver had lit up in my absence, but he snuffed out the cigarette against the dashboard as I clambered back into the car.

"All right now?" He wasn't unfriendly – just distant. I was a passenger, part of his day's earnings – nothing to do with him at all. I'd been glad he hadn't tried to engage me in conversation. Why should I expect any sympathy from him, just because I'd been childish enough to throw up?

"I'm fine. Sorry about that."

"Not far to go," he said, and we drove on towards the ever-receding line of light. I wound my window down and pretended to be a dog, sticking its nose out to sniff the swirling air.

I'd almost lost my balance climbing into the taxi outside York station. The driver had put out a hand to steady me, joking that I'd had a pint too many. I'd started to worry, as we wound through the city suburbs, that he could tell something was wrong with me and would start to ask questions. But he hadn't.

He was a wizened little man with deep creases in his face and weather-roughened skin, reminding me a little of my grandfather, the only grand-parent I'd known, who had died shortly before my father's accident. Just in time not to see his son smashed up in the terrible coach crash. I didn't think of my dad so often these days, but the rush of memory now brought tears smarting to my eyes. I turned so the driver wouldn't see me in his rear-view mirror.

I'd woken that morning with the headache I'd had for days, and a sense that my brain had turned into a huge dead slug curled up below my skull. I took a couple of aspirins with a glass of water, avoiding breakfast by my usual, now well-practised, combination of methods. Later, once my mother and Aunt Daisy had left the house, I rummaged in cupboards to find treats that Charity would enjoy – crisps, chocolate biscuits and a couple of cans of coke. I bundled them into a plastic carrier bag before the sight of them made me sick, and stuffed the whole thing inside my canvas backpack. I'd told my mother I would leave at three and walk to Claire's. She'd been delighted at my apparent recovery and suspected nothing.

Halfway to the station, which was less than a mile from home, my legs gave way under me. I sat down quickly on the pavement edge, willing the darkness to clear from my vision and my body to get its strength back. After a few minutes I felt better and scrambled to my feet. There were few people around and no-one seemed to be looking at me. I walked on, more slowly now, stopping every few yards for a rest.

Once settled in my seat on the train to York I'd felt much better and pushed the incident out of my mind. Opposite me sat a young mother with a baby of a few months who grinned and giggled at me. Doing my best to smile back, I thought of Charity on the train with Rosie. Had she really, truly, believed that the baby she had stolen was her own? Did she still believe that, and did she still think that Rosie was God's child?

I felt my face break into a real smile, as I remembered I'd be seeing Charity very soon. The baby opposite, watching me, broke into a delighted chortle.

I thought about Rosie again – the baby we'd believed was Rosie. I tried to imagine her back in Barnsley with her parents – with brothers and sisters, perhaps – all immensely relieved and happy to have her home. I shook my head to try to clear the image, and the baby's face creased with disappointment at my changed expression. With a little cry, she turned to her mother.

The mother, who could only have been eighteen or so, gave me a curious look as though trying to sum me up. I offered a weak smile, feeling some kind of apology was needed, then felt in my bag for Charity's letters.

I got off the train at York and asked at the enquiry desk about buses to Helmsall.

"There's only one bus a day, love, and it left at two-thirty," the woman told me, looking me up and down as though I wasn't fit to be out. I felt suddenly self-conscious and silly.

It was now ten past three. "How can I get there?" I asked.

She shrugged. "Taxi? There's a rank just outside."

I thanked her, glad I'd pocketed my mother's money.

As we sped on again across the empty moors, the taxi driver asked, "Did you say it was Helmsall you wanted, lass?"

"Yes. Well – just outside it. The residential unit. For teenagers with psychiatric problems."

"You mean the youngsters' loony bin?" He half-turned his head to me. "If you don't mind me asking, why would you be going there?"

"Visiting. My friend's in there. It's not a loony bin."

"Sorry, love. No offence, but it's easier to say than… what you said."

"That doesn't make it true."

"Course not. What's she in for, then?"

"She's ill. She'll be coming home soon."

It was almost dark, though not yet four o'clock, as he pulled in to a red-brick complex of buildings interspersed with tiny bushes that looked as though they might not survive the winter. We hadn't been through Helmsall itself – it lay, he told me, a couple of miles further on.

"Good luck," he said as I paid him. He'd said seven pounds fifty when I got in, but it turned out to be eight pounds forty. Perhaps because I'd made him stop for me to be sick. It didn't seem worth arguing, though I knew my mother would have done.

He counted out my change, then handed me a printed card. "Here's my number. Give me a call when you're ready to go home. I'll not be far away."

I wondered what had happened to the next job he'd mentioned, the one he was in a hurry to get to, but didn't like to ask.

As he drove away, I stood by the entrance in the freezing wind, feeling abandoned and suddenly afraid. Seeing Charity – the thing I'd longed for ever since the police had come to Louise's that evening and taken her away – was a frightening prospect now. There was so much to say and so much that could go wrong. Perhaps she wouldn't even want to see me. Or they wouldn't let me in.

As I hesitated outside the glass doors, a few stray flakes of snow appeared, buffeted sideways by the wind. I clenched my teeth and pushed my way in.

The girl at the reception desk looked about my own age or only a year or so older. Her long, dark hair was bound into a tight plait which hung down her back. She had a pretty but rather vacant face, as though her mind was somewhere else.

"Can I help you?" She barely looked at me, for which I was thankful.

"I've come to visit Charity Baker." I tried to sound self-assured, as though there was no doubt I'd be allowed in.

She turned her head to look at the clock behind her. "It's ten to four."

"I know."

"Visiting hours two to three-thirty on a weekday. Two to five on a weekend." She glanced down at her desk, where I noticed she had a pop magazine open. No doubt she expected me to go away.

"But I've come all the way from Castlehaven. By train and then taxi. I couldn't get here any sooner."

"Can't help it – I'm sorry." Her voice held no expression whatsoever.

"Please. I have to see her. It's really important."

She looked up from her page, as though she had suddenly remembered something. "Did you say Charity Baker?"

"Yes, that's right."

"She's that new lass, isn't she? Sister Evans said she can't have any visitors, except for a Mrs Watson."

My brain clicked into action. "Yes, that's right. They let Mrs Watson visit because Charity's relatives were all in France. But I've just got back to England. I'm her cousin. I can see her, because I'm related."

She gave me a disparaging look, as though noticing for the first time my untidy hair, white face, and, quite possibly, the traces of vomit on my clothes. "Thought you said you'd come from Castlehaven?"

"I have. I was in France before that. I got back yesterday."

"I'll have to check with Sister Evans."

"Can't you just let me in?"

She looked down at her magazine, obviously longing to get back to it. "No – I'd better go and ask. Wait here, please." She pointed to a row of chairs and walked away slowly, as though to make it clear she was doing me a favour and was in no hurry.

Once the door was closed behind her I jumped to my feet and set off down a corridor in the opposite direction. I'd no idea where I was going – all I knew was that Charity was somewhere in these buildings and I was going to find her.

Halfway down the corridor I met a boy with long, untidy ginger hair and a freckled face. His face brightened as though he recognised me. "Hey – it's our Mandy."

I decided not to argue. "Hello. I'm looking for Charity Baker. Do you know where she is?"

He thought for a minute. "Charity – that's the new girl. She'll be in t' day room. I'll show you, if you like."

He set off and I followed. "Thanks."

"What's your name?" I asked him as he darted along corridors and through double doors, leaving me breathless and a little worried I might fall over again.

He laughed. "You're a right case, Mandy. You know me – I'm your brother, Tim."

I laughed back, pretending it had been a joke. "How are you, Tim?"

"I'm great, thanks."

"That's good."

"You still going out with Pete Moulding?"

"No – I dumped him."

"Good for you – he were never good enough for you."

"That's what I thought."

Tim stopped by a doorway and pushed it open, then stood back. "She's over there, by the window. She always sits there on her own. I'll leave you to it."

"Thanks, Tim. You're a mate. I mean you're a great brother."

He scrutinised my face. "No, you're not our Mandy. But you're a nice lass. Ta-ra for now."

"Ta-ra, Tim."

I took a huge gulp of air which made my head swim and silver darts flicker before my eyes. Charity was in an armchair with her back to me, facing the window. I could see one hand and a bit of her reddish-gold hair. The curtains were open and a vista of moorland was just visible in the dusk, dusted with a thin covering of snow. I stumbled as I crossed the room, aware of several eyes on me and a television set blaring from one corner. The air was much warmer than in the corridor and there was an overpowering smell of lavender air-spray. The five or six occupants all looked young and there appeared to be no staff present. No-one spoke but a young man put out a hand to steady me as I passed.

"Thanks," I said, and Charity, hearing my voice, looked round.

"You've lost weight," she said. "And you've got those spots back on your chin."

She extended her arms and I hugged her, almost falling on top of her. We remained clasped together for several minutes, until she pushed me off, saying, "Move up a bit – you're suffocating me."

After that she gave me a long hard stare, her head on one side. "You really do look awful."

"I've not been well." I said. "But never mind me. Charity – it's so good to see you..."

We embraced again, and this time the tears flooded my eyes and streamed down my face, stinging as they ran into the not-yet-healed grooves I'd dug with my fingernails.

"Why didn't you come before? I've been waiting and waiting for you."

Charity looked much as she had at Louise's – her face pale and her hair scraped back into a tight pony tail. She had an odd smell about her that I didn't recognise – perhaps something to do with her medication.

"They wouldn't let me come. Louise said you weren't allowed any other visitors."

"So how did you get in?"

I told her about my encounter with the girl at reception.

She grinned. "Lucky you got Rebecca. She's new and she's a bit thick. If Annie had been on duty you'd never have got in."

"Where's your room?"

"Miles away in another block. I've only just learnt my way there."

"Can I see it?"

"I'm not allowed in it during the day. We have to stay in the day room. We're supposed to mix with each other."

"Do you?" I cast my eyes back over the other occupants, none of whom seemed to be talking.

"Not much. Some of them are weirdoes. There was a nice girl here the first day but she's gone home."

I opened my bag and brought out the rather squashed crisps and biscuits. "I brought you these."

"Thanks." She didn't look very interested.

"What's the food like?" I was aware of all the questions I'd meant to ask, but couldn't find a way to begin. We seemed stuck, instead, with talking about trivia.

"Not too bad."

I gazed out of the window. Snowflakes were tumbling, denser now, against the light. The moor was invisible in the near-darkness.

"How did you get here?"

"Train and then a taxi."

"How will you get home?"

"The same." Why wouldn't the words come – why couldn't I ask her about Rosie?

"Joanne, what's the matter? You look upset."

"Nothing. I'm fine." I tried to keep my voice level.

"There is something. Why are you crying?" She passed me a mangled tissue which I held against my cheek.

"Everything," I managed to say, though it came out muffled. "I've missed you. It's been awful. It must have been terrible for you…"

She shook her head slowly, with a little frown, slightly puzzled as though trying to remember something from years ago.

Then she gave a little cough, looked up to the powerful, greenish overhead light and down again and said, "God has been testing me."

"What?"

"I didn't realise at first, that I would have to go through fire to prove myself worthy to bear His daughter. But I understand now. It's like Herod killing all the baby boys. The forces of evil are ranged against Rosie and I have to show I'm strong enough to protect her before I can have her back."

I looked up at the light, too, as if it might hold a clue to what she was saying. "I don't know what you mean. Charity – she's not your –"

Charity didn't seem to hear me. "Mary and Joseph faced great danger – that's why they fled to Egypt with the baby Jesus. It's different for me – I had to come here on my own. But now *you're* here, it will get better. God's plan can move forward. First, you have to help me get Rosie back..." She sat back in her chair, folded her arms and looked at me.

"But I can't do that."

She shook her head, impatient. "Don't be scared, Joanne. God is on our side – He'll help us. As long as we have faith. He told me you were coming, to help me escape from here."

"No – I can't! That's not why I came." I hated saying it, but I had to.

Her eyes opened wide. "But you *have* to help me."

"I just came to visit. I wasn't even supposed to come. No-one knows I'm here. I've got to get back home..." I bit my lip hard to stop the tears.

She made a big effort to marshal her resources. "Listen, Joanne. I don't blame you for being scared. I was the same when they brought me here. But we have to be brave. We have to fight together against the forces of evil. Louise told me she'd pray for me. She's in the battle, too."

"I know, but –"

"Joanne, what's the matter with you?" She frowned, irritated for the first time at my refusal to cooperate.

"I *can't* help you, Charity. Not the way you want. That baby – it wasn't yours. You took it from its pram."

A hard note crept into her voice. "Only because God told me to. Because she *was* Rosie – don't you see? You sound like the people here, accusing me of stealing her. They don't understand, but *you do*. You're my only hope, Joanne – don't let me down." She had tears in her eyes now.

"I'll do anything to help you. Anything within reason. But we can't get Rosie back. What if God doesn't want you to have her any more? What it He wants someone else to bring her up? Maybe you're too young. Maybe..." I stopped, shocked by the look on Charity's face. It was as though I'd slapped her: pain, horror, disbelief.

"Joanne – stop it! That's what *he* said."

"What who said?"

She looked as though a bolt of lightning had struck her. "My dad. He said those same words. He said I wasn't fit to bring her up. When she was just born and they took her away. I could hear her crying. He said I wasn't fit to bring up a baby. That I was too sinful to have God's child, so they'd have to send her to someone else."

"No, Charity. That's not what I'm saying. All I'm saying is –"

"You're against me like all the rest of them. I thought you were on my side. I thought you believed me, about Rosie. You're no better than my dad. You think I'm too evil to have a baby – to look after my own child. I hate you, I hate you, I *hate* –"

Her voice rose with each repetition until she finished with a shriek. I'd grabbed her wrist and must have closed my eyes. All of a sudden she was wrenched away from me and I opened them to see a blue-uniformed nurse.

"Charity – Miss Baker – please calm down. It's all right. You're safe here. No-one's going to hurt you."

Another nurse, this one in white, was beside me. "Come with me, please. I don't know who you are, but Miss Baker is not supposed to have visitors."

"I didn't mean to…"

"Who are you, and how did you get in?"

I started to tell her my name but was drowned by Charity's voice, yelling, "I hate you, go away! You're evil, like him."

"Charity, no! I'm not evil, I'm your friend. I love you…"

"I *hate* you, I hate *him*…"

"Who do you hate, Charity?" the nurse asked.

"I hate him, the monster, the Terror by Night…"

"Please let me stay," I begged the white-coated nurse, who was trying to pull me away.

"He's the monster – he's the Terror…" cried Charity.

"Who is?" asked the nurse.

"The Terror – he's got his face…"

"Whose face?" The nurse's voice was insistent and calm.

"My dad's face. The Terror, he's got my dad's face…"

I pictured Charity's Terror, the figure from her nightmare, with a scaly outstretched hand or claw, gripping one of Mr Baker's cheeks as Charity's father struggled to get away. As the nurse tugged me towards the door, the last thing I heard was Charity's voice, raised again to a shriek, "He's got my dad's face!"

As we left the room my legs gave way again. My field of view shifted to the right by about three feet, my nausea returned and I was aware of tumbling into darkness.

I was sitting in a tiny room with dark wallpaper and a single, unshaded bulb hanging from the ceiling. Beside me was the blue-coated nurse, holding my hand.

"You're dehydrated," she said. "And we think your blood sugar may be low. You're not diabetic, are you?"

"No."

"The ambulance is on its way. They're going to check you over in hospital."

"Why?" I hadn't yet worked out where I was or remembered what had happened.

"Tell me, when did you last have something to eat?"

"I don't know."

"Was it today? Did you have some breakfast?"

"Yes. I had some toast. I mean, no." There didn't seem any point in lying to her. "I flushed it down the loo."

"Did you? Now why was that?"

I struggled to remember. "Charity." That seemed enough of an answer.

The nurse's voice was gentle. "Do you want to tell me what's going on?"

"They took her baby away. Rosie. But she wasn't Charity's baby. The other Rosie – the real one – they took her away, too. Charity's dad told her she was evil."

The nurse sighed and I realised I wasn't making much sense. "Sorry," I said, "I don't really understand it myself."

"All right, love. Don't worry. We need to call your parents to let them know what's going on. Can you tell me their number?"

"My dad's dead."

"Oh dear, I'm sorry. Your mum, then?"

"Mum and Aunt Daisy. They live together." I struggled to look at my watch. "Oh, help! They'll be worried. I should be getting home. I need to call a taxi."

"No – remember, I told you – we're taking you to hospital. The ambulance will be here soon. It's probably delayed because of the snow. Tell me your phone number and we'll phone home to let them know you're safe."

I reeled off the number and she wrote it down. After that I felt faint again, and the nurse told me to put my head between my knees. I stayed like that until the ambulance came.

"Joanne – I cannot *believe* you would do something like this." It was my mother, standing beside my drip, her face red and her eyes bloodshot.

I had a sense, not unpleasant, that my head was floating somewhere near the ceiling. My headache, I realised, had gone, and I felt as though I'd slept for a hundred years.

"Mum. Sorry."

Aunt Daisy appeared in view, sitting on the other side of my bed. She gave me her wide smile, as though it was an ordinary day and she'd come into my bedroom at home with a cup of tea.

"Hello, Aunt Daisy."

"Hello, Joanne. We're very glad to see you."

"I'm really sorry." I couldn't quite remember what I'd done, but I knew from the guilt welling in my stomach that it was something serious.

"It's quite a relief," Aunt Daisy added.

"The worry you put us through," began my mother. "Can you imagine how I felt when Claire's mother told me you weren't there – that you never went to their house at all? And then I found the money gone from the jar…"

It was all coming back to me. "Mum – I'll save up the money and pay you back. I didn't mean to steal but it was the only way I could get here. The taxi fare…"

"Don't talk to me about taxi fares."

"We came here ourselves by taxi," explained Aunt Daisy. "All the way to York. No trains at this hour. It turned out rather expensive."

"I'll pay that back, too."

"Don't be silly," said Mum. "It's not a question of money. It's… it's…"

I'd only ever seen my mother cry when reminiscing about my dad. It was odd to think that I had reduced her to tears. It struck me that, in spite of all her nagging, she probably loved me. An odd, uncomfortable thought that didn't please me as much as I would have expected. It was more embarrassing than anything else.

"I thought I'd never see you again. I thought I'd lost you, like your dad…"

A nurse appeared at that moment, plump and middle-aged, with greying hair cut very short. She silenced my mother with a stern look.

"Can I go home now?" I asked.

"Soon, when we get you back to normal. You'll have to stay on the drip a bit longer."

She adjusted something that was attached to me and went away.

My mother resumed her attack. "And they say you can't have eaten anything for days. Your blood sugar was at rock bottom. And you were dehydrated – no wonder you fainted. What were you playing at?"

"I couldn't eat. I just couldn't. I tried."

"But why couldn't you?"

"I don't know. Because of Charity – what happened to her…"

"I'd like to strangle Tom and those Crabbies," said my mother.

I remembered something else. "She was upset, when I fainted. What happened to her – is she all right? She was screaming about the Terror. Can you ask someone about her? I want to go back and see her."

My mother gave a strangled little laugh. "You'll be lucky. You're going nowhere near that girl again. She's caused nothing but trouble from start to finish. An asylum's the best place for her."

"It's not an asylum – it's a unit. It's not a loony bin."

"I didn't say it was. There's nothing wrong with an asylum. All I said was it's the best place for her. Let's hope they can get her sorted out."

"It's a nice place with a TV. Lots of young people. A boy called Tim thought he was my brother. He showed me where Charity was. I want to see her again – please let me go back!"

"Absolutely not."

"But she was so upset. She said the Terror had got hold of her dad's face."

"What are you talking about?"

"The Terror, the one she sees in her nightmares. I told you. The Terror had grabbed her dad's face. She was so frightened. I'm worried about her."

"I'm sure the staff at the unit will take good care of her," said Aunt Daisy. "They'll know what to do. She's obviously having some kind of delusions, poor girl. Louise will be able to tell you how she is, when she's been back to see her."

The nurse returned and said, "I think Joanne needs some rest now. Would you like to go and have some coffee?"

When my mother and Aunt Daisy had gone, I asked the nurse, who was still fussing with tubes and dials, what was wrong with me.

"Nothing that a few days in bed and some good meals won't put right. They'll let you go home soon. But you must start eating and drinking again or you'll have to come back into hospital."

"I didn't mean to stop. I wasn't trying to lose weight or anything. I'm not anorexic."

"What made you do it, then?" She sounded genuinely curious rather than angry.

"Because of Charity – my friend. She stole a baby. She really thought it was hers. She's the one I went to see, at the unit where I collapsed."

"That's terrible, about the baby. You must have been really upset."

"I was. I still am."

"But why stop eating?"

"I couldn't bear the feel of food in my mouth. Then I had Charity's nightmare. It's too complicated to explain."

"When you get home, maybe you should talk to someone about it. A counsellor or a psychologist, perhaps. I'm sure we can arrange something."

"I don't want to."

"It might help, to talk it through."

The nurse had a kind face, and I felt a sudden overwhelming desire to tell her. "I'm in love with Charity."

She broke into a broad smile. "That's wonderful, dear. Charity is very lucky to have someone who cares for her so much. I'm sure she'll be better soon. You both will."

"We're planning to live together, one day."

She beamed at me again. "I wish you both the very best of luck."

I felt a weight lift from me and my body seemed to float upwards to join my head at the ceiling. After that, I slept.

I woke from a vague, peculiar dream set in the art room at school. Charity, dressed in a long blue dress embroidered with white daisies, repeated her words to me: "The Terror – he's got my dad's face."

Her voice was calm, and this time I understood her to mean that the Terror's face was that of her father.

I lay awake for a few minutes, pondering how the same sentence could mean two such different things. Then I drifted back to sleep and had forgotten all about it by the time I woke up again.

Chapter 12

Tom's journal, Wednesday 19th December 1984

What a Christmas this is going to be.

Pattie is hardly speaking to me now. She laid into me a couple of days ago about the amount of time I'm spending on fellowship stuff. As if anything had changed! Up to now she's always been very understanding about my commitment to the Crabbies.

She mentioned, in particular, my visits to Louise. Is it possible she suspects something? Not that there's anything going on, of course. I've been trying very hard recently not even to think about Louise. Not in *that* way. Perhaps I spoke her name in my sleep? That's something I've dreaded for some time.

I've been struggling so hard and so long with these feelings – but they show no sign of lessening. The only way to destroy them, Jack tells me, is to cut myself off completely from Louise – never to see her again. But I can't do that. She's one of my flock and she's going through a difficult time.

What was I supposed to feel, when she told me, tears streaming down her face, that she'd asked Alan to come home and he'd refused? I had to pretend to share her sadness – while my insides curled into a sad cold little ball, confronted once again by her absolute indifference, in that way, to me.

Louise asked me if I would speak to Alan – try to persuade him to come back. I had to refuse. She didn't understand why. I had to try to tell her that I still had a suspicion that he might be the father. It was true, but she gave me a look I will never forget. Perhaps the way Jesus looked at Judas when Judas went off to betray him.

Enough of this. The real issue, the one on which I should be focusing all my energy, is Charity. And she, of course, is one of the reasons (though not the only one) I've been going to see Louise. I'm not allowed to visit Charity myself so Louise is my only contact with her. She's planning to see her every three or four days – as often as she can. It's a long, expensive journey without a car, and she has to arrange care for her children. But, being the strong, resourceful person she is, she is doing it anyway. I've offered to drive her up there next time. They won't

let me in but at least it will be company for Louise and save her time and money.

Louise tells me Joanne is in a bad way – due, she thinks, to the shock of all that has happened. I'm not allowed to see Joanne, either – Jean won't let me into the house. It seems she blames me in some way for what has happened.

Perhaps I deserve it. If I'd stamped down harder on this Special Blessing madness at an early stage, all this might never have happened. I've been a lousy pastor.

I feel so helpless – I can't even repair my own marriage. Jack says I must be honest with Pattie, but how can I tell her I'm love with Louise but trying desperately hard not to be? That's really going to work, isn't it?

God help me – please!

Just had a phone call from Louise. Still haven't properly taken in what she said. I'm shaking. I threw up in the loo on the way back to my desk.

Thank God I'm in the house on my own. I can't face Pattie at the moment. Or anyone else, except Louise.

I have to go and see Louise. And someone will have to tell Joanne. Louise tells me Joanne visited Charity two days ago. Travelled there alone, somehow got in to see her. There may be a connection with what has happened – apparently Charity got very upset. Maybe that's what set things off. Joanne collapsed and was taken to hospital. She hadn't eaten for several days.

I can't get my head round what Louise just told me. One of us should have *seen*. I should have seen.

I'm going to be sick again.

I picked up our phone, glad I'd got to it first.

"Joanne, hi. It's Louise. How long have you been home?"

"Since yesterday." How, I wondered, did Louise know I'd been in hospital?

They'd brought me home in an ambulance late the previous afternoon, Tuesday, after handing me a xeroxed sheet of dietary instructions and a letter for my GP. There was snow on the ground, still, and this added to the sense of unreality. I had a soft dizziness in my head that felt like swirling feathers every time I moved.

Louise's voice sounded shaky and strange. "Is your mum there?"

"No. She went out shopping with Aunt Daisy."

"I wondered if I could come round? I'd like to speak to you and your mum together. Tom's here with me – maybe we can both come?"

What was Louise playing at? She knew my mother wouldn't let Tom into the house. "That's not a good idea. Mum won't see Tom and she might be back any time. Can't you come on your own?"

"I... I'd rather Tom was with me."

"Why? Louise, what's the matter? What's happened?"

She was, I realised, close to tears. My stomach gave a lurch.

"There's some news, Joanne. I'd rather tell you in person, with Tom there, too."

"Is it about Charity? Is she all right? What's happened to her?"

I heard Tom's voice for a moment in the background, then Louise said, "Yes, it is about Charity. Tom just suggested he picks you up in the car and brings you here. Is that all right?"

I knew my mother wouldn't like it – I was not supposed to leave the house, let alone talk to Tom. But I was worried enough about Charity to say, "Yes, okay, come straight round now, before they get back."

I yanked off my dressing gown and pyjamas and pulled on my jumper and jeans. Then I tore a sheet off the shopping pad on the fridge and wrote a quick note to my mother: "Gone to Louise's."

Minutes later, Tom's car pulled up outside. His face was white and I was more scared than ever.

"Please tell me," I said, hearing my voice shake. "Is Charity dead?"

There was a horrible pause which went on forever. In it, I recalled everything that happened when Dad died.

"No, she's not dead."

"Is she very ill?"

"No, it's not that. Nothing like that. Joanne, I'm sorry to delay telling you like this. But I want Louise to be with us. You'll see why."

We drew up outside Louise's house and Tom opened her back door without ringing the bell. Louise's face was pale and she had tears in her eyes. She was holding David, who was trying to tell her something about his truck. Alice must have been at school.

"Come and sit down, Joanne," Louise said. "Here, beside me on the sofa."

Tom sat down opposite, in the armchair. David began to run his truck around Tom's feet but Tom, for once, ignored him.

Louise took a breath. "I had a phone call from the unit this morning," she said. "It was about Charity. They've found out what happened. The baby, I mean. How she..." She looked at Tom as though asking him to take over.

Tom said, "Okay, I'll explain. Charity got very upset – but I think you know about that."

I'd been dreading this – whatever awful thing had happened, it was my fault. "I'm sorry – I shouldn't have gone there. I just wanted to see her. I didn't mean to make her worse..."

"You didn't make her worse, Joanne. You're not to blame for this at all. Your visit may have been a good thing. It got her talking..."

"How do you mean, talking?"

"She said some things that made the staff start to think. She mentioned her father."

"She did that while I was there. She kept screaming that the Terror – that's the creature in her nightmare – had got hold of her dad's face."

Louise and Tom looked at each other.

"No, she didn't mean that," said Tom. "She meant it *had* her father's face. Looked like him."

My dream came back to me. "Yes, I realised that later on. But what...?"

"They asked her lots more questions and it gradually came out that..."

Tom stopped as the kitchen door rattled, the living room door swung open and there stood Alan, looking bigger than ever. His teeth gleamed as he opened his mouth in a kind of snarl. "What the hell is going on?"

Tom jumped to his feet. "Alan! I don't know what to..."

Alan's face screwed up with rage. "What are you doing in my house, with my wife? Get out, you bastard. Right this second – now!"

"Please let me explain," said Tom. "I'm here because Louise got a phone call – about Charity. They know what happened to her now."

"Oh they bloody well do, do they? Well, Mr the Reverend Tom know-it-all, perhaps that'll get you off my back after all this time! How you've got the nerve to sit here in my living room after accusing me of child abuse... Get out, now, or I'll make you!"

Alan towered a good three inches above Tom, but Tom stood his ground. "Just let me say something, Alan. Let me tell you how sorry I am. I was never sure, but yes, I did suspect you for a time and I see now how mistaken I was. Please, please forgive me."

Alan's lip curled and he pushed Tom to the door.

Tom looked at Louise.

"I think you'd better go," she said.

"We're in the middle of telling Joanne what happened," said Tom. "It's – it's pretty bad. That's why we're here. Let me just finish – then perhaps you'll understand."

"Tom – just go." said Louise. "I'll finish telling Joanne. Alan – no!"

Alan's punch landed hard on Tom's jaw. Tom almost went down with the force of it, but somehow regained his balance, one hand cradling his injured face, and stuttered, "Alan, please, let's talk – "

The second blow, on the nose, caught Tom even harder and this time he collapsed to the floor. Louise went to support him but he wrenched himself out of her grasp.

"Okay, if that's what you want, Alan, I'm going," he said. "I'm truly sorry. And I don't blame you for…" he stopped as the blood started pouring from his nose and clasped the bundle of tissues Louise offered him, "… for hitting me."

The door slammed behind him.

"I'll go as well," I said, overwhelmed with a sense of not belonging. At least I knew Charity was alive. Could the news of who had been the father of her baby really be so bad?

"No, don't go," said Louise. "Alan – just leave us for a minute. Make yourself a cup of tea. You realise you probably broke Tom's nose? In front of Joanne and David, too." David was on Louise's knee, looking bemused. "He could report you for assault."

"It'd be worth it for the pleasure I got from those punches." Alan disappeared into the kitchen.

"Why has Alan come back?" I asked Louise.

"I phoned him just after I got the call from the unit. He said he'd come home this evening after work. Oh, Joanne – I'm so sorry about all this."

"I still don't know who the father is and why it's so awful."

"You haven't worked it out?"

I felt very young and stupid. "No. Should I have?"

"Of course not. I just wondered if you might have guessed. That thing we were saying about her father's face..."

"What about it?"

We were sitting down again on the sofa and she took my hand. "Joanne, the father of Charity's baby... It's Charity's own father."

My head spun as I tried to make sense of this. "Mr Baker? But he can't be. That would make Charity and the baby sisters. It's impossible."

"No, it's not, I'm afraid. You see, he..." Louise's voice caught on a sob in her throat. "Charity's father sexually assaulted her. Forced her to have sex with him." She looked at me, still squeezing my hand, as understanding very slowly dawned.

"No."

"I'm afraid so. The staff at the unit seem very sure. Charity broke down in the end and blurted it all out. How he used to come into her bedroom at night, for years and years. Starting from when she was quite small."

I shivered. "The Terror."

"What?"

"The Terror by Night. Her nightmare. It was real."

"Yes. I'm afraid it was real."

There was another pause, one that seemed to go on forever.

Eventually I managed to speak. "But why didn't she tell someone? Why did she pretend it was a nightmare?"

"They don't really know. Perhaps it was her way of trying to cope with it. By pretending it was a dream."

Now I'd started asking questions, I couldn't stop. "But why did she let it keep happening? Why didn't she tell her mum? Why didn't she tell *me*?"

"I don't know about her mother. Maybe Charity tried to tell her and she didn't believe her."

"*I'd* have believed her. Why didn't she tell me?"

"Darling, I don't know." Louise had her arm round me now. "I'm sure she'd have told you if she could. Perhaps by the time she met you she'd convinced herself it was a nightmare, to make it more bearable."

I was conscious of sick rising in my throat, of the need to keep talking, to make it stay down. "She used to pray that prayer every night. She gave me a copy. If she got the words right, the Terror didn't come. If she made a mistake, he did come…"

Louise shook her head. I could see she was fighting back tears.

Mine wouldn't flow, somehow. I felt emotionally frozen but mentally alert, as though all I could do was ask questions, find out every last detail. "So the thing about getting the words wrong?"

"I suppose that was her way of explaining why the Terror sometimes came. She could always tell herself she'd made a mistake."

"But when I started praying the prayer for her, she stopped having her nightmare. Almost."

Louise was silent.

I supplied my own answer. "I suppose her father must have stopped what he was doing, for some reason." An image of the horrific events suddenly filled my head. "Louise – it's horrible. The thought of it."

Alan opened the door and peered in, but Louise shook her head and he retreated.

"Try not to think about it," said Louise, as though she was speaking to Alice. "Try really hard to put it out of your mind."

"I can't. I keep seeing the Terror, with her dad's face, coming towards her bed."

"The police are looking for him. They'll try him and he'll go to jail."

"For life?"

"I hope so."

I wrestled myself out of Louise's grasp, all of a sudden not wanting comfort any more. "Can I see Charity now? Now that I understand – she can tell me about it. They *must* let me see her, now."

"I don't know. She's still in quite a state. She's going to need a lot of care and help."

"But I'm her best friend. I can give her that. I love her."

"I know you do, Joanne. There'll come a time when she needs you. But it may not be just yet."

I was feeling sick again. "How *could* he, Louise? How could her dad do that?"

She shook her head. I noticed how white her face was. "I don't know."

"When I met him, he looked like a normal man. Anyone's dad. I quite liked him. I can't believe he took me in."

"He took everyone in. He's sick – sick and evil."

"He did it right from when she was small…"

Louise took me in her arms again. "I know. It's absolutely awful. That's why I wanted tell you in person, with Tom there and your mum as well."

"I'm glad Mum wasn't here." I tried to imagine her reaction and couldn't. "Will you tell her, Louise? I don't want to."

"Of course I will, if that's what you want."

"Please. But she'll still find a way to make it my fault, or Charity's."

"No, she won't. No-one is to blame but Mr Baker. Your mum will understand that."

"Poor Tom. I hope he's all right."

She hugged me tighter. "I hope so, too."

"He thought that Alan was the baby's father, didn't he?"

"He half-believed it, at least. For a long time."

"And I ended up thinking it must be that boyfriend of hers from Barnsley. I was so angry with her – so jealous."

"That's understandable. She's your girlfriend."

"Yes, she is." I remembered the nurse's words and felt a tiny measure of relief.

"Will she ever get better from this?" I asked.

"I hope so. But it may take a long time. As I said, she'll need lots of counselling and support."

"I'll be there for her."

"Of course you will. So will I, and lots of other people."

David pushed his way between us and Louise hoisted him onto her knee.

"I still don't understand about the baby," I said.

"What don't you understand?"

"The way Charity told us it was God's child. That the Spirit had fallen upon her, like Mary, and made her conceive. Why did she think that? She really believed it – I'm sure she did."

Louise thought for a moment. "Perhaps she convinced herself – the same way she convinced herself that her father's visits were a nightmare. It was an explanation she could accept without having to face up to the truth about the abuse."

"But how can you make yourself believe something like that?'

'I don't know. Maybe we do it all the time, in smaller ways. Perhaps some of our faith is like that."

"You think so? You know, I sometimes find it hard to believe that the Holy Spirit came to Mary, the way is says in the Bible. That He was Jesus' father. Do you think it's really true?"

"I don't know. Alan would kill me if he heard me say it, but I sometimes doubt it, too."

"Maybe the same thing happened to Mary as to Charity."

"It's possible, I suppose. Though it needn't necessarily have been Mary's father."

I pulled away from Louise and seated myself on the chair opposite. "So the whole story of Jesus might be based on a girl like Charity making up a story because of something awful that happened to her?"

"We'll never know. Of course, many Christians do believe in the virgin birth. They'd be horrified at what we've just been saying."

"But surely it's worse to cover up the truth – for it never to be found out?"

"Maybe. But what good would it do now, after all these years? Even if there was a way of proving it?"

"I suppose Jesus' father could just have been Joseph."

"I'd prefer to think so."

"And me."

We fell silent for a few minutes. David, on Louise's lap, had gone to sleep. The grandfather clock ticked away in the corner.

"Louise – are you and Alan going to get back together?"

"I hope so. I think there's a chance, now."

"I hope you do."

The doorbell rang and I heard Alan's voice in the hall. The living room door opened and there stood my mother, her eyes blazing at us all.

Tom's journal, Thursday, 20th December 1984

I just tried to call Alan but he put the phone down when he heard my voice. All I want to do is apologise – try to explain. Ask him to forgive me.

I'm very sore, especially around the nose and jaw, and my head is throbbing like crazy. Having staggered home (I left my car outside Louise's – couldn't see well enough to drive), I managed to stop the bleeding by squeezing my nostrils for ten minutes. But when Pattie came in and found me, she insisted on picking up the car and taking me to casualty, where we waited for two hours only to be assured my nose wasn't broken and sent home.

It wasn't easy, explaining things to Pattie. I told her the truth – that Alan hit me when I tried to apologise for not trusting him, for suspecting him of being the father. Pattie gave me a funny look as though she didn't quite believe me.

"What were you doing at Louise's in the first place?" she asked.

I then told her the news about Charity's father. She was shocked and upset. We shared a hug, or the closest I could get to one in my battered state.

"I never understood why you thought it was Alan," she said after a minute or so, pulling away from me.

I didn't want to think about it. "It was the way he used to look at Charity."

"I think you exaggerated all that. He just admired her and was interested in all the Special Blessing stuff."

I shook my head, which was a mistake. Darts of pain shot out from my nose into my cheeks and neck. "It was more than that. He was infatuated."

"Even if he was – it's a big jump from that to fathering her child."

"I know. I was mistaken and I'm terribly sorry about it. What more can I say?"

"That poor, poor child." Pattie got up and went into the kitchen.

Louise called me later – thankfully Pattie had gone out with Juliette and Craig. She wanted me to know that Joanne is back in hospital. She cut her arms with a razor blade in her bedroom yesterday evening. And she is refusing to eat again.

I rang Jean to ask if there was anything I could do to help.

"No," she said. "You've done enough damage already." Her voice was tight and bitter.

I asked what she meant, exactly.

"You and your Crabbies." A great deal of venom in those few words.

I'm sick with worry about Joanne, now, as well as Charity. Louise is going up to see Charity tomorrow. I won't be able to drive her there now. Perhaps Alan will take her. He has, I gather, come back for good. Or rather, in Louise's words, they are going to "try and work things out."

I hope they succeed. I really do.

Tom's journal, Friday, 21st December 1984

Louise rang again to give me an update on Joanne. Pattie picked up the phone and her voice turned cool when she discovered who it was. What does she think we're doing – having a secret affair?

When I got to the phone, Louise said. "Joanne's under sedation. Very woozy. She hardly seemed to know who I was – started talking about elephants or something."

"Elephants?"

"She's confused. Her arms are bandaged up – she cut them quite badly."

"But why?"

"The shock of it all, perhaps? Remember, she and Charity are very close."

"I feel responsible. We broke the news to Joanne so badly – especially with Alan arriving out of the blue like that. Perhaps we should have let Jean tell her about Mr Baker."

"We did our best. There's no point blaming ourselves."

"Sorry – I wasn't blaming you. I feel it's my fault."

"Tom, stop it. It's not your fault. Get that into your head. This is all the fault of that evil Mr Baker. But there's some good news there – the police have tracked him down in Belgium. He's on his way back to England to face charges."

"Thank the Lord they've got him. Does Charity know?"

"I don't know what they've told her."

"How is she now?"

"I don't know until I see her. They didn't say much. But they gave me a bit more information."

"Yes?"

"It's rather shocking. They're charging Mr Baker with other offences. More child abuse. Some of it in Barnsley, before he came here. And some incidents in France."

"Incidents?"

"Other young girls."

I couldn't speak for a minute.

"Tom, are you all right?"

"Not really, no."

"It's terrible, isn't it? All the harm he's done. Unbelievable."

"Louise – I don't think I can go on."

"What do you mean?"

'With everything. With Crabbies – after this. It's knocked me for six. Knocked all the faith out of me."

She was silent for a moment before saying, "I understand. But isn't this when we need our faith, times like this?"

I thought of Charity's father, an elder in the Barnsley church, attending services week by week, no doubt prayer meetings, too – participating with fervour, hands in the air, eyes glazed like Charity's. Once again, I could not speak.

"That's Alan just come in," said Louise. "I'll have to go."

The phone went dead. I hobbled back to my desk and sat here for ten minutes, head cradled in my hands. Having failed to speak to Alan on the phone I've been trying to write him a letter. Not that he would read it. I suppose I'm doing it to make myself feel better. But I can't find the right words.

Chapter 13

Louise told me much later that for a few days I thought I was an elephant. I kept muttering about needing to reach the waterhole – I was thirsty and had to find a drink. She poured me a glass of water but I wouldn't take it – I was an elephant and I couldn't drink until I got to the waterhole.

I think I was in hospital seven or eight days, including Christmas. The nurses hung decorations all around the ward and my mother twined a piece of silver tinsel around my drip stand. A Santa person tried to give me a present, which I refused, protesting that I was too old. My mother told me I was ungrateful but she seemed so far away I didn't care.

One visiting session when my mother left to go to the bathroom, Aunt Daisy said that she had a message for me from Louise.

"She's been to see Charity."

"Is Charity all right?"

"Louise says they had a long talk, and that Charity seemed quite normal. No shouting or screaming, anyway. Charity sends you her love and wants to see you."

That made me feel much better, until Aunt Daisy told me that Charity was due to be moved in the next few days to another unit up in the Scottish borders. They had found some relatives of hers up there – a cousin and aunt of her mother – who would be able to visit her and provide support.

My heart sank, hearing this. It seemed unlikely I would see Charity for a long time.

"You can always write to each other, keep in touch that way," said Aunt Daisy, seeing my face.

I turned away from her and shut my eyes.

Tom's journal, Friday 28th December 1984

I didn't think things could get any worse, but I've been proved wrong. While I was walking on the cliff top this morning, trying

to clear my head, Pattie, it turns out, was rooting through the contents of my desk drawer.

We've always had an unspoken agreement not to read each other's diaries, letters and so on. She must have been desperate to find something.

She read my journal for the last few months and discovered all my feelings for Louise.

I sensed the atmosphere as soon as I opened the door. She had emptied two or three kitchen cupboards and their contents were spread out over the worktops. Her hair was tied back, her face flushed, and she held a dishcloth in her hand which she was using to wipe the outside of a spice jar.

Pattie doesn't clean out cupboards very often. Her eyes, as she turned to face me, were icy cold.

"What's wrong?" I asked.

She gave a sniff that caught in her throat and exploded into a sob.

"Pattie, what is it?"

I tried to touch her but she pushed me away and banged the spice jar down onto the draining board.

"Get off me."

"I don't understand."

"Go back to Louise, then. That's where you've been, isn't it?"

"No, I've been on the cliff path, like I said. I –"

"Go on, go back to her. Back to your lover. Just keep away from me." Her eyes flashed a message I'd never seen in them before.

My heart was thudding hard now. "My lover?"

She pointed to the floor, in the corner where my journal was lying open, face down.

"Pattie – no! I didn't. I haven't..."

She came towards me, more frightening than Alan, eyes blazing. "Don't lie to me, Tom. I've read all that stuff you wrote. You and Louise – I might have guessed. I did suspect – I just wasn't sure, until now."

"Nothing ever happened. We held hands once, on the beach. For a few minutes. Then she pulled away and said we shouldn't. I agreed. That's all, Pattie – honestly..."

Her expression softened for an instant, then her face closed up again. "I don't care what you did or didn't do. It's what you thought. It's what you wanted to do. You're in love with her, aren't you? Don't try to deny it."

I wished she would punch me in the face like Alan, so I could collapse to the floor and be out of it. I sank, instead, onto a kitchen chair.

"Pattie, please let me explain. I love you, you're my wife. I didn't –"

"Tom, are you stupid? I've read your diaries. I know how you feel."

"I'm so sorry. All that stuff I wrote. Let me try to explain. Louise and I spent all those hours talking, when I was counselling her. No – please let me go on. It was counselling, it really was. Nothing else. I see now that I should have stopped it, but at the time... she was so grateful. And you were so, so... I mean you and I were going through a bad patch. You seemed so distant. I felt I was helping her, especially after Alan left and she was upset."

She banged two jars together so hard I was surprised they didn't shatter. "So Alan's leaving gave you licence to fall in love with Louise?"

"No, of course it didn't. It was wrong of me – I shouldn't have let myself..."

"Let yourself what?"

"Let myself start to have feelings for her. Or gone on with the counselling once I'd started to feel that way. But I tried so hard, Pattie. If you've read my diaries, you'll know. I wrestled and struggled and begged God to take the feelings away. Pattie – I didn't even kiss her."

Her whole body contorted at the word, her face in a grimace. "And does she feel the same about you?"

"No. Not now."

"You mean she did?"

"I don't know. I suppose she might have, for a while. But she wanted Alan back, I know she did, as soon as she stopped suspecting he was the father. And now he's back."

"And does he know about this?" She gazed at my injuries as if for the first time. "Is that why he hit you?"

"No. I don't think he knows about me and Louise. The reason he hit me – I told you – was because I'd mistrusted him."

She gripped the edge of the work surface, head down as though she felt faint. I got up to offer support but she wouldn't let me anywhere near.

"I'm going – I'm leaving you – as soon as I've put these jars back."

"Leave the stupid jars. Don't go, Pattie, please. We need to talk this through."

"I've said all I want to say. I'm taking Juliette and Craig to my mother's We'll stay there for the time being. As soon as possible, I want a divorce."

"But Pattie, you and I –"

"You and I don't exist any more. Not as a couple. We haven't for a long time, in case you haven't noticed. We haven't made love for months, we never talk, we don't go out, we don't spend any time together..."

"But that's only been just recently, since all this trouble. I haven't felt able..."

"It's been Crabbies, Crabbies all the way, ever since we came to Castlehaven. They come first and last in your life and all points in between. Juliette and Craig and I don't get a look in – we never have. In spite of all your preaching about family values and Christian love. If this is what being a Christian means, I don't want any more of it. I'm leaving you, Crabbies, possibly even Castlehaven. All I care about now is my kids."

"Where are they?"

"Since you see fit to ask, they're at the swimming pool. I told Juliette I wanted a private talk with you when you came in. She knows something's wrong – she saw me crying. I gave her the money to take Craig swimming. They didn't want to go – they're both worried. I'll let you explain all this to them when they come home."

"Pattie – please. Let's go out for a walk together, you and me – have a proper talk. I thought you understood about my work. You've always been so supportive. Being a pastor's wife is one of the hardest roles – with your own job, too, and the house and the kids."

"Yes, it's always been hard work but I never minded that. I only ever wanted us to be happy. To find time for some family life. Not huge swathes of it, necessarily – just some time – but you wouldn't. There was always something you had to do first. And when that was done, there'd be something else. You made out you were putting God first and I believed you, for a while, at least. But you weren't – I see that now. You were putting yourself first – it was a crazy ego-trip to prove yourself indispensable to a group of nutters – one of whom, it turns out, was practising incest."

There was a charged pause. Then I said, "Mr Baker was never a Crabbie."

"As if that makes any difference." She picked up one of her spice jars and stared at the label. "Why didn't someone notice what was happening to Charity? You, with your so-called spiritual wisdom – shouldn't you have spotted that a girl in your fellowship was a victim of abuse?"

That hurt more than anything. "Yes, I should. I should have realised."

"But instead, you blamed Alan."

"I didn't. I wasn't sure. I only thought it might be him."

Pattie shook her head, picked up her cloth and began wiping the jars again, putting them back in neat rows in the cupboard. I thought of all the meals she had made with them, coming in each day from work exhausted. Meals we had eaten as a family around the kitchen table.

"Pattie, if it's any comfort, I blame myself a hundred per cent for not seeing what was happening to Charity. I can barely live with my conscience."

"And you blamed Alan for looking at Charity, when all the time you were plotting to get into Louise's knickers..."

"I wasn't!"

"I've no more to say, Tom. I've no more to say to you, ever. Except to remind you that this house is half mine and of all the work I've put in to support you. Now go away and let me finish these cupboards."

Tom's journal, Saturday 29th December 1984

So my marriage is over. Pattie has finally had enough of me. Reading my journal was what prompted her to leave, but I think it was just the last straw.

I've been pushing too hard and too long at the boundaries of what it is reasonable to expect a marriage partner to endure.

Pattie is right that I have put her and the children way too far down my list of priorities, for much too long.

There is no doubt that I love them. I believe that, should circumstances require it, I would die for them. But, it seems, I couldn't give up an afternoon's work to take them ice-skating on Boxing Day. Pattie had no trouble coming up with a hundred similar instances.

I've been a lousy husband and father and I deserve every word she said to me.

But that doesn't make it any easier to bear.

Looking back through my journal (those words – I can hardly bring myself to imagine her thoughts as she read them!) I see all too clearly where I went wrong. I should have given up those counselling sessions with Louise as soon as I started having feelings for her. Instead, I kidded myself I had to continue because I was the only person she could talk to. That was rubbish. All she needed was someone kind and sympathetic. It could have been anyone.

But no, I managed to convince myself it had to be me. As Pattie said – I had to be indispensable. Especially to the woman I was falling in love with, and who I fantasised might have similar feelings for me. I actually wrote in my journal that I thought I was good for Louise because she felt rejected by Alan and needed to talk to a man who found her beautiful, so her morale could be restored. Who was I trying to fool?

I fooled myself, that's for sure. Made a fool of myself. Far worse than that, I've ended up hurting the people I love most. Wrecking my marriage. Misjudging my closest colleague and friend, Alan. It's quite possible that my poor judgment was a result of my feelings for Louise. As well as my failure to deal properly with the Special Blessing. I let Alan have his own way too long – then I got scared. Started to question his integrity, to fear his infatuation with Charity. Perhaps it was right to fear that. But I should have dealt with it calmly, not ended up accusing him of child abuse.

I should have talked to Pattie about my worries – about the Special Blessing and about Alan. Yes, she was busy and didn't need burdening with all the details. But she's always supported me, given me sound advice. If she had known what was bothering me she might not have taken it all so personally and started to think I no longer loved her.

Even if neither of us had the energy to make love, I could at least have cuddled her in bed. We could have gone on some walks. I could have spent Saturdays with her and the kids, the way we used to.

And now it's too late – she's gone, with Juliette and Craig. I've no idea what she's told them. They know something's wrong. They both gave me reproachful looks as they left. They know they are not just visiting their grandparents in Whitby for a holiday.

All this, on top of the burden of guilt I already feel over Charity. Pattie was right to say I should have suspected her father. Okay, there was no obvious reason to, but something should have told me. Am I so spiritually blind I can't recognise evil in a person?

I met Mr Baker at least twice – surely I should have sensed something wrong? I didn't like him much, that's true, but so what? I meet plenty of people I don't like. It's my job to see the good in them, to focus on that. Mr Baker appeared to be a hard-working businessman. I don't like gambling but I consider amusement arcades pretty harmless. He didn't appear to have a lot of time for his daughter, but it's not easy being a single parent, which he effectively was. And anyway, who am I to speak?

Charity appeared to be well fed and reasonably well clothed. It can be very difficult to get your teenage daughter to wear clothes you approve of. I'm on the brink of that problem with Juliette. Or I was...

Yet all the time Charity was here – and, it seems, for years before that, going back to when she was a little girl – her father was subjecting her to sexual abuse.

The unimaginable horror of it. How can I, a grown man, have the remotest idea what life must have been like for that child? The suffering, the web of lies she spun to try to convince herself it wasn't happening. The 'nightmares' that transferred her father's terrible actions from the domain of reality to the world of dreams. The Spirit-induced pregnancy that allowed her to believe she was still a virgin.

I'm worried about Joanne, too. Louise tells me she has been cutting herself and refusing to eat. That she has retreated into a world of her own. Hearing what Charity's father did was too much for her to handle. That, and being apart from Charity,

unable to see her. Joanne is a bright, imaginative girl and she must be trying to envisage what it was like, all those years, for Charity. Jean is a loving mother but not the gentlest of souls. I can't imagine her talking all this through with Joanne. Perhaps Daisy will help. And thank God, as always, for Louise.

"Hi Joanne – how are you doing?"

Mark, from Crabbies, came to see me the day after I came home from hospital. I was surprised my mother let him in, but glad she did. I'd started to feel bored and fed up, especially when she told me I wouldn't be going back to school until after Easter at the earliest.

When Mum had shown him into the living room and disappeared, Mark gave me a hug and then went quiet. I guessed he didn't know whether he was allowed to talk to me about Charity or not. I wasn't sure how much he'd been told, so I gave him the details. He hadn't heard about her father and was horrified.

"I'm not surprised you're ill," he said. "It must have been an awful shock. Specially when you two are so close." He looked at me and I knew it was time to tell him.

"We're in love, Charity and me."

He raised his eyebrows. "Really? Well. I did wonder."

"Did you?"

"You were always together. But it wasn't just that – oh, I don't know. I had an idea you might be. I knew there was someone and it made sense for it to be her."

"Are you okay with it?"

He frowned, puzzled. "Of course – why wouldn't I be?"

"I thought, last Christmas – remember the party? You seemed interested in me."

He grinned. "Back then, yes – it hadn't clicked with me. I hoped for a while you might go out with me."

"Sorry. I did enjoy our dancing."

"Me too." He paused and looked down at his legs. "Actually, there's a new girl at Crabbies I'm quite interested in."

"That's good."

"She's the only reason I'm still going. Crabbies is weird these days. No Tom and no Alan, no you and no Charity."

I looked at him in surprise. "Where's Tom?"

"They say he's ill. He hasn't been there for the Sunday service the last couple of weeks. People are taking it in turns to lead the worship. It was quite funny when Mr Streatfield had a go."

"What happened?"

"He made all the women wear hats. Warned them all beforehand – turn up without a hat and you won't be allowed in."

"You're kidding me."

"It's true! My mum put a handkerchief over her head and asked if that would do. Mr Streatfield was a bit foxed, really. Went purple in the face. Let her in eventually to shut her up."

When I'd stopped laughing, I said, "I'm giving up Crabbies. I'm not going back."

"I'll probably give up, too. It's only Sarah, at the moment, keeping me going." Mark's eyes lit up as I'd never seen them. This was unmistakably love.

"What's she like?"

"Slim, dark-haired. Makes me laugh. A bit like you, really."

"Stop teasing me."

"I'm not. She *is* a bit like you." He glanced at my skinny arms. "Though I preferred you with a bit more weight on."

"Skinny doesn't suit me, does it?"

His tone became serious. "Are you eating again?"

"I'm getting back to it. Who told you I wasn't?"

"Can't remember. Someone at Crabbies. We've been praying for you."

"Bloody hell."

He grinned. "It's not like you to swear."

"I'll have to practise, if I'm going to stop believing. Have to learn to become a normal person."

"Some hope of that."

"Thanks, Mark." I grinned back at him.

He wheeled himself a bit closer. "Know what I think? Seriously? You should come out as gay and then keep going to Crabbies. That would show all those homophobes."

I put my hand on the arm-rest of his chair. "Maybe I should. But it's not because of being gay that I'm leaving. I've known what I am for a while. It's because of all that's happened with Charity's dad."

"Why should that make you stop?"

"Mr Baker was a Christian."

"No, he wasn't. Not a real one. He can't have been."

"Charity said he was into all the Special Blessing stuff," I said.

"Was he? Well, it can't have been genuine. Not in his case."

"I also feel I've grown out of Crabbies."

"It's partly that with me, too. They believe so many stupid things."

"You're telling me. I'd quite like to be a Christian without having to believe all that stuff. But maybe you can't."

"No, maybe not. I don't really know." Mark was clearly tiring of our theological discussion. "I'd better go in a minute," he said. Your mum said I could only stay until five."

"You're lucky she let you in at all. Louise is the only Crabbie she's allowed to see me since it all happened."

"Not even Tom?"

"No. I wish she would. I'm worried about him, now."

"Someone said he was suffering from stress," Mark said.

"I'm not surprised, after all that's happened."

"I'll miss Tom if I leave Crabbies."

"And me."

Mark leaned over and kissed me on the cheek. "Get better soon, Joanne. I'll be back."

"See you around, Hot Wheels."

"Ta-ra, little Miss Skinnyribs." With another grin, he hurtled towards the open door and into the hall.

Tom's journal, Friday 4th January 1985

I have written my letter of resignation. It's on the hall table, waiting to be posted.

The house is silent as death. I will go mad if I stay here alone any longer.

I have tried to talk to Pattie, but she won't. I've seen the children twice. Pattie has told them we are going to live apart. Juliette is furious with both of us. Craig has gone quiet, clammed up or rather closed down – will hardly say a word. His face expressionless. Stunned, can't take it in. Neither can I.

My family is beyond repair.

I've just checked my documents. Everything's up to date and I have reasonable life insurance. They would be better off with the money than with me. I am seriously considering it.

I still haven't seen Joanne. Jean won't let me in the house.

I passed Louise and Alan a couple of days ago on the High Street. Louise gave me a cool hello. I suppose the coolness was because Alan was there – but still, it hurt. Alan didn't speak, wouldn't even look at me.

I'm officially on sick leave, not taking services or doing any other work. Numbers have fallen. This could be the end of the Crabbies. Not that I care. My faith has gone.

Most of Castlehaven appears to know what has happened. The press have got hold of the story. Charity and her father can't be named, but everyone seems to have worked it out.

They are transferring her to a new unit in the Scottish Borders. Her mother has gone up there to stay with relatives. I suppose it makes sense for Charity to be near her family, but it means Louise will only be able to visit occasionally, now. It's our last link broken.

I saw my GP and he prescribed anti-depressants. I should take them but I can't bring myself to. I don't deserve to get better. I have nothing and no-one to get better for.

Louise and I, strolling on the beach back in June, got into a discussion for some reason about what it would be like to swim out to sea and drown. How long it might take. It was a warm, calm evening – that time we held hands and Joanne almost spotted us. We decided that drowning could take several hours – but that was summer. On a bitter day like this it would be much less – a matter of an hour or only minutes, even. The cold would get you.

Not a pleasant way to go. On the other hand, no mess for anyone to find, and the children could be told it was an accident. I don't want them to know I killed myself.

I used to think I would never have the courage to end my life. But I see now that, in some circumstances, it's living that takes the greater courage. I don't have that courage any more.

I can put up with an hour of agony if it leads to oblivion. I realise that I never did believe in hell. Not hell-after-death. Nor heaven – not in the traditional sense. All I ask of heaven is respite from my guilt, my shame – the unbearable knowledge that I have let down my family, my friends, my congregation – all those who trusted me.

I'm sorry, Father. You backed a loser when you called me to Your service. I'll get out and make room for someone better.

Chapter 14

"Can I go for a walk, Mum, on my own?"

My mother frowned. I'd been home from hospital just over a week and it was the Monday I should have gone back to school after Christmas. I'd started eating small portions of Mum's carefully prepared, tempting meals, and my face had begun to fill out again. My dose of sedatives had been reduced and my brain was beginning to wake up. I was bored senseless and longed for a change of scene.

The pain of missing Charity and the hollow, sick feeling inside me when I thought of her ordeal, now came in waves rather than being constantly present. Two or three times a day I was overwhelmed and found myself in tears or (much worse) lying with my face to the wall, frozen into a timeless agony that blocked all rational thought. I don't know how long these episodes lasted, but each one felt as though it would never end.

Every time I emerged, it was like waking from a dream. I was aware of the pain and fear slowly dispersing like mist in the sun, giving way to a blissful emptiness of mind. But I learned that the darkness might return any time, and when I saw it coming there was nothing I could do.

Frightening images formed and reformed in my head as in a turning kaleidoscope, each more vivid than the last. I had so many questions, most of which I didn't dare ask my mother or Aunt Daisy. Nor did I trust them to know the answers.

"Shall I come with you?" asked Aunt Daisy as my mother hesitated. "We could call in at the café for tea and doughnuts."

"No thanks. I really want a walk by myself. Sorry," I added, seeing the disappointment on Aunt Daisy's face.

"Where were you planning to go?" asked my mother, looking out of the window. It was early afternoon and there was a streak of lemon January sunshine in the sky.

"Along the promenade. Or on the beach if the tide's out."

Aunt Daisy looked at her watch. "It should be low tide about now. You'll get a good long walk along the sands. Put your walking shoes on and wrap up warm – there's a bitter wind out there. And be careful."

“Okay.” We had somehow bypassed my mother and it would be difficult for her to object now.

“Take your umbrella in case it rains or even snows,” said Mum.

It was exhilarating but also frightening to leave the house on my own. The cars came along the road unexpectedly fast and it took me forever to get across. I’d lost my confidence and it was a relief to meet no-one I knew.

Once on the beach, I felt better. I headed towards the sea, where the tide-wrinkled sand was deserted apart from a dog-walker and a small child in wellingtons making sand pies while her mother stood a few feet away, arms folded against the cold. I kept well back to make sure no-one looked at me or spoke. I’d grown self-conscious in the past two or three weeks, blushing if anyone addressed me, aware of how thin I’d become. At the shops with my mother, several acquaintances asked what was wrong with me. Those who had heard about Charity and knew she was my friend gave me pitying looks which made me cringe.

The retreating tide had left shallow bands of water which gleamed silver in the weak sunlight. The rocks where children climbed in summer were uncovered and I stopped for a moment, thinking I saw a child sitting on one, quite a long way out. I walked closer, concerned, as he or she appeared to be alone, and the tide came in fast.

As I approached I saw it was not a child but a man, sitting on a rock with his back to me, looking out to sea. Seconds later, I realised it was Tom.

“Hello, Tom,” I yelled. “Hi there!”

Perhaps he hadn’t heard – there were seagulls shrieking all around. He didn’t turn his head, anyway. I called again and this time he stood up and looked towards me. But he still didn’t reply.

I was on the rocks myself now, scrambling towards him, stumbling as I tried to hurry. “Tom, it’s me – Joanne.”

Could he possibly have forgotten me, I wondered, in so short a time?

He answered with a flat “hello”, as though he had known it was me all the time. Was he angry with me for some reason?

Then I noticed that his face didn't look right. I could almost believe he had been crying. For a second something glinted on his cheek, then it vanished as a dark cloud passed over the sun. An icy gust of wind caught me and I almost lost my balance on the slippery rock. The sea had turned black, oily and threatening.

"Are you okay, Joanne?" His voice was heavy and lifeless, like a slug of seaweed pushed onto the rocks by a wave.

"Yes, I'm fine. Much better, thanks."

"That's good."

"I'm still off school, though. Probably until after Easter."

"Really?'

"They want to make sure I'm properly better. And they're worried that people will upset me."

"Yes, I see."

I wanted to ask Tom all the questions that had been welling up inside me, but it was impossible to start. He looked so bad himself that it didn't seem right.

Then I noticed he had taken his shoes off. They rested on a nearby rock, in danger of being washed off by a wave. He wore black socks with a small hole in the left big toe.

I wanted to ask about the shoes, but again I didn't feel I could. There was something odd going on here. I sensed he wanted me to go away, but some mix of curiosity and concern kept me there.

"Are you all right, Tom?"

"Me? Yes, of course." He gave me a quick glance, then turned his eyes out to sea again.

"Are you sure?"

He sighed. "To be honest, Joanne, I'm not coping too well, either, with all that's happened. And as you may have heard, Pattie and I have decided to go our separate ways."

"I haven't heard anything. What do you mean?"

"We are splitting up. Pattie has taken the children to live with her mother for the time being."

"But why?" I tried to picture Tom and Pattie together, to remember the last time I'd seen them, but failed. Instead, what came to mind was Tom walking on the beach with Louise in the summer. The two of them holding hands.

Tom gave a grunt. "I'd prefer not to go into detail."

"Sorry, it's none of my business."

He looked me full in the face for the first time. I expected him to comment on my still-sunken cheeks, but he didn't. Instead he broke into a warm smile, as though he was suddenly pleased to see me.

"Have you been to see Charity?" I now felt able to ask.

"No. I tried, but they wouldn't let me."

"I'm not allowed to see her either. Not after last time."

"They think visitors might upset her. It's nothing personal."

"It is with me. It was when I was there that she went crazy." I felt better, having said this to Tom.

"From what I hear, your visit helped her open up. That's when the truth came out. It had to happen."

We sat down on adjacent rocks. I dabbled my hand in the water, then withdrew it because of the cold. I thought of Tom's feet, which must have been freezing in his wet socks.

"Don't you want to put your shoes on?"

"No."

I dried my hand on my jeans and pulled my woollen glove back on. "I'm worried about Charity. No-one will tell me anything."

"She's in good hands. The staff at the unit will know how to help her."

"It's not just the abuse. She lost her baby, too. The real Rosie, not the one she brought here."

"I know."

"That baby died, didn't she, Tom?"

"We must assume so. Apparently she was a few weeks premature. Her lungs wouldn't have developed properly."

"Charity heard her cry before they took her away. That's what Louise said."

"That's terribly sad."

"Why wouldn't they let Charity see her?"

"I don't know. I expect they took her away to try to revive her."

"Mum said there must have been something wrong with her, because of Charity's dad being her father. She thinks that might be why she died. Is that right, Tom?"

Tom took a breath and expelled it in a long sigh. A single bird screamed, far out at sea. "I don't know, Joanne. It's possible, I suppose, that she had congenital abnormalities. That can happen when a baby's parents are very closely related."

"So was that why she died?"

"It may have had something to do with it. Or perhaps not. I don't know much about these things."

The lump in my throat made it difficult to form the words, but I had to ask. "You don't think she had two heads or something?"

Tom turned quickly towards me, his brows knitted, shaking his head. "Joanne – have you been imagining things like that? No – I think that's incredibly unlikely. I expect she looked just like any other baby, but very small."

"But they wouldn't let Charity see her. I thought that might be why."

"As I said, they would have taken her away to revive her. Put her on life-support, perhaps."

I breathed out, overwhelmed with relief.

We were silent for a few minutes, watching a couple of seagulls circle above our heads. Then Tom said, "This has been awfully hard for you."

"Not as bad as for Charity."

"No – but very difficult, all the same. You've been very brave."

"I don't think I have. She's the brave one."

"Both of you are. I'm so proud of you."

I felt tears pricking my eyelids. "Did you know that Charity and I are in love?"

He replied slowly, as though thinking hard or being careful. "I had some idea. Louise mentioned that you were – an item. If that's the right way to put it?"

"Yes, we are. Before all this, we were planning to live together. We were going to be joint parents to Rosie."

He looked me in the face again. I noticed for the first time how bloodshot his eyes were. His face was thinner, too – like mine had been but not as bad.

"Joanne – that makes it even harder for you. I'm so sorry."

"It's making me feel better, talking to you."

He wriggled his toes, which must have been half-frozen. "Is it?"

"Yes. Do you remember when my dad died, how you talked to me then?'

"Of course I do." Tom's voice had warmed up a few degrees – he sounded a bit more like himself.

"Can I ask you something else?"

"Anything at all."

"It's a 'why' question."

"They're always the hardest. But go ahead."

"I used to think I understood about sex. Both homo- and hetero-sexual."

He gave a little smile. "Did you?"

"I mean, how people are attracted to each other and all that. It kind of made sense."

"I used to think I understood it, too."

"What do you mean?"

"Never mind. Go on."

My throat began to constrict but I forced the words out. "How can someone have sex with his own child?"

Tom didn't answer for several minutes. Then, gazing at the nearly-black folding waves, he said, "I don't know. I can't imagine and I don't even want to try."

"If he wanted sex, he could have paid to have it with a prostitute. That's what people do, isn't it?"

"Some of them. I've heard it said that child abuse is not about sex – not primarily. It's more to do with control. A kind of bullying."

"But when it's your own daughter…?"

"I know. It's horrible, Joanne. I've got no answers."

"How *could* he?"

"His mind is distorted, sick, perverted – he's mentally ill."

I felt a shiver of fear. "But I'm mentally ill. So is Charity."

"Not in that way. Nothing like that. Neither of you. What Mr Baker has is something different. A kind of disease, perhaps? I don't think anyone really understands. Perhaps *he* was abused, as a child…"

"So he was trying to get his own back?"

"Not exactly. But it seems to make some people that way. Like people who bully in other ways – they've often been bullied themselves."

The sun emerged for a few moments, falling on Tom's greying hair and making it glisten.

"If Mr Baker is ill, does that mean that what he did is not his fault?"

"That's another difficult one. No, I believe we all have to take responsibility for our actions. But if someone has been treated badly themselves, or they have an illness or some dreadful compulsion, perhaps we should feel some compassion for them. Or at least we should bear it in mind."

"I can't feel any compassion for Mr Baker."

"I wouldn't expect you to."

The sun had retreated and the sky was darker than ever now.

"Do you feel compassion for him?" I asked.

"Not at the moment, no."

"What about forgiveness? The Bible says you have to forgive."

"I'm not sure it's always possible. It can't be forced, and I don't believe it should be rushed."

"So God doesn't expect me to forgive Mr Baker?"

"All I can say is, if I were God, I wouldn't."

"Wouldn't expect me to, or wouldn't forgive him yourself?"

"The first. Possibly the second, too."

We sat in silence again. The seagulls had departed. Then Tom said, "But those are just my thoughts. Others may disagree. Before this happened, I might have told you we should always forgive."

"So you've changed your mind."

"Possibly. I don't know."

I was beginning to feel I could say anything at all to Tom. "I'm not sure whether I still believe in God."

"Really?"

"Not after this. It doesn't make sense any more, any of it. Charity's father was an elder in the Barnsley church. At the same time, he was doing those terrible things to Charity."

Tom said nothing, but stared out to sea and shook his head.

"He *was*."

"I know he was." Tom still didn't look at me.

"You know all that Holy Spirit stuff Charity used to talk about. Do you think she meant it?"

"I'm sure she meant it. She believed all of it. So do lots of other people."

"She believed that God made her pregnant with Rosie," I said.

"I think that was her way of rationalising what her father had done. She was trying to change reality – leaving out the abuse. Trying to find an alternative explanation for the pregnancy."

"Those nightmares she had – where the Terror came into her room – they were real, weren't they? I mean, it was her dad coming in, to abuse her."

"At least some of them must have been real."

"And, all the time, she was praying to God to stop them. She gave me a prayer she'd written out, so I could pray it, too."

Tom sighed. "I sense another difficult question coming up."

"Why didn't God answer her prayer? Why didn't He stop Mr Baker doing it?"

"I don't know. I really don't." He looked at the sky for inspiration. "One answer is that He gives us free will. If He didn't, we'd be robots. The idea of goodness would make no sense."

"Then why pray about anything?"

"I could try to give you an answer – but I think it's more honest to say you've got me there."

"Good."

"Why good?"

"Because you see the problem."

"I see the problem, all right."

"Do you still believe in God, Tom?"

He gave a deep sigh. "Unfortunately, yes."

"Why unfortunately?"

"Because it feels very uncomfortable at the moment. I'm conscious of having let Him down."

"How have you let Him down?"

"In more ways than I can possibly explain. But, believe me, I have."

I trailed the edge of my glove in the water. "You're a good person, Tom. You help everyone and you don't pretend."

"Thank you, Joanne. I only wish those things were true."

"They are true. You haven't let anyone down. It's not your fault, what happened to Charity. You've done your best all along. Are you upset by this stupid gossip about the Crabbies?"

"A bit. But the problem is mostly my own conscience. I've been selfish and stupid and messed everyone up. Someday, when you're older, I'll explain, if you still want to know."

I imagined being grown up, being an adult alongside Tom. The idea was intriguing. "I'll always be your friend, Tom."

"Joanne – that's the nicest thing anyone's said to me for a long time. Thank you." He raised his hand to his face – was he brushing tears away?

"You're welcome. By the way, I may stop going to Crabbies."

"That makes two of us."

"What?"

"I'm resigning my post as pastor. I can't do it any more. But never mind me. Why are you leaving? Because of all this?"

"In a way. Can you be a Christian and not believe all the crazy stuff?"

"What crazy stuff?"

"Miracles and all that. That God made Mary pregnant with Jesus. That Jesus died and came back to life."

"People attempt it, to various degrees. Not all believers take the Bible as literally as some of the Crabbies do. There are bishops who don't believe in a physical resurrection."

"I'd like to believe in a God who is just sort of there. Not one who answers prayers and gives people the Holy Spirit. Is that possible?"

"Only you can decide that."

"I think I might try."

"Is it something you really want to do?"

"It's something I have to do, I think."

"Then I'd say go ahead. But don't leave any bits of yourself behind in the process. Do you see what I mean?"

"Like Louise, having to give up her physics because of Alan?"

"That's exactly what I mean."

"I won't give up my maths, if I ever get it back. My brain won't work at the moment."

"You could have fooled me. Don't worry – your maths will come back, in its own good time. There's no rush. You can repeat the school year if you need to."

"Yes. Maybe. I'll be okay. It's Charity I feel sorry for. Will she be able to go back to school?"

"I hope so, in time, if that's what she wants."

All of a sudden I felt very frightened. "She will get better, Tom, won't she?"

"People do recover, Joanne, with the right kind of help. Which she's getting. She'll always have scars, of course, mental ones. But she's young and strong and resourceful."

"Like we were saying, she lost her baby. Without even getting to see her."

"She'll have to go through a grieving process for Rosie."

"I still can't forget the baby she brought here. I think of *her* as Rosie. I miss her."

"That baby's safe, with her own family."

"I know. But it feels all wrong."

Tom offered me a rather damp tissue. I saw that his fingers were almost black with cold. He reached across and laid his bare hand on my gloved one. Then he withdrew it. "Sorry. I probably shouldn't."

"It's okay. I trust you, Tom."

Then he started crying, too, and I had to hand him back my soggy tissue.

After a few minutes, he said, "Sometimes I feel guilty, as an adult, especially as a man – towards every child on the planet. For all the suffering we inflict on them."

"It's not just men. Women do some terrible things, too."

"I know."

A dark shadow seemed to have fallen across us. I said, "I feel ashamed to be human, sometimes."

"You don't need to. You're still a child."

"I don't think I am, any more."

"Joanne – I don't know whether I should tell you this."

"What?"

"When you found me just now, with my shoes off, looking out to sea. I was going to…"

"It's all right. I know."

"You know?"

"It was kind of obvious – what you were planning to do."

"Was it?"

"I'm not stupid. And like I said, I'm not a child any more. I understand, now, why people want to do themselves in."

"Do you?"

"Completely."

"Doesn't it frighten you that I was planning to do that?"

"Not now. As long as you promise that you won't ever do it."

Tom sighed. "All right. I promise."

"Good."

"Now what about you?"

"How do you mean?"

"Cutting your arms and not eating."

"How do you know?"

"Louise mentioned it. I've been worried about you."

"I wasn't trying to kill myself. It's different. I can't really explain."

Tom was trying to push his frozen feet into his shoes. I held one shoe open to help.

"Try."

"The cutting makes me feel better, for a while. When I can't bear how I feel. Seeing the blood – it helps."

"I don't understand."

"Mum is making me see a psychologist on Fridays. He asks me loads of questions."

"Good. And what about the eating?"

"I'm starting to eat again. I am, really. The not-eating thing is more to do with my mother now. I hate her."

"Your mother's a good person. A little over-protective, perhaps."

"You haven't seen her when she gets mad."

"She's had a hard time, losing your dad. You both have."

"She was always like that, even before Dad died."

"I think part of the problem is that you're very different. You get on better with your aunt, don't you?"

"Yes, Aunt Daisy's okay, when you get her away from Mum."

He stood up, both feet now firmly inside his shoes, and winced. "Shall we walk along a bit? I need to get my circulation going."

We set off, heading in towards the promenade, Tom rather unsteady on his feet.

I held out my arm for him and he took it. "Tom…"

"Yes?"

"I wish you and Pattie would get back together."

"I wish we would, too."

"Can't you persuade her? Tell her you really, really love her? It's horrible to think of you two splitting up."

"I have tried. I'll try again. But it's a lot to ask of her. I made some bad mistakes. I thought, for a while, that I loved someone else."

"Louise?"

"What?"

"Was it Louise? I saw you holding hands that time here on the beach."

"Ah. Well, yes. I didn't realise…"

"I tried to tell myself you were just being friendly. But it didn't look like that."

"I'm sorry, Joanne."

I knew what he meant, but I said, "What for?"

"I let you down. You and all the Crabbies. As your pastor. I tried so hard *not* to love Louise – well, part of me did. But I failed. I'm so sorry."

"But falling in love isn't something you can help, is it?"

"I could have helped it. I should have stopped seeing her. For counselling, I mean."

"When I fell in love with Charity, it just happened. The second I saw her."

"That's different. You were single and free."

"Mum still doesn't know I'm gay."

"Are you going to tell her?"

"I daren't. She'll kill me."

"What about your aunt?"

"I think she's guessed. I've often wondered if she's gay herself."

"Perhaps you could tell her first? Try to get her support."

"Mum will still kill me. If ever there's anything on TV about homosexuals, she goes mad."

"That's a great shame."

"I think I'll tell her when I get home, Get it over with."

"Want me to come with you? Would it help?"

"No, I don't think she'd see you. And you've got wet feet. But thanks for the offer."

"I'll pray, then."

"Okay. Are *you* all right with it, Tom?"

"With what?"

"Me being gay. Some of the Crabbies don't approve. Do you approve?"

"Of course I do. You know I do. We've discussed this before."

"Some of them are like Mum – they think it's evil."

"I'm afraid so. Much as I love my fellow Crabbies, some of their beliefs are primitive, outmoded and riddled with prejudice."

"Can't you tell them?" We had reached the edge of the beach and turned to walk up the cliff path. Tom was still hobbling on his numb feet.

"I can't tell people what to believe."

"You can try."

"I have tried."

"Louise says Alan thinks gay sex is against God's will."

"Alan, in my opinion, is wrong."

"He's our assistant pastor."

"I know."

"Can't you sack him?"

"I have a lot of respect for Alan, even though we disagree on some things."

"Even since he punched you?"

"Yes. Even since then. You know, Joanne, there are churches that welcome gays. And where people don't interpret the Bible so literally. You might find a home in one of them."

"You think I should try?"

"If you want to, yes. There are churches with gay leaders, now. I have a lesbian friend who wants to enter the ministry. Knowing her, she'll succeed. Things are slowly beginning to change. You could be part of all that."

"I'm not sure I want to. It might be easier just to give up."

"It's your decision."

"Aunt Daisy says that people believe in God to give themselves comfort, but I'm beginning to think it's the least comfortable thing there is."

"That may be an exaggeration, but I think there's some truth in it."

We stopped halfway up the cliff path to look down at the sea. The tide had made some headway now, and the rocks we'd sat on were almost submerged.

"Are your feet still dead?" I asked.

"I don't think they'll ever recover."

I laughed, then said. "Better to lose your feet than the whole of you."

"Yes. You're right."

"Tom – you know that Charity is going to be moved to a new unit in Scotland?"

"Yes. I wasn't sure if you'd been told."

"Louise told me. It's going to be impossible for me to see her now. But I was wondering – could you find out her address for me?"

"I'll do my best."

"Thanks. I want to write – to let her know I haven't forgotten her. I won't expect her to reply. She might not be able to. But maybe one day, when she's better..."

"I'm sure she would love to hear from you."

We'd reached the top of the path.

"This is where we go our separate ways," said Tom.

"I'd invite you back for a cup of tea, but I can't."

"Don't worry. Listen – good luck."

"And you. Hope you can get Pattie to come home."

"I'll try my hardest." There was a long pause. "Joanne – thanks."

"You're very welcome. See you, Tom."

As I turned in at my gate a little further along, I looked back and saw he had stopped and was watching me. We both raised our hands to wave.

Tom's journal, Tues 8th January 1985

What would have happened if Joanne hadn't met me on the beach yesterday? I'll never know. Best not think about it.

I've offered Pattie a new start. A new life – away from the Crabbies, away from Castlehaven. Away from the ministry. I will look for an office job. Brush up my accountancy skills and try to get back into it. If I'm earning a bit more, Pattie may be able to go part-time, if that's what she wants. Or give up work altogether. Or retrain for something new.

She's considering my offer.

I broke down, at home, after my walk with Joanne. It was her trust in me that did it. I phoned Pattie in tears. She came straight round and we talked for hours.

Father – please, please, please. Let her say yes...

PART 3

Chapter 15

May 2006

A couple of weeks ago, I typed 'Charity Baker' into a search engine and up came the familiar pattern of results. I've been doing this once a month or so ever since I got my computer and went online. That must be seven or eight years ago.

Scrolling down the list, I spotted an entry I'd not seen before. 'Charity Baker – *The Marvellous Sea* – Centre for Natural Health and Healing, Cornwall.' My heart quickened as I clicked to bring up the page. On my screen was a photo of a woman with wild golden hair caught in the wind. Without doubt, it was Charity.

Except that she looked far too young. She must be thirty-seven now. Maybe it was an old photo. She was holding a girl of two or three, with the same green-flecked eyes and untidy hair, a shade or two lighter than Charity's. Behind them was a white cottage and beyond that, steep cliffs and blue sea.

'Welcome to *The Marvellous Sea*. I'm Charity Baker and this is my daughter Silver. We hope you will find something to interest you in these pages. If you are seeking healing of any kind, or just a rest from your hectic life, perhaps you would like to consider visiting us.' There was lots more, but I was fixated on the photograph.

I didn't return to preparing my weekly sermon, but sat gazing at her image until darkness fell. Then I started typing an email.

The journey seemed endless. Charity's cottage was on the edge of a tiny village a few miles south of Newquay. As the road slipped beneath me, edged by moorland, hills and the occasional glimpse of sea, I slowed down.

It wasn't that I didn't want to see Charity. It was that I'd waited over twenty-one years for it, and now my adrenalin was way beyond excitement, almost at panic level. I feared our meeting would be a disappointment – that one or both of us would be awkward, that we'd have nothing to say. Or that she (or I) would have changed beyond recognition and prove an enormous let-down to the other.

That all my dreams would dissolve away on seeing her again, and all my memories, too. That I would no longer love her (could that be?) or that I would discover that she never had loved me. That was the deepest fear – that the most cherished moments from our past would be destroyed.

And yet I *had* to see her – to see her whole and fully recovered from her terrible ordeal.

She had replied to my email the day I sent it. Her tone, like mine, was bright and chatty. Yes, of course she remembered me and would love to meet up again. Would I like to visit? The next week or so would be perfect as she had few guests at present. Things would hot up when the summer season began.

Reading her message, I realised that only part of me wanted to meet her, but that part would win. Before I knew it I had checked out the route from Nottingham to Newquay and asked Charity for details of the last few miles to her cottage. Four days later, early on a Thursday morning, I was on my way.

Charity's home was easy to find, but I stopped half a mile short to compose myself, comb my hair and try to stop my stomach churning. I wound down the window and took deep breaths of the sweet seaside air. She had found a beautiful place for herself, her daughter – and whoever else she lived with.

One of the many reasons for my pounding heart and disturbed stomach was the thought of meeting Silver's father. I prayed for a generosity of spirit I knew was beyond me. I would, I knew, have to rely on my acting skills.

Being a Church of England vicar prepares you for many things, but not this.

I took a further breath, closed my window and started the engine.

"You look wonderful, Joanne. Just as I remember you."

We hugged. Charity must have heard my car – she had run out of the door and along the drive to meet me. Silver was beside her, jumping about with an energy that reminded me of her mother.

"I eventually got rid of my spots."

She released me and looked at my face. "I always said you would."

"It took a while. Charity – you look hardly a day older."

She laughed and called Silver, who had run off. "Come and say hello to Joanne."

I said, "Hello, Silver," and she put her fist in her mouth and retreated behind her mother.

"Don't be shy," said Charity.

"It's fine, don't worry. She can say hello when she's ready." I wanted to ask about Silver's father but I couldn't – it was too soon.

"Come in and have something to eat. You must be starving. Have you driven all the way today?"

"Yes, I set off early. Stopped for a meal at a service station somewhere in Devon. But I am quite hungry now."

"I made some scones. Go on, in you go. Leave your bags in the hall. That's it, right through to the living room – make yourself at home. Silver, show Joanne your boats while I put the kettle on."

Silver forgot to be shy in the excitement of being reunited with her family of toy boats, all of which had names. I amused her by trying, without much success, to remember them and how they were related to each other. I noted that the daddy boat had his own house behind the sofa, and came to visit the mummy and baby boats at the weekend. My spirits rose in a ridiculous surge of hope.

"She's got a fantastic imagination," said Charity, returning with a tray. "Here – I've made a traditional Cornish cream tea. Get stuck into it. Sugar in your tea?"

"No thanks." I reached for the cup, conscious that my hand had started to shake. This was awful.

If Charity noticed anything, she ignored it. We sipped our tea and I spread a scone with thick cream and what tasted like home-made raspberry jam.

"My neighbour makes it," said Charity. "Mrs Brown from the next cottage along."

As we ate, Silver entertained us with stories about her boats. It was a relief to delay the inevitable mutual questioning. I was glad to see Charity looking so well and happy, but a tide of dread swelled inside me as I anticipated hearing about her life. Her personal life. Silver's father – who might at any moment come into the untidy, sunlit room with its blue cotton curtains billowing in the open window.

Had I really, all these years, held onto a hope that Charity might still be homosexual (if, indeed, she ever had been), or that, even if she was, she would still be interested in me?

I told myself to stop being so pathetic, to grow up and be at least professional if I couldn't manage anything else. It didn't work of course. I started to feel sick and wished I hadn't come.

Silver thrust a red-sailed yacht onto my knee. "This is you-boat."

"U-boat?"

"She means it's your boat," said Charity. "That it represents you. She's welcoming you to the family."

"Wow." I was close to tears. "Thanks, Silver." I put out my hand to take the yacht and made it sail across an imaginary sea.

"You can have my bedroom," she said, giving me a huge grin just like Charity's.

"No, you don't need to give me your bedroom. I can sleep on the sofa. I've brought my sleeping bag."

"We've got lots of spare rooms but Silver wants to give you hers," said Charity. "It was her own idea. Don't turn her down or she'll be upset."

"Sorry," I said. "I just didn't want to take your room from you, Silver. But if you really want me to have it, I'd love to. Thank you very much." I smiled and Silver's face lit up again. She was so like Charity it was unnerving.

"Come and see my bedroom," said Silver, pulling on my arm. "Come on, get up. Come and see it."

"Let Joanne finish her tea first," said Charity, but I got up to go with Silver.

Silver's ground floor window was wide open and looked out over the bay – granite cliffs, a narrow stretch of sand (the tide appeared to be high) and sparkling sea. The room was full of boats – they were lined up on every available surface. Old and new, plastic and wooden, even a few origami ones.

"You like boats, don't you?"

"I want a big one of my own to go sailing in."

"Do you go out sailing with – with Mummy? Or…?" I couldn't ask about Daddy, however much I wanted to – it wouldn't be fair.

"No, I go in a boat with Sam and Mary."

Who were Sam and Mary?

"Here." She reached for a rather beautiful wooden yacht with a canvas sail, and put it into my hands. "It's very careful."

"You mean I have to be careful with it? Don't worry, I will." I held the boat with reverence, giving its wooden deck a gentle stroke.

"That's Nana-boat."

"She's beautiful."

We returned to Charity, who was just topping up my cup of tea.

"So, how long have you been here?" I asked.

I'd unpacked and had a brief lie-down on Silver's bed, which had, needless to say, a boat-themed duvet cover and pillows. We were now taking a stroll across the wet sand left by the retreating tide. The sky had half-clouded over and the sun bobbed out from time to time, casting a brilliant sheen on the bands of shallow water that lay across our path. We had all three of us taken off our shoes and socks so we could splash through, regardless. Silver ran ahead, picking up shells and pebbles to bring and show us.

"Just under two years," said Charity. "But *The Marvellous Sea* only opened its doors last summer. It took nearly a year to make the place fit to live in."

"I like the name."

"It comes from a poem by Jean Ingelow. Jon introduced me to it."

"Jon?"

"Silver's father."

"Oh, I see." I looked away from her, over the gleaming sands.

"I'll tell you all about him soon. But first, let's hear about you. What have you been doing all these years? What's this about you being a vicar? Were you kidding me?"

"No – I'm afraid it's true." It was clear I wasn't going to get any information about Jon without telling Charity about myself first.

"For the last seven years. Before that I was a maths teacher in Nottingham."

"That makes sense. You were good at maths."

"I always liked it."

"I remember you helping me with my homework, explaining it to me. I bet you were a great teacher."

"I think I was okay. I enjoyed it, anyway. It was thrilling, getting some of the kids interested – especially the disaffected ones. Doing statistics on football scores. The chance of life on other planets. Stuff that grabbed their interest."

"So why did you give it up?"

"I got a nagging feeling I should be doing something else. I resisted it for a long time but in the end it got to me. I gave in and applied to train for the ministry. It came as a shock when they accepted me. But I joined up, as it were, and here I am – vicar of a church in a rather run-down district of Nottingham."

"Are you happy there?"

To my surprise I hesitated. "I think so."

"You don't sound sure."

"I am sure. I mean, I'm sure it's what I'm meant to be doing. It's quite demanding at times. Even more than teaching, in a way."

"You kept your faith, then?"

"Sort of. Not the kind of faith we had in Crabbies." After a pause, in which I gazed at the distant sand dunes, I said, "How about you?"

"I suppose I have a kind of faith. But not in God, not really. I believe in natural healing – that's why I started this place. I'm probably closer to Buddhism than anything. And I sometimes go to meetings of the Society of Friends in Newquay."

"You say you've been here two years? What made you come?"

"My mother died. I'd lived with her for some time, in southern France. She left me some money she'd saved over the years – enough to buy this place and do it up. Well, not quite. I ran out part way through. Jon helped me a bit, though I'm still not out of the woods."

"That was good of him."

"It was an investment on his part. He owns a share of the cottage."

"Right. And is he – are you…?"

"Are we what?"

"I just wondered if you and he…?"

She looked puzzled. "We're friends, Jon and I. Good friends."

The sun emerged at that moment and the beach lit up golden as my heart soared with relief. Then I bumped down again. Jon was Silver's father. The fact that he and Charity were no longer together meant nothing much. Charity was straight now – that was the truth I had to assimilate.

She continued. "I dreamed for years of doing something like this. All my life, really – ever since my illness."

"You seem to have made a good recovery."

"I've had a lot of help."

"I'm so glad."

"That's why I want to give something to other people who need it. At first I planned *The Marvellous Sea* to be for people who'd suffered sexual abuse. But it turned out to be broader than that. It's for healing of any kind, emotional, mental, physical. I'm not a crazy amateur – I've had quite a lot of training, mostly in France. People seem to find coming here helpful. Though I sometimes think it's the chance of a bit of peace and quiet by the sea that does most of the work."

"It sounds wonderful."

"You're welcome to come down here yourself, any time."

"Thank you."

'Silver loves you already.'

"I love her. She's gorgeous."

We watched Silver as she scuttled towards us, holding what looked like a dead crab. "Yes, I'm very proud of her. Aren't I, *mon petit chou*? What's that you've picked up?"

When Silver had run off again, I said, "You mentioned that your mother died two years ago? I'm very sorry to hear that."

"Yes, I miss her. We got quite close towards the end. It took a long time, though. She battled with her alcoholism for years. It was liver disease that killed her. But her main problem was that she couldn't forgive herself."

"For what?"

"Leaving my father and me. She blamed herself when she discovered what he'd done. It turns out she'd suspected something years before but my father denied it when she challenged him. Apparently I denied it, too. I don't remember. I expect he told me to keep it secret. That part is all a blur now."

"So your mother didn't have any part in what happened… to your baby?"

"No, definitely not. She knew nothing about it. I hardly saw her when I was pregnant. Some of the stuff in those letters I sent you was invented."

I wanted to ask more, but didn't feel I could – not yet. "I'm glad you and your mother made up, in the end."

"It took me a long time to forgive her for leaving me with my father."

"I understand."

"It was only when I had Silver that I began to let go of my resentment towards her."

"Silver showed me her Nana boat."

"Yes, my mother bought it for her just before she died. Silver doesn't remember her nana but we look at photos."

We walked in silence for a while. Then, when Silver was some way off, I said, "It can't have been easy for you, having a baby, after what happened back then?"

"No, it wasn't easy. But it was something I wanted to do, very much. I was dreading labour so they gave me a Caesarean. I was in quite a state. It brought it all back, what happened with Rosie..."

I found myself putting my hand in Charity's, the way I used to years before. "Rosie," I repeated.

She accepted my hand. "Silver and I have made a little garden for Rosie."

"Does that mean that you know for sure that she…?'

Charity brushed her hair back from her face in a familiar gesture and sighed. "It took me a long time to accept that Rosie was dead. There was no way I could look for her while I was in the unit in Dumfries. My mother told me she was trying to find her but I didn't believe it at the time. It wasn't easy in those days – no internet or anything."

"I know."

"It's only in the last few years that I've come to accept that Rosie must have died at birth or very soon after."

I squeezed her hand but said nothing.

She continued. "I try to believe that she died naturally. The thought that my father might have harmed her…"

"Surely, not even he…?"

"That man was capable of anything." Her voice cracked and I sensed rifts, rents – dried-up places inside her that would perhaps never fully heal. "All I know is that she is safe now. Once I'd started to forgive my mother, we hunted together, high and low, but never found a trace. He couldn't have hidden her as well as that. He wasn't clever enough."

"So you've told Silver she had a big sister who died?"

"Yes. I'll show you the garden when we get back."

"I'd love to see it."

"Silver helps me keep it tidy. On Rosie's birthday, we are going to plant a tree for her." After a pause, she said, "It's so sad I have no photos of Rosie. That I never even saw her."

I said, "I still remember the baby you brought to Louise's. I think of *her* as Rosie."

"So did I, for a time. I really believed she was my baby, you know."

"I know you did. I never doubted that."

Charity pulled her small rucksack from her shoulder and unzipped one of the pockets, pulling out a faded photograph which she passed to me. It showed a girl of about two with dark curly hair and a mischievous smile.

"Turn it over," she said.

On the back was written, "Love from Anna," followed by a toddler's scrawl.

"Anna?"

"That's her, the baby I stole. They got me to write a letter to her parents as part of my rehab. To say sorry for taking her. The family were so kind – they replied to me and sent that photo. I've always treasured it."

"Gosh. I'm sure."

"I felt so guilty, once I realised what I'd done."

"You didn't hurt Rosie. Anna, I mean."

"I was temporarily insane, they said. I could have done anything."

"But you didn't. You cared for her. You took her to Louise – that was probably the best thing you could have done."

"I'm amazed, looking back, that Louise didn't catch on that something was wrong."

"I didn't, either."

"You were only a kid."

"I knew something wasn't right, I just didn't know what. I was so hurt – I thought you didn't love me any more."

The words fell between us and hit the sand with a thud. I regretted them as soon as they were out of my mouth. There was a long silence during which I felt my cheeks pinken and prayed that Charity wouldn't see.

She said, "Have you kept in touch with Louise?"

"We exchange emails every now and then. She's in America – got a job at Princeton University a couple of years ago. Before that she was a senior researcher at York. She studies dark energy."

"Dark energy?"

"A mysterious force in the universe. No-one understands it, not even Louise. Not yet."

"So she went back to university?"

"Yes, a year or so after… everything that happened. I'm not sure how she managed, with two young children, but she did. Finished her degree and went on to a PhD."

"Did she and Alan get back together?"

"They tried, for a while, but it didn't work out. Louise had begun to assert herself and Alan didn't like it. He left Castlehaven – I'm not sure where he went. I haven't seen him since."

"Are the Crabbies still going strong?"

"They folded when Tom left. A new group started up called the Castlehaven Christian Fellowship. It's still thriving. Do you remember the twins, Ray and Tony? Tony is its leader."

"No! Wow. And what about your mother and your Aunt Daisy?"

"My mother's fine. Pretty much the same. Aunt Daisy died of cancer three years ago. Very sad – but you know what? She found happiness in her last few years. Remember our head-teacher, Margaret Dodd?"

"Miss Dodd – of course I do."

"She retired and the new head who took her place, Maisie Smith – well, she and Aunt Daisy hit it off. Fell in love, in fact."

"Goodness! I remember, now – you used to wonder if your aunt might be gay."

"I was right."

"How wonderful that she found someone in her last few years."

"It took Mum a while to get used to it."

"Your mum was always quite – er…"

"Homophobic."

"I was going to say outspoken."

"That, too. She's mellowed to some extent. We get on better now. She kicked up a hell of a fuss when I first came out. That was just after you went to Scotland."

"Did she blame me?"

"I don't really remember, now."

"I bet she did."

"She had to accept me in the end."

"Does she still run the guest house?"

"No, she sold it when Aunt Daisy died. She lives in a little bungalow further along the same road."

"I've never been back to Castlehaven. Perhaps I should, sometime."

"We could go together."

"I'd like that. Though who would I know there, now? You said Tom had left, didn't you? Where are he and… what was his wife's name?"

"Pattie. They split up, too."

"Really? Now that does surprise me."

"Pattie left him when she found out about Louise. You didn't know about that, did you? Tom fell in love with Louise."

"No!"

"Well, yes. That summer you were in France. I don't think anything ever really happened between them. But Pattie found out and stormed off with the kids. Tom persuaded her to come back and try a new start. They moved to somewhere near Doncaster and stayed together for a few more years. I don't know why they broke up in the end. Perhaps Tom was impossible to live with."

"Do you ever see him now?"

"Quite often – he lives about a mile from me. He pops in all the time. We even tried living together for a while."

"You and Tom?"

"Just as friends. It didn't work. After he moved out we soon made up."

Charity's face was thoughtful as she took all this in. "Pity he and Louise couldn't have got together."

"I'm not sure they were ever really in love. Not she with him, anyway. She was looking for an escape from Alan."

"That makes sense. Who wouldn't want to escape from him?"

"I'm not sure how I feel about Alan now. He had lots of faults but he loved his family, I've no doubt. And he got a bad deal, with everyone thinking…" I stopped, embarrassed.

"That he was Rosie's father?"

"Well, yes."

"Yes, that was unfortunate."

I took a deep breath. It had to be asked. "What happened to your father?"

Her voice was neutral, almost matter-of-fact. "He was arrested, charged and convicted of child abuse. Not just of me. Other girls too. Some of them very young." She was silent for a few moments, then added, "He spent eight years in prison."

"And then?"

"He died there. I think someone attacked him. We never properly found out."

Silver had got some way ahead, almost out of earshot, and she didn't look round when Charity called her name. We set off after her at a gallop.

Charity caught up Silver in her arms and we all three collapsed onto the sand. Silver asked for a sandcastle and we dug with our hands in the damp sand, scooping out chunks of it and shaping it as best we could into turrets and towers. Our clothes were damp but it didn't seem to matter.

"So what does Tom do now?" Charity asked, as Silver busied herself with sticking shells to the castle walls.

"Stacks shelves in a supermarket. He's had a whole string of casual jobs – never sticks at anything for long. Long periods on benefits, too. Several bouts of depression."

"Why did he ever give up his ministry? He was so good at it."

"I think he felt he'd let all of us down."

'How? Oh – because of Louise?"

"Well, partly. And because of not being able to help you more."

"Help me? How could he have done that?"

"He thought he should have worked out what was going on."

"That's ridiculous."

"He doesn't see it that way. He still blames himself."

"For what happened to me? That's ridiculous."

"I've told him that a million times over the years."

"Perhaps I should speak to him?"

"That's not a bad idea."

"You think he'd come down here? He could stay a few days."

"He might. He was pleased when I told him I was coming to see you."

"Tell him I'd be delighted to see him. And tell him I'm all right, now."

"Yes, I will. You are all right, aren't you?"

'Of course I am. It took a long time, but I've got over it.'

"I'm so glad."

"I've still got scars, of course – they'll always be there. But scar tissue can grow strong. Not pleasant to look at, but strong and tough."

"You're lovely to look at. You're still beautiful." Perhaps the sun and sea were going to my head, but it didn't seem to matter what I said any more.

"So are you."

"I was never beautiful."

"You are now. But more importantly, you're happy. Like me. We're both doing what we want – and what we're meant to do."

"I suppose that's true."

"That's what you told me."

"It's true in part."

"Joanne, are you close to anyone? In a relationship, I mean?"

"No. I had a couple of lovers in succession when I was teaching. But no-one since. Tom asks me to marry him every now and then."

"Tom does? But you're gay!"

"That doesn't stop him. He lives in hope, or he says he does, that I'll become straight just for him."

"That's crazy.'

"He doesn't really believe it. He'd die of shock if I accepted. But we're very close friends."

"Do you see yourself finding anyone for life?"

"It's probably too late."

"You're only my age – a bit younger, even. Thirty-six? You've loads of time to find the right person."

"Have I?" I gazed out to sea, heavy with sadness. "What about you? You told me about Jon. Is there anyone else?"

"Anyone else?"

"Since Jon?"

After a pause, she said, "Joanne, you didn't think that Jon and I were lovers?"

"But he's Silver's dad."

"Daddy," said Silver, looking up for a moment before returning to her castle.

"Jon's gay. I thought I told you. He donated his sperm."

"Oh, I see."

"I wanted a child and he liked the idea of being a father. Not a very involved father, as it turns out, but at least he comes down to see Silver once or twice a month."

I took a deep breath. "So, is there anyone else?"

"No. I've had a few casual flings. But like you, no-one stuck." She glanced at me. "Joanne, what's wrong? My God – you don't know, do you?"

"What don't I know?"

"I can't believe you sometimes. You're trying to ask me whether I'm still gay, aren't you?"

"Sorry. I didn't like to assume anything. I was never quite sure, even back then."

Eyes wide, she shook her head. "You daftie! Of course I was gay. You knew I was. All the stuff we said – and did."

"But you used to talk about being bisexual."

"Did I? I don't remember. Perhaps I was probably teasing you. Or maybe I was confused for a while. I'm sorry."

"And now?"

Another pause. "You haven't changed at all, have you, Joanne?"

"Haven't I?"

"Didn't I just tell you you were beautiful?"

"Yes, but that could mean anything. It's the sort of thing a friend might say."

"I *am* your friend. At least, I hope I am."

"Of course you are. I'm sorry. I was so worried – and I'm making such a mess of things."

"No, you're not." She leaned towards me and kissed my cheek. "If we were alone, I'd do more than that. If you'd let me."

"Would you?"

She laughed. "Joanne, fancy you thinking I was straight."

I was trying my hardest not to blush. "I didn't know for sure. But I couldn't very well ask."

"Why on earth not?"

I didn't reply, and we watched Silver is silence for a few minutes. My heart was thumping as it did on the evening I first met Charity.

Then she said, "I've had an idea, Joanne. It may not appeal to you at all. But I'll say it, anyway."

My heart pounded even harder. "What is it?"

"You're probably so wedded to your job – your vocation, whatever you call it – that you wouldn't consider this. But if you wanted to – I'd love it if you came to live with me."

I gasped. "What, here?"

"Well, yes. I can't go anywhere else – not now I've got this place going. Would you like that?"

"I don't know. It would be a huge step. I can't just leave my job…"

She sighed. "Of course you can't. Sorry. It was a crazy idea."

"… Not just like that. But perhaps I could give it some thought."

"Could you? I'm not trying to rush you. And even if you did decide to, I don't mean as lovers. Not necessarily. Unless we both decided that's what we wanted. We could take our time."

I couldn't find a single word, but managed a croak of assent.

"Of course," she went on, "in your job, you may need a partner more religious than me. As I explained earlier, I'm not exactly what you'd call a Christian these days."

'Do you really think I care about that?'

She appeared to relax, her hand flopping on the sand beside her, the slight frown she'd had throughout the conversation melting into her smooth brow. "Don't you *have* to care about things like that?"

"I have my priorities. And anyway, as I told you before, I'm not the kind of Christian we used to be in Crabbies. I don't have a list of requirements for a partner."

She grinned. "Thank God for that."

"But…" I had to say this. "I can't make snap decisions. Much as I'd love to live here near you – whether as lover or friend – I'll have to give it some thought."

"Of course you will. You'll have to pray it through, as Alan used to say."

"I will. Though I suspect my way of praying wouldn't pass muster with Alan."

"Who cares about him?"

Alan's face with those gigantic teeth filled my vision as it used to do in the old days, provoking not fear any longer but a fervent hope that, wherever he was, he'd found a way to serve his God and be happy.

"I'd need a job, of course," I said.

"There must be C of E churches somewhere around here needing vicars."

"I could have a look."

"It would be great for me to have you here. I do get lonely sometimes. We could reminisce about the past."

"I'd love that."

"You could live here, if you wanted to."

I looked back towards the white cottage nestled half way up the cliff. "I haven't lived by the sea for years. I didn't realise how much I missed it until I came here."

"It's addictive. I couldn't leave it now."

"I can see why."

"Whatever happens, please think of this as your home. Stay whenever you like, for as long as you like. Preferably for ever."

"I'd pay rent, of course."

"There's no need."

"Don't be silly. I could even…" I thought of the money Aunt Daisy had left me, lying almost untouched in my savings account. "If you wanted, I could perhaps buy into the cottage. Or a share of your business. Free up some money for you to get on with the renovations."

"You'd want to do that?"

I told her about Aunt Daisy's legacy. "It's quite a lot. She'd been saving all her life."

"I couldn't possibly accept."

"It would be a business investment, like the one you already have with Jon."

"I suppose…"

"But we're forgetting Silver in all this. It might be upsetting for her to have me come to live with you."

We watched Silver for a few moments. She picked up a couple of pebbles and presented one to Charity and one to me.

"There's your answer to that. She loves you."

"She hardly knows me yet."

"She'll grow to love you even more."

I laughed and felt the rest of my life opening up, stretching ahead of me like the puddled sands, now dappled with red striations in the sinking sun.

"Tell me something, Charity."

"Tell you what?"

"All your enthusiasm for the Special Blessing. All that joy you had in the Lord, in the Spirit, way back then. Was it real?"

She paused and then replied, "Real? Yes, I think so. It felt real. Why do you ask?"

"I've wondered, since, if it was all part of your delusion. Your trying to cope with what happened – with what your father did. If it was some sort of pretence…"

"No, it wasn't pretend. It's hard to recapture the feeling, now – but I loved God so much, sometimes, I could have burst with it. You think that was a delusion?"

"No. Not at all. I'm just asking what you think."

"Other people have suggested that perhaps all the Special Blessing stuff, the way I went over the top with it, was a kind of extreme reaction to what my father did. I don't know. But plenty of other people believed it. People who weren't abused."

"Lots still do. People like Alan, if he still does."

"Not you?" she asked.

"Not any more. The God I believe in now is much more prosaic. Not very supernatural at all."

"How can God not be supernatural?"

"I'll try to explain it sometime. Not just now."

"Okay. I'll wait."

"Tom once told me not to leave any bits of myself behind, in my pursuit of God."

"You mean, like your common sense?"

"Yes, exactly."

Silver was down at the water's edge, trailing her hands in the foaming wavelets, her form in shadow against the setting sun.

"Silver!" I called, and she turned and ran towards us.

I woke in the night with the unmistakable conviction that all was not well. As each new shot of adrenalin hit my bloodstream I felt increasingly sick. 3.30am. I was in that disoriented, jet-lagged state where I knew light would be painful, yet I was afraid of the darkness. I reached for the bedside lamp, only to find it wasn't working.

My memory thrashed around without much success, retrieving only a sense of guilt. Had I hurt someone; had someone hurt me?

Flickering images danced in my eyes and shutting them didn't help. My visual field jerked every few seconds as if I'd detected a hint of movement at its edge – an insect or a mouse? There were beastly crawlings in my head, the click-click of the carotid pulse and a cold clutch of fear around my shoulders and throat.

Something was badly wrong. Was this the residue of a dream? I'd gone to bed thrilled as a child the night before Christmas. Charity and I had kissed and I was certain of her love. Now I'd awoken in the dank early hours with the cold suspicion of a wrong decision made, a false path taken.

Bits of dream swam into view. Pebbles – no, big boulders, over which I was scrambling, on one of those seashores that don't exist in reality but are the well-known settings of whole families of dreams. Smooth boulders with insufficient footholds to retain my grip. The water was rising and my feet were soaked and freezing cold. I bent forward, trying to crawl my way to the shore, but the boulders increased in size and number and I had a sudden sense that all was lost.

That was where the adrenalin and the fear had come from. I banished the dream to its proper place in my brain, but the physical sensations remained, as did the conviction that I'd made a wrong move.

But why? I'd lain awake for hours last night, happy in my plotting. Finding Charity was the best thing to happen to me ever – or second only to meeting her the first time. For over twenty years I'd yearned for this.

Long after midnight, I'd lain awake planning our future. I'd made a decision to look for a job down here, as near as possible to Charity. If no church wanted me, I'd give up my vocation and do something else. Some of my pastoral and planning skills might even be useful to *The Marvellous Sea*. I could soon drop the more overtly religious elements if required.

Perhaps Charity and I could even have a child together? Would Jon agree to be the father, so that the baby and Silver would be half-siblings? Could I, perhaps, be the one to carry and give birth to this child?

It hadn't felt right to me that we should sleep together last night and I think Charity felt the same. Nothing was said, but after a long kiss I'd gone to my bedroom – or rather Silver's bedroom – and Charity didn't try to stop me. All that was still to come. We both needed time – and I relished the opportunity to lie alone and revel in anticipation.

So what had changed in two or three hours of darkness? Was I merely the victim of a silly, meaningless dream that had left me in a bad mood but would disperse once I had slept again?

If only that were true. If only I could turn over and go back to sleep, safe in the certainty that I would wake up to the same state of pleasure I'd experienced last night. But something told me this could not happen. Doubt had crept in and there was no going back. Was it a warning from some deep part of myself that knew far better than my conscious mind what was good for me?

I had no doubts about Charity. She was as vital and beautiful and fascinating to me as ever. She was still herself – the girl and woman I had loved for years. And it was gloriously obvious that she felt the same about me.

Was it just a natural fear of the unknown? No, it was more than that – it was the fear of taking the wrong path and of losing something bigger than my future – of losing my past as well. It was one of those occasions when you know that time is not linear but fervently wish it was.

I recalled my fanciful idea of Tom's visiting Charity, of her assuring him that what happened to her was in no way his fault. Of his life and calling finally restored. The stuff of fairytales, I saw now in the pre-dawn darkness. Did I really think I was God, able to create happy endings for myself and my friends?

All of it now seemed impossible. I wanted to run out of Silver's bedroom, get into my car and drive off before mother and daughter woke up – to be miles away, out of Cornwall and heading for the motorway home before they started to look for me, puzzled, bewildered, then upset.

I pictured Charity trying to explain my disappearance to Silver. Of the tears. I imagined trying to explain my flight to Tom.

No, I couldn't go without an explanation. I had to find the courage to tell Charity that I was confused and unhappy.

For over two hours I tossed about, not with indecision but with the pain of what I had decided.

At 6am I left the warmth of my bed and crept into her room, expecting darkness and a figure lying asleep, hair spread across the pillow as of old.

But the light was on, Charity's bed was empty and the window half-open, letting in cold damp sea air. She was sitting at her laptop in a pink candlewick dressing gown, sobbing. My entrance didn't appear to surprise her.

"Look." She pointed at the computer screen.

I moved closer and read the message displayed there.

Dear Ms Baker,

I believe you may be my mother. I hope very much it is so. Her name, like you, is Charity Baker. For a long time, I look for her, but now I find your name on the internet and I begin to hope.

My name is Marie St Thérèse and I live in a small village near to Nantes, in a house of people who are dedicated to serve our Lord and Saviour, Jesus Christ.

I was born in September 1984. Did you, Ms Baker, give birth to a baby girl in that month? I understand you were a very young woman at that time. I do not know who is my father.

I found on the internet your photo and that of your daughter. Both of you bear a great resemblance to me. As well as your name, this comforts me that I have found, at last, my true mother.

I hope the shock is not too great. Let me tell you, as you already know, that I am twenty-one years and have no need that you will take care of me. But I hope very much that you will desire to meet me. I have added my photo to show you that there is a powerful resemblance.

I have a happy life with many kind friends, the sisters. Together we serve our Lord. Since two years I believe that God gives me a purpose, to tell His message to the world. I do not know yet how I will do this. The sisters tell me they hear that my mother when she is young has great faith and she will understand and help my task. I hope, my dear mother, if you are so, that you are happy to do this.

Mother – may I call you 'maman'? – I know that you did not give me away without love. The man, he who found me and brought me to this house, told the sisters that my mother abandoned me, but I do not believe it. I think you have wished good for me and perhaps you look for me since many years, without a result. Or perhaps you believe that I am dead?

Dear maman, if it is so, please know I am very well alive and I hope that you will be pleased to hear it.

If you are not my mother, pardon me for too much boldness and my error. Excuse too, my poor English.

With warm regards,

Marie St Thérèse Baker.

Charity and I read together in silence. Then she looked at me, her face expressionless, to check I'd finished. I nodded and she clicked on the attachment and scrolled down to reveal the photograph of Marie St Thérèse Baker.

It was Charity as I had known her at sixteen – the same brown limbs and sturdy figure, the same grin, the same profusion of untidy hair. She wore a simple, shortish skirt and cotton top.

There was no doubt.

"How did she know your name?" I asked.

Charity shook her head. "I've no idea. I don't understand. If she knew my name, you'd think she'd have traced me earlier."

"Perhaps she only just started wanting to."

"Maybe that's it. Since her… " Charity's voice tailed off.

"Revelation?"

"Or whatever. Oh God – Joanne…" She was crying again.

I had no idea what to say but I cradled her head in my arms while she continued.

"I can't cope with this. I should just be happy but I'm not. I'm frightened. And I feel so bad for not looking harder. She's been on her own all these years."

"You did your best to find her."

"And she thinks she's the new Messiah or something. Oh God! What did they do to her?"

"Charity, I'm here. I'll help, if you want me to. We'll deal with this together."

"Are you sure?" She turned her face to look at me. "I woke in the night and began to wonder…"

Did she have an idea of the doubts I'd been wrestling with? Had she experienced similar thoughts to mine in the darkness?

I shut my eyes for a moment, thinking of the young woman in France – of how Marie needed not only the love of her long-lost mother but the dual strength of two committed adults.

But could I do it? Was I sure? I opened my eyes, ready to set limits to the support I could offer.

Then I saw the curve of Charity's wet cheek, glistening in the pale light from the monitor. I knelt down and took her in my arms.

She gave a further sob and I held her tighter, absorbing her warmth, feeling her soft hair against my face.

"I'm sure," I said.

~ The End ~

Circaidy Gregory Press

Independent Books for Independent Readers

What do we mean by independent? For readers, it means having the courage and imagination to find your own favourites, rather than reading whatever reviewers tell you is the number one this week. For writers, it means being given the chance to take a bit of responsibility for your own creation: To have a hand in the design, the marketing and the development of your books.

We are told that more books are being published than ever before. Well, I suppose it depends what you mean by 'published'. When you compare what's in the mainstream bookshops up and down the country, or when you talk to the average reader, you get the feeling that just about everyone in the world is reading the same few books.

A book stored in an electronic file on the Internet by a company who plan to print a copy if and when someone stumbles across it and orders one is, I suppose, published: A few dozen copies printed, unedited, unreviewed, and sold to the author at cover price is another form of publication – but we at Circaidy Gregory Press are looking for something better than that – something smaller than mainstream publication, but a form that allows authors to produce a book of their own, to have it evaluated, edited and published without losing control of it, and to have a chance of benefiting from sales.

Working outside the mainstream book distribution industry, Circaidy Gregory Press, a small press with high editorial standards, aims to raise the profile of worthy authors and to bring something different to the adventurous reader: Not famous names, not high street best sellers, but carefully selected works by writers who have proved themselves through freelance work, small press anthologies, little magazines and Internet publications: Writers who live in the real world, have something to say, and the talent to say their piece in an entertaining and thought provoking manner.

Kay Green December 2007

To Independent Readers

You won't necessarily find our books reviewed in the Guardian. They may not be in the windows of the big chain bookstores, but you can find them in independent bookshops, on our website – www.circaidygregory.co.uk – and at a book fair near you. Wherever you find them, you will find something different from the top 100 fastsellers – but something well worth reading.

To Independent Writers and Illustrators

If you would like to get involved in our future publications, come along and have a look at www.earlyworkspress.co.uk, the home of our Writers and Reviewers Club, and the workshop where our projects take shape. Our books are written and illustrated by club members or competition winners discovered at Earlyworks Press.

Short Stories from Circaidy Gregory

Jung's People

Collected Short Stories
by Kay Green

Kay Green draws on Jungian philosophy to create a compelling and intellectually stimulating collection. This is another excellent collection ... and well worth reading. Jung would, I think, be proud of this child. – *Review from Prism: The magazine of the British Fantasy Society*

Light in the Shade

Selected Short Stories
by Pam Eaves

How do you escape from a morass of debt? How do you help someone who is desperately seeking a partner? Everyday problems – world-shattering to those involved –these stories illuminate the basic instinct of us all to overcome obstacles thrown in our path and continue to strive – and survive.

Poetry Collections from Circaidy Gregory

wormwood, earth and honey

Selected Poems
by Catherine Edmunds

This, her first poetry collection, is accessible but never trivial: warm, earthy, intelligent and – just when you begin to snuggle into the intimacy of it – spiked with fire and venom.

Coming soon:

Dark Matters

Poems by
David Dennis

To find out more about Circaidy Gregory Press publications,

visit

www.circaidygregory.co.uk

or write to
Circaidy Gregory Press, The Creative Media Centre,
45 Robertson Street, Hastings, Sussex TN34 1HL